Mountain Cowboys

A Dusty Rose Series Book 2

Paul,
Hope you enjoy the ride!

Susie Drougas

Susie Drougas

Mountain Cowboys

Copyright © 2015 Susie Drougas
All Rights Reserved

Except for brief quotations for purposes of review, no part of this publication may be reproduced in any form or by any means, electronic, mechanical, recording or otherwise without express written permission from the author.

This is a work of fiction. Any resemblance to persons living or dead is entirely coincidental.

ISBN-13: 978-1496154361

Layout and design by Katherine Ballasiotes Rowley
Edited by Heidi M. Thomas
Cover Photo by Susie Drougas
www.SusieDrougas.com

Published in the United States of America

Dusty Rose, an attorney, and Mike Dracopoulos, his sidekick, head to the mountains again. Julie Wolfe, a friend from the Eagleclaw Backcountry Horsemen asks him to represent her in a divorce. Paul, her abusive husband, does not want the divorce and Dusty becomes the new focus of his anger.

Going on a Backcountry Horsemen work party up to Buck Creek, Dusty hopes to clear his mind from the stresses of his law practice. He's still never gotten over the beautiful attorney he crossed trails with in the Pasayten, Cassie Martin. Then in she rides—with a dark haired stranger, Roy. Dusty realizes he needs to do more than just think about her or he's going to lose his chance.

"Dusty bent his head down to kiss her. Cassie raised her head to meet his lips and the feeling washed over her that they had known each other for a very, very long time. The electricity and heat poured between them and Dusty pulled her closer. Cassie never wanted it to stop."

Feeling overstressed, Dusty and Mike escape on a pack trip to Cougar Lake to relax. Dusty knows somebody is trying to kill him, but he's not sure who.

"The bullet whizzed in front of him and hit the rock a few feet away. "What in the hell? Gunfire, Mike." He saw Mike drop to the ground and heard some more bullets zing by, he wasn't sure which happened first, but he prayed Mike wasn't hit."

Acknowledgments

Once again, I want to thank my friends for all your help and encouragement on this book.

My Yak Writers group for your critiquing, inspiration and keeping me on course.

April Laine Oostwal, my dear gifted friend in Amsterdam. You never cease to amaze me with your ability in grammar, punctuation and story. Thank you so much for being my "final eyes" on this book.

Katherine Ballasiotes Rowley, once again, your hours of hard work, artistic talent and graphic design brought this book to life. I can only hope to write a book well enough to fill your cover.

Dedication

I am dedicating this book to two adventurous women, both of whom are outstanding examples of a life well lived. This year they are observing their 91st birthdays.

My mother, June Anderson. Living through the depression as a young girl, she met my father at age 18 at a Port Angeles USO. My mother served in World War II as a WAVE. This came in handy, as she spent over 50 years sailing the Puget Sound and beyond with my father. My mother is an inspiration to me. She has the ability to always see the positive side in life and people. To this day she is so busy with friends and activities that she is rarely home. Thank you for your support and unwavering belief in me as a writer and a daughter.

My aunt, Vicky Due. Aunt Vicky has a life filled with adventures—gold mining in Alaska, camping and fishing with her best friend and husband, Dave Due. After many years of high adventure, they settled on the K-D Ranch, 180 acres nestled near Mount St. Helens, where she was finally reunited with horses. She is a kindred spirit in the appreciation of the *smell* of horses. It is my pleasure to put you in the saddle again for another ride with Dusty Rose.

MOUNTAIN COWBOYS

Prologue

The early-morning sun was bright and the sky a sharp blue. Dusty wondered why he was heading into town on a day like this one—instead of back into the mountains. He parked his truck on the main street of Eagleclaw, grabbed his briefcase and slammed the door shut. As he approached his office, shouting on the other side of the street caught his attention.

A silver Land Rover was pulled over and a petite woman stood next to it on the passenger's side. "I told you before, it's my fucking business! Who I hire is up to me!" The man, wearing a suit and tie, appeared to be somewhere in his forties. He wasn't particularly tall, but he towered over the diminutive woman.

The woman visibly flinched as he raised his voice and stepped closer to her, pointing at his chest. The man was using his size, as well as his volume, to bully her.

The woman looked familiar. Dusty's hand clenched his briefcase. It was Julie Wolfe from the Eagleclaw Trailriders. He felt his stomach tighten and heat flashed up his back. He could not stand seeing women treated like that by men. It was cowardly and pathetic. He fought with himself over whether he should get involved and stood a few feet from his office door watching the scene. He turned to walk across the street, then hesitated and stopped.

The man slammed his hand on the car next to where Julie

cowered. She screamed and covered her face. An ugly voice snarled, "I'll deal with you when I get home."

Hearing the scream, Dusty dropped his briefcase and started towards them. Almost simultaneously, the woman darted around the car, jumped into the driver's seat and drove off. As Dusty stopped in the middle of the street, the man in the suit sneered at him, "Mind your own damn business," he growled. And stalked off.

As he stared after the man, Dusty had to hold himself back. There were such things as assault and battery, he reminded himself. But boy, this would have been the perfect guy to blow the charges on. His own adrenalin was pumping and he willed himself to calm down.

Watching the Land Rover drive away, Dusty saw a child seat in the back with little arms flailing. His heart sank. He picked up his briefcase and walked into his office.

Chapter One

Dusty sat at his desk reading over the file for the third time. He just wasn't concentrating. Since he didn't have any meetings or court today, he was wearing jeans, a faded blue western-cut work shirt and his packer boots. He'd just gotten back from a pack trip into the Pasayten Wilderness two weeks ago, and he felt like he was ready to leave again. The trip hadn't been as restful as he had hoped. A couple of criminals had crossed the border and attacked a family. He and Mike had ended up rescuing the kids. And if Cassie hadn't shown up just when she had, he shuddered, not even wanting to think about what might have happened. His thoughts were interrupted when the bell jingled as the front door to his office opened.

"Good morning, Mike. You're in luck today. Mr. Dustin Rose is in his office." The older woman receptionist gave her familiar greeting, as always, using his full name. Mrs. Phillips had worked for Dusty's father, so when Dusty came along, she had to distinguish between the two of them. She had tried "Junior," but Dusty had quickly put his foot down on that, so he had become *Mr. Dustin Rose* from that point forward.

"Thank you, Mrs. Phillips." In a few moments, Dusty's investigator knocked on his door and stepped in.

"Come on in." Relieved for the break, Dusty looked up and smiled.

Mike smiled back. "Hey, Dusty." He passed the desk and sat at his usual chair by the window. He had on a ball cap, navy Carhartt vest, blue-and-black plaid shirt, jeans and packer boots. Mike leaned back, picked up an *Outfitters Supply* catalog and began thumbing through it.

"So, to what do I owe the pleasure of this visit, or are you just interested in shopping for horse tack?"

"They do have great mountain gear in this catalog. I like *Trailhead Supply* too. I was actually here for a different reason—I was wondering if you had heard anything from the Ross family," Mike asked, referring to the terrifying experience of their Pasayten pack trip two weeks ago.

"As a matter of fact, I have." Dusty handed Mike an envelope that contained a card. Mike opened it and read a young girl's perfect scribe. The letter thanked Dusty and Mike for all they had done in the rescue of the Rosses. Mike's eyes appeared misty as he read. Sally wanted Dusty to know that she planned to see if she could get a job with Bob and his outfit when she was eighteen. She and her brother Scott had recovered completely. They missed their dad, but knowing he was in one of his most favorite places made his absence easier.

"Well, that's sweet. You think she'll hold that thought for three more years?" Mike rubbed the corner of his eye.

"I don't know, but Bob would sure love to have her work for him. Getting younger people interested in horses and packing has really gotten to be a challenge these days. She would be a great asset to the outfit," Dusty said earnestly, as he collected the papers he was reading into a pile on his desk.

"I'm glad they're doing okay. They were really nice kids," Mike said earnestly.

"Yeah, they were. And tough too!" Dusty put the papers in a file and tucked it into the drawer of his desk.

"What about Cassie? Hear anything from her?" Mike was referring to the beautiful attorney they had run into on the high mountain trails, and in the courtroom of Seattle.

Dusty sighed, "As a matter of fact, I got a notice for her motion for reconsideration. It's going to be a week from Friday at three o'clock."

"Is that it?" asked Mike, raising his eyebrows.

"That's it," Dusty said dejectedly.

"Well, I guess it's another day, another dollar."

Dusty had placed a call to Cassie when they got home from their week in the Pasayten Wilderness. The only response he'd gotten was in the mail. He hadn't realized how much he'd wanted to talk to her—until he never got a call back.

"I did actually have another reason for stopping by today."

"Enlighten me, please."

"Are you planning on going on the work party this weekend?"

"I haven't even been paying attention. Where is this one?"

Mike leaned forward, warming to the topic. "They've got a bridge out up at Buck Creek. I was thinking about going up, spending the weekend. Maybe we could hit the Naches Tavern on the way down and get one of their really great hamburgers."

"Sounds good to me. Who's heading that one up? Val?"

"Yup."

"Boy, that guy does keep busy, doesn't he?" Dusty pushed back from his desk.

Mike set the catalog down. "Well, you know, he's retired. Not like us hard-working guys."

"Yeah," agreed Dusty.

"Speaking of working hard, you want to head over to Maude's place and grab some lunch?" Mike stood up.

"I thought you'd never ask." Dusty walked around his desk, grabbed his hat and slipped into his brown corduroy suit coat.

The gray-haired, heavy-set receptionist smiled, "Have a good lunch, Mr. Dustin Rose. Mike."

"Thank you, Mrs. Phillips. You enjoy yours too," said Dusty. Mike smiled as he followed Dusty out the door.

Since it was still a few minutes before noon, the café hadn't started filling up yet. Dusty and Mike walked to the back and took their usual places at the lunch counter.

Maude bustled up, swishing her pink waitress uniform, a pencil in her dyed-red hair. "What will you boys have? The usual?"

"Let's see," said Dusty. "What day is it?"

"Wednesday," said Maude.

"Okay. I'll have the usual then."

"You're so hard to please, Dusty." Maude laughed and rolled her eyes.

"Make that the same for me too," said Mike. "I don't want to be any harder to please than Dusty is."

"My pleasure." Maude smiled and hurried off to the window to put up their orders.

Dusty and Mike were talking about their last pack trip and were just getting to the upcoming weekend when their food came.

"Here is your hump day chili." Maude set two steaming bowls of chili with a homemade side of cornbread on the table in front of them.

"Smells great," Dusty said, inhaling the spicy aroma.

They had just started to dig in when a soft feminine voice spoke next to Dusty's ear. "Mind if I sit down?"

As Dusty looked up, the smile froze on his face. "Well, of course, Shelley. Have a seat. What brings you here?"

A woman in her early forties stood next to him. She was about 5'3" with silverish-blonde hair with a black stripe down the middle, wore plenty of mascara and blue eye shadow. A large silver buckle adorned the front of her too-tight jeans. Her T-shirt was tucked into her jeans, and she carried at least 20 extra pounds around her middle. Her low-cut shirt allowed her more-than-ample bosom to be on full display. Her short, cropped jean jacket with silver accents didn't help hide the extra weight.

Dusty quickly looked back at his food. Shelley plopped down on the seat next to Dusty. Her silver bangles rattled as she placed one freshly-manicured hand on the counter and set her jeweled western purse next to her.

"I had the day off and thought I would take care of a few things in town." She gave him a huge smile.

Mike seemed to be enjoying the whole thing immensely, watching Dusty squirm uncomfortably as he tried to eat his chili.

"So what would you boys recommend?"

"We just got the hump day chili," offered Mike.

"Well, that sounds wonderful. I would love to have some of that!" She eyed Dusty and set her menu down on the counter.

Maude rushed up with a glass of water. "Are you ready to order, honey?"

"Yes, I would like the hump day special." Shelley laughed at her own joke.

"You got it. Anything else?"

"No, that will do for now. Thank you."

"Coming right up." Maude raced back to the order window. The café was quickly filling up.

Shelley cocked an eyebrow. "Are you guys going to the work party this weekend at Buck Creek?"

"As a matter of fact, yes, we are," said Mike.

Dusty seriously thought about giving him a kick, but figured it would probably be obvious if he did.

"Oh, finally, you're going to come to something," said Shelley. She laid her hand on Dusty's arm, her bracelets jangling.

Dusty managed to wolf down his chili and cornbread. He hurriedly wiped his mouth with a napkin. "Great seeing you, Shelley. I've got to get back to the office. You know, pressing business." He threw some bills down on the counter as he turned to go.

Mike had a huge grin on his face.

"Later, Mike."

"'Bye, Dusty. Wish you didn't have to leave." Shelley's chin stuck out as she looked down at her food, her face quickly forming into a pout.

Dusty hurried out of the restaurant. *Geez, there is just really no escape sometimes.* He hoped the work party had a large turnout so he could lose himself in it. And why did Mike always seem to find so much humor in his discomfort? Dusty was so glad to be able to provide him entertainment. He shook his head and walked back into his office.

Chapter Two

Dusty managed to get out of the office in the early afternoon on Friday. He loaded both of his horses, Muley and Cheyenne, in the trailer and threw in his sawbuck packsaddle. This time he was taking his living quarters horse trailer. After having a camper for weekend trips for a number of years and having to load and unload, with swaying trailer jacks and mishaps of bumping into it—not to mention tearing off the jacks on trees—he'd bought a Trails West LQ a few years back and it was the best investment he had ever made. Being a gooseneck, all he had to do was back up and hook onto it. That left his truck free to drive around. Talk about easy! He left it plugged in and ready to go. Whenever he wasn't packing in or day riding, he used it.

This was another perk of being divorced. His ex-wife never understood his love of horses and riding. She had argued about the hay bill and just about everything else—including the time he spent riding. She never would have supported his buying a new living quarters horse trailer, let alone the new pack equipment and all the great trips he had been on since the divorce. Dusty chuckled. Let her have Hawaii or Mexico. There was so much unexplored territory in the USA—he'd do his vacationing here. Washington, with its craggy mountains in the Glacier Peak Wilderness, the arid beauty of Eastern Washington's desert, the Sawtooth Mountains by Lake Chelan. The list went on and on. And that still left to explore the neighboring states of Oregon,

Montana, and even beyond when he hit Arizona in the wintertime.

The afternoon sun hovered low in the sky as he wove his way up Highway 410 to Buck Creek. As the houses became farther apart and the pastures and trees more plentiful, Dusty felt the tension leave his muscles. He passed through the little town of Greenwater; once a bustling logging community, now more or less a stopping point for skiers and hikers accessing Mount Rainer. Highway 410 became Chinook Pass. The majestic presence of the snowcapped mountain surrounded by thick green fir trees made Mount Rainier National Park a memorable experience. Dusty felt exhilarated coming so close to the mountain it looked like you could practically touch it.

The views were awe-inspiring. It definitely was not for drivers who were faint of heart. After several hairpin switchbacks, the road topped the pass and then began a steep territorial view-filled descent into Eastern Washington. Due to the altitudes, the pass was closed in the fall, depending on snowfall, and reopened in the spring. Again depending on snowfall, but usually by Memorial Day weekend. It helped with the mass exodus of vacationers from the rain-soaked West Side to the very low-precipitation, sunny East Side of the Cascade Mountains. Memorial Day weekend, when everyone had their fill of rain and dreary weather, boats, campers, trailers, ORVs and horses came pouring over the mountains.

Dusty slowed and signaled for a right-hand turn into the Buck Creek camping area. As he pulled in he could see five or six rigs already set up. A Forest Service vehicle was there, and a couple of men were talking to a uniformed ranger. He left his engine running and walked up to the group.

"Hey, Val," Dusty greeted the Eagleclaw Back Country Horsemen work party coordinator. Val was a big man, over six feet, wearing a red-and-white plaid western shirt, brown Stetson, boots and jeans. He stood with a couple other men in cowboy hats talking to the forest ranger.

Val left the group, walked over to Dusty, stuck out a big paw and the men shook hands. "Hey, Dusty. Glad you could make it up.

I heard you might. You came just in time. We have gravel up there we can access, but we need to get about twelve planks packed in. Would you be up for a trip this afternoon?"

"Sure, I can do that. How far is it?"

"It's actually only a couple of miles. So about a four-mile round trip. Eddie just showed up with his mules. I've got Sunny, and he's got Johnny Walker, so with your packhorse Cheyenne, we can get it done."

"Sounds good. I'll just pull in and get ready to go."

"Great. We'll get this wrapped up and then hit the trail." Val turned back to the group.

Dusty drove over to the treed camping area, backed in and unloaded his horses. Scout didn't get to make this trip, much to his disappointment. Dogs were not allowed on work parties with the Eagleclaw Trail Riders and most chapters of the Backcountry Horsemen. The distractions by the dogs increased the risk of accident and injury to people as well as the animals.

Dusty tied his horses to trees while he threw up his highline. With any other horse he would tie him to his trailer, but Muley already put some dents in his rig by striking it with his hooves, so Dusty hoped to preserve what he had left. In no time at all, Muley and Cheyenne were saddled and Dusty tied on his rain slicker as Val and Eddie rode up with their packhorses in tow.

Dusty swung easily into the saddle. "Go ahead and lead out, Val."

"I'll take the rear," said Eddie.

Dusty, Muley and Cheyenne took the middle as they rode over to where the planks had been placed.

"I brought the duct tape," said Dusty.

The men taped the ends of the planks together. The Forest Service trail crew had cut the planks to four-foot lengths for this project with a chain saw. They were milled planks, thick for the bridges. By taping the ends together, the men could load two planks to a side on their animals, for a total of 140 pounds. An old rule of thumb for packing horses was they carry no more than twenty percent of their weight. This included the weight of their own packsaddles. So 140 pounds plus the saddle was under the allotted weight, but with the bulkiness of the boards, it was better to be too light than too heavy.

Horses were versatile when it came to packing in stuff for work parties. A favorite was to hitch a couple of garbage cans on and then put different implements in them for cutting, chopping or digging, or just loading up with debris, if need be. One of Dusty's favorite work party packing stories was loading up Whiteman, an old packhorse of his, with a garbage can on one side and a gas-powered weedeater on the other side. This was a work party to work on trail tread outside of the wilderness. Whitey took it all just fine and made his way to the portion of trail that needed work. For whatever reason, at exactly the point that Dusty was going to stop, Whiteman noticed the weedeater on his back. In the attitude of *better late than never*, the horse quickly unloaded his pack with tools flying everywhere and the weedeater sailing through the air. Nothing was damaged because it fell in the soft grass, and everything was ready to go for the work party. Dusty chuckled, remembering. A person could never forget that just because horses allowed you to put things on their backs once, they could still change their mind at any point.

The men finished tying the last of the planks on Eddie's mules, and they were ready to go. Val had gaited horses, so he rode in front and set a good pace. Dusty followed. He shook his head as he watched his horse. Muley didn't know he wasn't gaited, so he was pretty happy to keep up, and Cheyenne was going wherever Muley went. Eddie's mules in the back did what mules did best; whatever they wanted. As near as Dusty could tell, a good mule rider was someone who was able to convince his mules to do what the rider wanted them to do. In Eddie's case, his mules usually did—the key word being *usually*. It seemed to work well for them. And off they went down the trail.

The sun was setting in the afternoon sky; they would probably be back just before dark. Time didn't matter up in the mountains.

Dusty's shoulders relaxed, as they always did. The tension slid off his back. The tangy smell of thick, green fir trees combined with the aroma of fresh dirt and leaves on the trail. The birds were chirping and it was nearing the end of a beautiful late-summer day. None of the men talked. They didn't need to—they were all exactly where they wanted to be. Streams were plentiful, even though it had been an unusually dry summer for the West Side. Val stopped and let his animals drink at the first creek. They were careful to do it one at a time. Getting in a wreck with planks and horses or mules would be a painful experience everyone would rather avoid.

After about forty-five minutes, the group came up to the bridge site. Not far from the creek were two large trees that had been precut and limbed by the Forest Service. These would be stripped and used for stringers on the bridge. Stringers were the long logs that were seated in the dirt to which the planks were eventually spiked. It didn't take long for the work party to unload and they piled the planks on top of a pile already there.

The men remounted and headed back. Buck Creek was close to the base of Mt. Rainier, but the mountain usually was not visible because of the dense growth of fir trees. The closest town of Greenwater had an elevation of 1,699 feet, so it was accessible later and earlier than the high mountain country.

"So, Val, how many people do you expect to have up here for the work party?" Dusty asked.

"I'm not really sure. We announced it at the meeting, and I called a few people, but it kind of came up last minute. I think a lot of people are holding out for the steak feed next weekend. Hopefully we'll get some of the hard-cores up here."

"Mike is coming up tonight."

"That's great. We can sure use him. We'll have a potluck tomorrow night with Dutch-oven cooking." Val pushed a branch out of the way as he rode.

"That sounds really good," said Dusty. "I do get tired of my own cooking."

"Just you and Marie Callender in the kitchen, right?" said Eddie.

"Hey, you're giving away my trade secrets." Dusty gave him a look of mock concern.

Val's booming laugh bounced off the trees. "I think he's giving away all our trade secrets." Val's wife had passed away a few years back, and after more than twenty years of marriage, he found himself back in the dating pool. "I've got to say, Marie's been in my kitchen too."

"Well, she's staying out of mine. I don't think my wife would like it!" Eddie chimed in.

Laughing, they headed down the trail in the fading light.

Chapter Three

Dusty noticed several more rigs had pulled in since they left. Horses were highlined out in the trees and they had their heads in their hay bags munching away. A highline is a long rope with seat-belt-material straps which encompass the trees on either end. The ropes can be pulled tight high in the air, as tall as a man can reach, and the straps protect the trees from burning and chafing. The horses are tied to the highlines by their lead ropes, and it gives the animals a lot more room to move than just being tied up. Feed bags are hooked onto the highlines.

Dusty put up his highlines to keep his horses away from the trees. He filled his hay bags and clipped them onto the highlines. The horses plunged their heads into the bags. The idea was to keep the hay off the ground. The feeders were made of a porous material, such as scrim, so the horses can breathe as they eat. The system works, for the most part, but horses are grazers and they tend to root around, pushing and grabbing hay out of their bags, so a good amount still fell on the ground. Dusty always brought a small wheelbarrow and pitchfork to pick up the soiled hay and manure so he could later disperse it for quick ecological breakdown. In some camps dumpsters and portable wheelbarrows are provided to transport the excess hay and manure for disposal. Those campgrounds are a pay-per-night to help cover the costs of waste transport. Buck Creek was not that kind of camping area and only required a U.S. Forest Service trailhead pass.

A campfire was roaring and several people were seated around it in the twilight. Dusty recognized a few of the rigs. Mike's blue, older-model Ford was parked by Dusty's truck and his wall tent was up. The horsemen used a lot of different modalities for camping. From tents, campers, sleeping in their horse trailers or truck beds on cots, RVs pulling a trailer behind, to a living quarters RV. It really depended where they were in their hobby and financial means to pursue it. Dusty had learned over the years that the horses and the mountains were what made him who he was— so he invested completely. He felt fortunate to be able to afford the living quarters and the diesel fuel to go to the places he dreamed of going. Dusty stripped off the saddles, took his horses over and tied them to the highline. They nickered to him as he walked away.

"All right. All right. Hang on, boys. I'm almost there," he said good-naturedly.

Muley and Cheyenne wanted to make sure he didn't forget to feed them. Horses had different pitches in their speech. Panic was an alarmed shrill neigh. A low-pitched neigh to a friend—new or old—leaving them. And the endearing low-throated little nicker, which said, *Hey, buddy, don't forget about us!*

Dusty still chuckled when he remembered the one exception to the rule of horse voices; poor old Diamond, a horse Dusty had many years ago. If there were a horse choir, Diamond would have been asked to leave. His neigh sounded like an old tire that was running out of air. It was several octaves lower than the other horses and completely out of tune. When Diamond was left behind and calling to the other horses, you couldn't help but feel for him. The poor excuse for a neigh made him particularly soulful as he looked forlornly at his departing friends.

Dusty loaded up the hay bags and clipped them to the highline. Muley was first. He laid back his ears and tried to look as ferocious as possible. Dusty ignored him, calmly walked by and clipped on his bag. Cheyenne waited patiently to one side while Muley put on his show and then eagerly jammed his head in the feed bag as soon as it was close enough.

"Hey, Boss." Mike came up to Dusty as he stood watching his horses eat.

"Hey. When did you get here?"

"Well, I like how I tell you about the work party and then you beat me to it." Mike pushed his hat back on his head.

"Yeah? I liked that part too." Dusty smiled and dusted off his gloves. "What was the holdup?"

"Well, I have this crazy thing called a job."

"Really." Dusty feigned interest.

Mike shook his head. "I was trying to get a photo of Paul Wolfe leaving his girlfriend's house. I sat out there all day! These women who want photographic proof of their husbands' infidelities. It really gets old. But it does put diesel in the truck."

"I hear you on that one. Divorces make up way too much of the law practice these days; a byproduct of the times, I guess."

"So how did the work party go so far?" asked Mike.

"Val, Eddie and I got the planks moved up there. Looks pretty good. They have the gravel and stringers all laid out," Dusty said. "How many people are here?"

"There are about fifteen so far. Not a bad turnout for short notice."

"No, that's pretty good."

"Oh, yeah," added Mike, "Shelley is here. You left kind of quick the other day at Maude's place."

Dusty sighed. "Oh, great."

"Yeah, I tried to pick up the pieces. She really has a thing for you. You may have to have a little talk with her."

"If it comes to that, I will. I guess I was really hoping it wouldn't."

"Yup. Well, you know, when you're such a good-looking guy and all, it's bound to have repercussions." Mike laughed.

"Oh, puh-leez! You got any coffee going?"

"As a matter of fact, I do."

"I'll get my cup." Dusty went to his rig to grab his coffee cup, and Mike went in his tent to get the coffee simmering on his camp stove.

Chapter Four

Dusty held his steaming cup of coffee in one hand, carried a lawn chair in the other and followed Mike over to the campfire. Val was already there and his girlfriend Mary had arrived. People were sitting around the fire. Eddie was in the middle of a story about his pack trip up in the Pasayten with Val and another buddy.

"I woke up in the morning and I couldn't find my hat. I walked out of my tent and there it was, half eaten on my chair. After that we just called the place *Half a Hat Valley*. A big laugh resounded around the campfire.

"There's a lot to be said about having a dog in camp," said Dusty.

"Yeah, if I would have had one up there, well, I would have probably still had a hat. No mules anymore, but a hat for sure." Everyone laughed again.

"That's okay, Eddie. A loose dog in camp is a cougar attractor, anyway," said Mike.

"Always something, isn't it?" said one of the women.

Lloyd and his brother Frank were really good workers; it was nice to see them there. They did cement contracting for a living. Digging and setting logs in dirt was going to be a breeze for them. Some of the retired guys were there—Russell and Bob would probably beat them all up in the morning, as usual.

Dusty noticed Shelley for the first time. She seemed rather subdued and just smiled at him sadly from her seat by the fire. She was holding a drink, and that made him a little nervous. The other girls, besides Mary, were married, but their husbands didn't ride horses. The Back Country Horsemen chapters always had a high percentage of women who came alone or sometimes together, determined to pursue a sport their husbands weren't interested in. As independent women, they were very capable hands with their horses and had strong backs for hauling. Robin and her best friend Sheila always turned out for work parties.

A few more people that Dusty didn't know showed up, but it looked like they had a good group for the job. The campfire lasted until around ten. Stories from the past and present were told with lots of laughing. Dusty enjoyed this group socially because they didn't have a lot of serious drinkers in it. He didn't mind, but when people really wanted to imbibe, he stayed away from it. He had spent too many wasted nights and days drinking; he didn't want to spend any more time watching other people do it.

Mike didn't drink, either. It had nothing to do with Dusty; he had quit before he met him. Mike was one of those people that everybody had told Dusty didn't exist—the people that just quit. Mike said after blacking out one night he had to call a friend to find out what he did and how he had acted. He had absolutely no memory of the night before. When the friend told him he was just like he always was, that was it for him. If Mike was anywhere near his next drink, he sure didn't seem like it; it had been about twenty-five years since his last one.

The fire was burning low and people were starting to yawn. Val stood up. "The ranger, Danny Conger, and some Forest Service trail crew workers will be here at eight-thirty for a safety meeting. If everyone could be saddled up, we'll ride out right after that. We are going to have to pack in tools. We've got shovels, rakes, pulaskis, axes, saws and hoes. The planks are already up there and the gravel has been hauled in. Make sure and wear your chinks, work boots, gloves, eye protection, if you need it. Bring your lunch." Val was all business.

"Am I too late for the campfire?" A petite woman with long

auburn hair came hurrying in, carrying a camp chair and a bottle of pop.

"Well, no, Terri, the campfire is still here," answered Val.

"Well, thank goodness. I was on a deposition and it just didn't stop. I didn't think I was ever going to get out of there."

Dusty perked his ears. This was Cassie's sidekick from the Pasayten. Funny, he'd never picked up that she had a career in the legal field. Maybe she didn't. Maybe it was her deposition? He couldn't stop himself from asking. "What were you doing at the deposition?" He knew it was none of his business, but out it came, anyway.

"Oh, I'm a court reporter."

"Fun job," he said.

"Yeah, I like it. I guess you would know how fun it is." Terri laughed.

"Is that how you and Cassie met each other?"

"No, we met at an Eagleclaw meeting. It's funny because we both work in the same field. Maybe that's why we get along so well."

"Is she coming up to the work party this weekend?" Why did he just ask that? "It's good to get all the help we can for this bridge, right?" He looked to Mike and Val for support.

"Yes, Boss." Mike nodded and smiled.

"Oh, absolutely. We're going to have some help from the Forest Service trail crew on Saturday, but we've still got to move those logs and they're pretty heavy," said Val.

The edges of Terri's mouth turned up. "She said she was going to try."

"Well, I think I'm going to turn in." Dusty folded his chair, grabbed his empty coffee cup and headed toward his rig. He felt heat creeping up under his collar and figured the best thing to do was leave.

"Right behind you." Mike folded his chair and dropped in beside Dusty as they walked away from the fire.

The surrounding hills blocked out a lot of the night sky. A

three-quarter moon hung over them. The stars were visible, twinkling above the treetops. The fir trees were thick and dark.

Dusty put his lawn chair under the truck to stave off morning dew. He grabbed a bucket and watered his horses. They didn't usually drink much on the first night of a ride, but the weed-free hay was pretty dry. Dusty had to buy the compressed bales—which he hated. Muley stuck his large head in the five-gallon bucket and it just fit. When he was done drinking, it was mostly gone, so Dusty went back to his fifty-five gallon barrel on the back of his pickup and refilled it for Cheyenne. The simple tasks of caring for his horses and breathing in the mountain air made Dusty feel so grounded.

He thought back to his conversation with Terri at the campfire. He liked Cassie, but he wasn't about to admit it to anyone. What to do about it was another thing, and he was at a complete loss. Maybe he'd ask her if she'd like to go riding. He'd have to think about it. *Why do women always make things so difficult?* He turned back to his horses.

Setting his buckets down by his truck, he saw the campfire area was emptying out. Only a couple of silhouettes remained seated by the fire. Burning red coals glowed in the distance. Dusty looked up at the night sky. It was clear, and the bright stars looked like it was going to be another good day tomorrow. He filled his lungs with cool evening air and exhaled. His back felt light and his arms were loose at his sides. He opened the door to his living quarters and went inside for the night.

Chapter Five

Dusty woke early to his alarm. He needed to give his horses at least an hour and a half to eat before he saddled them, so he'd set it for 6 a.m. As always, first things first. He lit his stove and started his coffee pot. He quickly washed his face and brushed his teeth. Taking a quick look in the mirror when he brushed his hair, he saw he'd already acquired a 5 o'clock shadow from the day before. He gave the mirror a white toothy smile, put on his hat and turned to go out the door. It was so nice that the unshaven look was back in vogue. *Sure makes life easier.* He put on a fleece-lined jean jacket, slipped on his Romeos and headed out the door.

The minute he came outside, Muley and Cheyenne greeted him with deep neighs as if to say, *Hey, what's taking so long? We've been standing here waiting for you.*

Dusty smiled as he peeled off four flakes of hay and headed over to the feed bags still hanging on the highline. He put two flakes in each bag. The horses just about knocked him over in their excitement to eat. It was like this every morning. The time to be concerned was if they didn't want to eat. That was a sign of colic or some other ailment that would need immediate attention. Dusty's horses were, as a rule, healthy, and he didn't have problems with them tying up and becoming sick.

He returned to his LQ and the perking coffee. Filling his big coffee cup, he went back outside. A small group had already gathered at the morning fire. Dusty grabbed his chair and headed down there.

"Good morning," they all greeted as he sat down. Mike was already there and, sure enough, the old-timers, Eddie, Russell and Bob, were also seated at the fire.

The sun peeked over the tops of the fir trees. The crisp early-morning mountain air mixed with the smell of campfire smoke smelled like home to Dusty. The only thing to top it off was the cup of coffee in his hand and his friends around the fire.

"Hey, we were just talking about you," said Bob. "Sounds like you had quite the adventure in the Pasayten a couple weeks ago."

"Yeah, I guess you could say that." Dusty took a drink.

"Terri filled us in last night after you went to bed. It was her first pack trip."

"Yeah, I guess it was."

"Glad to hear that it mostly worked out okay," said Bob.

"Yes, those were some tough kids, that's for sure," agreed Dusty.

"All the years I've been going up there and the most excitement I got was a half-chewed hat." Eddie feigned a mournful look.

"Oh, get off your pity pot. You almost got burnt up by lightning too. That was a good one!" Bob slapped Eddie on the back. Everyone laughed just as Val walked up.

"Hey, what's so funny?"

"Oh, poor Eddie didn't think he had as good a story as Dusty about the Pasayten, and I reminded him about that lightning you guys got into that time," said Bob.

"Oh, yeah. I was there for that one." Val set a coffee pot next to the fire. "Fill up your cups. I've got plenty here."

More people arrived around the fire, having fed their horses. The circle was getting larger.

"Refresh me on the lightning story. That seems like it happens a lot up there. Did someone get hit?" asked Dusty.

"Well, not exactly," Eddie said, "but close."

"Oh, yeah," boomed Val. "My first pack trip into the Pasayten. We were camped over at Spanish Camp and decided to try our luck fishing over at Tungsten Lake, just below the old mine over there."

He took a drink of coffee. "Me, Eddie and Matt. We had a good time fishing and caught quite a few. The sky had been kind of dark that day, but we hadn't paid much attention to it. As we packed up and mounted our horses, a light rain began to fall. No big deal. Rain happens. We put on our slickers and headed out. After just about a mile or so, the thunder and lightning began. Our horses and Eddie's mule didn't like it, but they kept going. Everything was fine right up until it struck a tree about fifty yards away. Darned, if the thing didn't burst into flames right in front of us."

"It burnt it clear to the roots, just like a big fire cracker," added Eddie.

They had the group's attention now.

"So what happened?" Terri stepped up to the fire ring with her lawn chair and coffee. "What did your horses do?"

"Well, I always wondered what they'd do," said Val. "Mine just planted and stood still. We all had our jaws dropped open staring at the bonfire in front of us. Not Eddie's mule, though; he took off bucking. I don't blame him."

"He bucked like a son of a gun," agreed Eddie. "I think I got a free spinal adjustment on that trip."

Everyone laughed. For some strange reason, Dusty mused, horsemen got a big kick out of horses bucking, kicking, going wild, as long as nobody got hurt. And indeed, the idea of poor old Eddie being bucked into the distance on his beloved mule would have been a comical sight.

"So then what happened?" prompted Terri, eager to hear the next part.

"Well, there wasn't much else," said Val. "We just rode back to camp and cleaned our fish."

"Nothing else happened?"

"No, but we did look up a lot when the lightning was striking. And we did count the seconds to make sure that we were ready if it was going to strike near us again."

"Well, how do you be ready?" Terri asked, who appeared to be gathering information for future reference in the mountains.

Val said, frowning with his eyebrows closely knit, "You hang on!" He let out a loud laugh and the rest of the group joined in. "I better get my horses saddled. See you guys at eight-thirty for the safety meeting in the meadow." Val tossed out the rest of his coffee and headed back to his trailer.

Dusty stood and folded his chair. Everybody else followed suit, and the fire ring emptied out quickly.

Chapter Six

Dusty checked his packsaddle one more time. He had brought his sawbuck; the crossbucks made it a lot easier to pack the planks on than his decker. He figured he'd help with the tools. He untied Muley and swung into the saddle, pulling Cheyenne's rope behind him. As he rode into the meadow, other horsemen were already there. The ranger, Danny Conger, stayed to do the safety meeting, and the rest of the Forest Service trail crew of about five people left hiking to the work site.

The safety meetings were pretty boring and repetitive, but a necessary evil. With new requirements in insurance and procedures, the Back Country Horsemen had to comply. The information was good for new volunteers—eye protection with the power tools, chinks for leg protection, heavy boots, work gloves, making sure you checked your space before swinging a tool or running a chainsaw. The meeting lasted for about a half hour and they went over the plan they would follow to build the puncheon bridge.

When all the questions were answered, Danny finished it with, "Okay, see you all up there then." He pulled his pack on his back and hiked out, leaving the horsemen to follow.

"Those of you with packhorses meet me over at the tools and we'll get loaded up. I only need about five," said Val.

Val had divided the tools into approximate weights for each side of a packhorse and set them in piles by his pickup. Dusty and

Mike rode up and tied their saddle horses nearby. Looping the packhorse lead rope off the saddle horn, they walked over to check out the loads.

Dusty picked up tools in a large rubber garbage can. He took it over to his horse, emptied out the can and began to form a basket hitch to cradle it to one side of Cheyenne. He then picked up another bunch of pre-weighed tools and placed them in his 7 x 9 canvas mantie he laid out on the ground. In no time he had them rolled and tied. Even though the loads were very different, an experienced packer like Dusty had no trouble tying a garbage can on one side of his horse and a pack on the other—the key being equal weight and position.

Usually the open cans were used on trail work so the different implements were readily accessible when needed. Today they had spikes and mallets and other small but heavy articles that were easy to place in the rubber cans. The one cautionary measure when loading a horse with loose material; you better have a well-broke, unexcitable packhorse. Loose tools clanged and banged and horses had a tendency not to appreciate all that noise on their backs. Once they didn't like something, the next step was to get rid of it. Cheyenne had been there and done that, so it was no big deal to him.

Mike had a different scenario in front of him. It was the dreaded griphoist. "Man, I hate packing this thing."

"I hear you," agreed Dusty.

The griphoist easily weighed 70 pounds. The weight was daunting, but the job it could do was amazing. The ability of the hoist to move thousands of pounds by just turning a crank was a real asset in the wilderness, where only non-motorized tools were allowed. And *non-motorized*, by definition, included a wheel of any kind in the wilderess.

Mike got underneath the hoist and loaded it into a reinforced canvas pannier on one side of his packhorse. Duke leaned heavily, trying to rebalance himself under the load.

"Hang on a second, Duke. I'll get the other side." Mike quickly grabbed a loaded mantie with tools of equal weight rolled into it and tied it on the off side of his packhorse. Having gained equilibrium once again, Duke stood balanced with all four feet planted on the ground.

"Hey, you guys, what can I bring?" Terri rode up, pulling her white Pony of the Americas packhorse. Since Terri wasn't very tall, this worked out really well. The POA packhorse was either a really small horse or a very large pony. This made it easy for Terri to pack her load without having to stand on anything.

"Well, we do have one more thing we need taken in." Dusty eyed the white horse speculatively.

"Bring it on. Moose here can handle anything," Terri said, looking at her horse fondly and stroking him on the neck.

"Okay." Dusty turned and picked up the six-foot culvert lying in the dirt. "We'll just load this up."

"What the heck is that?" asked Terri. Her mouth dropped open and her eyes widened in surprise.

"That is a culvert," said Mike. "We need to bury it underneath the bridge to allow for runoff."

"Okay," said Terri hesitatingly. "Let's load him up!"

She tied her Paint horse to a tree and led over her packhorse. While she held the lead rope, Dusty and Mike loaded the culvert. It wasn't heavy, but it did take up space from in front of the crossbucks of her packsaddle to square in the middle of her horse's butt. Mike held the long pipe steady while Dusty arranged a network of knots to secure it.

"There. That ought to do it." He stepped back. "Why don't you walk him out for a little test run and see how it goes."

Terri looked tentatively at her horse. Moose stood patiently. If having a six-foot pipe on his back was bothering him, it sure didn't show.

"Come on, boy." She clucked to him and set out walking, not daring to look back. As the horse walked, the pipe would slap him on the butt every few steps. At first Moose perked up his ears, but since it didn't hurt, it apparently didn't seem like a big deal and he let it go. He walked quietly behind Terri.

"I think you got it, Dusty," said Mike.

"Wow, is there anything you can't pack?" asked Terri. Her eyes bright.

"Well, there has been a few things," said Dusty, pushing down on his hat.

"Yeah, those bathtubs and pool tables have been a real challenge to him," joked Mike.

Dusty slapped him on the back. "I'm sure with your help I could still get it done. Let's hit the trail."

Chapter Seven

"We're going to head out in groups of twelve heartbeats," said Val. "So you guys need to split up." The twelve heartbeats was a rule that had been imposed sometime back by the Forest Service. The Back Country Horsemen complied with it, but it greatly limited their sport. Twelve heartbeats meant that each horse and rider was two heartbeats, so you could only have six riders. If you were each pulling a packhorse, then you were limited to four riders—or any combinations that equaled only twelve.

It was one more unfair discrimination against horsemen that chafed Dusty. The Forest Service could give a special permit for more stock use when the BCHW was doing trail work. If you had a family of four and two packhorses, you had already used up ten of your heartbeats, and it left room for one more rider and no packhorse. There were hefty fines for violating this rule. Basically it meant families were not allowed to pack in together. The regulation didn't seem to have the same effect on the backpackers, however, and more than once Dusty had seen groups of twenty-plus Boy Scouts hiking. On one trip he saw more than fifty boys in a huge encampment, right on the lake at the Sisters. To Dusty, the solution wasn't to stop the Boy Scouts or the backpackers from enjoying the back country, but to stop the overregulation and instead focus on responsibility and equality.

As Dusty was lost in thought, Terri rode up to him, pulling her packhorse. "Would you guys mind if I rode in with you?"

"No problem." Dusty smiled.

"Yeah, Terri. We're Pasayten survivors; we've got to stick together," added Mike.

"I guess we are." Terri laughed. "I wonder what we can stir up on this work party?"

"I don't know. The day is young." Dusty kicked Muley and they headed out of the meadow and down the trail. Mike followed on his bay, Toby, pulling his Appaloosa packhorse, Duke. Terri brought up the rear on her short-brown and white Paint, Sugar, pulling her white packhorse.

The early-morning air was cool and it felt good on Dusty's face as he rode. The rhythm of the horses as their hooves hit the trail and the smell of horse sweat and fresh earth brought him home. He felt like one of Bev Doolittle's paintings. Dusty was just a guy on a horse, but when he went down the trail, he became invisible, back where he belonged. He was so camouflaged by the forest that one would have to really look to see him and his horses. At least that's what happened in his mind, anyway.

Dusty could hear Mike and Terri talking behind him about bridge building. She had an unstoppable enthusiasm and just as many questions. Mike's patient, amused answers brought a smile to his face. When he and Mike rode they usually didn't talk much, but having Terri along brought a new component. Mike seemed to be enjoying himself.

There were several groups of horsemen, and Val had them spaced out so they would not violate the twelve heartbeats. When they got to the worksite they would tie up. They may have more than the allotted heartbeats there, but it was permitted in a work area.

Dusty's group moved along and they arrived in what seemed like no time at all—and it basically was—two miles compared to the usual rides he and Mike took of fifteen to twenty miles. They found a place, tied their horses up and unloaded the packs. Since they were going to be working for a while, they took the bridles off their horses and loosened the cinches on their saddles. Might as well have the horses be comfortable while they waited. Dusty, Mike and Terri carried the tools they had brought over to the bridge site. Danny and the Forest Service crew were just arriving and people were standing around waiting for directions.

They split into different work areas. Some of the women began stripping the bark off the stringer logs. Terri got to work on that right away. The trees were green, so the bark was easy to take off. Using a sharp ax, she worked on it, and once she got a little piece free, she set down the ax and pulled the strip off as far as she could.

Terri finally announced, "Boy, I'm glad we're not trying to build a whole log cabin here. I think at the rate one log is going, it might take me about ten years to finish!" The other women laughed and agreed.

Dusty and Mike were digging out an area to place the stringers. It was a whole lot more difficult than it sounded. There were so many tree and plant roots that Dusty could hardly get a shovelful of dirt without having to grab a pulaski to chop something before he could continue. Several of the men were working on digging, so he had to be really careful not to hit anyone—or get hit himself. That was where the safety zone really came in handy. Dusty tried to look all around him before he swung his tool. Even with that, Lloyd got so enthusiastic chopping one root, he almost whacked Dusty.

"Whoa, there, Lloyd," Dusty cautioned.

"Oh, sorry, Dusty. I didn't see you there."

"No problem. We're all working hard."

Dusty moved a little farther away from where Lloyd was working and took another look around to make sure he hadn't gotten into anyone else's space.

Mike dug a little way down the trail where the Forest Service had indicated was accessible gravel. As Mike filled the five-gallon buckets, Shelley, Mary and the other girls would take two—one on each side for balance—and transport it down to the bridge foundation. It was grueling work and pretty hard on the body.

Riding and caring for horses definitely made for strong backs, and the group was able to transport several buckets, resting only as they waited for the fill.

The morning flew by and in early afternoon Danny finally called out, "How about a lunch break?"

"Thought you'd never ask," said Shelley. Several women echoed agreement. Everyone set their tools aside and went to their saddlebags to pull out their lunches and drinks. Sitting either on the ground or on logs and dirt around the bridge site, they surveyed their work so far.

"Hey, Val, how long do you think this is going to take?" asked Mike.

"We had today and tomorrow slated for it, so hopefully we'll finish up by tomorrow afternoon." Val took a big bite of his sandwich.

"If it's mostly done, the trail crew will be able to finish it off, no problem," said Danny. "We really appreciate your help out here. We couldn't have done it without you."

"It's our pleasure," said Mike.

"Yeah, Danny, we are always interested in helping out," added Dusty.

Shelley walked up as they spoke and plopped down on the ground next to Dusty. "Mind if I join you guys?"

"Not at all, Shelley." Dusty moved his lunch over to make room for her.

Mike smiled and bit into his sandwich.

The humor he always seemed to find at Dusty's discomfort was a conversation Dusty was thinking about having with him—soon! He turned to the woman beside him. "So how is it going down on the gravel-hauling end?"

"We're getting it done. I'm not sure what's going to run out first, though, the gravel or the places to put it. By the time this is over, I am really going to need a back rub." She glanced sideways at Dusty.

"Oh, yeah?" Heat rose up Dusty's neck. He hurriedly took

another bite of his sandwich and washed it down with his water.

Before he could think of anything else to say, a couple of riders came down the trail and stopped short of the bridge. A dark-haired man with a black Stetson, brown jacket, and black boots rode a very large black horse with a white blaze. The rider behind him was difficult to see, but as he stepped aside, the large gray Walker stepped up and the woman who dismounted was unmistakable—Cassie Martin.

Chapter Eight

Cassie dismounted and smiled. She flipped her light-brown hair back over her shoulder and moved her horse away from the man.

"Hey, Cassie." Terri walked up to her. "I wondered if you were going to show up."

"I've been on the way. It's just taken a while," Cassie answered.

"Who's your friend?" asked Terri.

Dusty loved that about Terri. He didn't have to ask anything—all the questions and answers would be forthcoming.

"This is Roy Perry. I met him at the trailhead and he was interested in helping out with some trail work, so I invited him along."

Roy smiled at the group, a big crooked-toothed smile. He wore his black hair slicked back with his big crumb-duster moustache on full display. He was particularly attentive to Cassie.

Watching the way that Roy was looking at Cassie, Dusty could see that he was willing to help her out with a lot more than trail work. The back of his neck tightened.

"Well, I guess we'll just tie up and get our lunches, since it appears to be that time," said Cassie.

Cassie and Roy walked a short distance from the group and found some suitable trees for tying up their horses. As Cassie slipped her bridle off and loosened the cinch, Roy seemed to watch her and followed along with his horse. Getting their food from the saddlebags, they walked side-by-side to the area where everyone was sitting for lunch.

Next to Dusty, Shelley wore a big smile. "Hi, you guys," she happily greeted Cassie and Roy as they sat down. Shelley scooted a little closer to Dusty.

Dusty sat quietly taking it all in. He wanted to move away, but he wasn't quite sure how to do that. His focus remained on Cassie and the dark-haired man. This was a new guy, not anyone he'd seen around before. *Is this the kind of guy she likes?*

Roy sat comfortably on the ground with his dirty wooly angora chaps. His boots were black and didn't look like real leather but in contrast, he had Garcia spurs with very large rowels. He crossed one foot over the other in front of him. His light-weight red and white snapped western shirt fit loosely with his denim vest. And a blue handkerchief hung around his neck.

Dusty glanced at him out of the corner of his eye. *Kind of dimestore cowboy, if you ask me.* They were all just about finished with their lunches, so he stood up and brushed himself off. "Guess I better get back to it."

Shelley said in dismay, "Already?"

He ignored her and walked back to the bridge.

Seeing Dusty get up, several of the other volunteers also stood to head back to the worksite, including Mike and Terri. They all filed back, leaving Cassie and Roy alone to finish their lunch.

Cassie ate her sandwich. Roy seemed like a nice enough guy—he liked horses and that was ten points in his favor. But she didn't know him and that wasn't a major thought to her. The work party was the reason she'd come and that's what she wanted to go do. She finished the last bite of sandwich, stood, and headed back to Prince to put her lunch bags away.

"You leaving me already?" Roy looked up at her.

"Yeah. Sorry about that, but I came up here to work." She smiled and went to her horse.

Roy quietly finished his lunch. He stuffed the remains in the sack and, making sure no one was looking, he tossed it in the bushes behind him. He reached for his cigarettes in his front pocket, then dropped his hand and walked over to the work area. "So what can I do?"

Dusty overheard him and thought about a couple of suggestions, but he figured he should probably keep them to himself.

"You can grab a grub hoe and see about getting some of those roots out of there." Val pointed to the far end of the bridge site. "We are going to be hauling the stringers over in a little while, so we need to get the foundation area set. Thanks a lot for your help."

Cassie had walked over and started helping carry buckets of gravel. She didn't ask what she could do. Cassie just saw what needed to be done and did it.

Dusty snorted. *Calling them work parties seems a contradiction of terms. There's a lot of work and no party.* But he enjoyed it. The work seemed like nothing compared to what he got out of the wilderness. Dusty was happy to put back. Digging in the dirt and carrying logs was second nature to him. He had spent many years working on Uncle Bob's outfit and clearing trails for the dude trips. He looked over at Roy. This wasn't the case for everyone, though.

Roy was bent over, spending a lot of time chopping on a stubborn root. In between all the chopping was a lot of sweating. He appeared to not have experienced a lot of hours in physical labor—of any kind. Roy took a big swing back with his grub hoe and there was a huge roar.

"Hey! Watch what you're doing with that thing! You almost took my head off!" shouted Eddie. He stepped back, feeling the back of his head for any damage. His look was a cross between horrified and disgusted.

Roy seemed unfazed. "Oh, sorry 'bout that, bro," he said insincerely, and turned back to his root.

You meet all kinds up here, that's for sure. Dusty looked over and caught Mike's glance. They both shook their heads.

Cassie, meanwhile, was hauling gravel and had missed the

whole thing. Terri was peeling the stringers. The rest of the volunteers kept working on the roots.

Pretty soon Danny called for everyone's attention. "Okay, we're ready to move the stringers down. We're going to need everyone's help on this. Just make sure you have no back problems and come on over."

They had packed in log carriers, which consisted of long bars with hooks attached. The men set the apparatus on top of the log and they kicked in the hooks that hung down on either side of the log. People assembled in pairs on each carrier. They had about twenty people on a log, the Forest Service trail workers included.

Danny said, "Okay. Now, on the count of three, we're going to pick up the log and move it a couple of feet. Okay. One, two, three!" Everybody picked up the log and moved forward two feet. On the command of "Down!" everybody set the log down. Using this method, they slowly moved the log down the hill and jockeyed it into position on the short logs laid perpendicular to the trail, also known as mud sills.

Moving the stringers that way was slow, arduous work. It really gave Dusty an appreciation for what his forefathers had gone through—the smallest things today were a major task in the old days. Having set one stringer in place, everyone headed up the hill to get the second one.

Roy bent forward and groaned. "Whoa. My back's starting to act up. I think I'll sit this one out."

Dusty gave him a sidelong glance as he and everyone passed by him, including the women. The remaining group picked up a handle on the log carriers and got ready to go again.

"That's just fine, Roy," said Val. "We don't want any broken backs up here." He grabbed a bar opposite Mary and, on the count of three, everyone began the process for the second log. It went faster than the first, the crew having gotten their job down pat. After getting both stringers set on the mud sills, they checked them one more time. Terri set the leveler on top of the log while Mike checked.

"Lookin' good," Mike said.

Terri blushed, and picked up the level.

"The log too." He smiled.

Dusty walked by, carrying a plank. "You dog!" Both men laughed heartily. Terri joined in.

Val brought over the spikes and, with Lloyd's and Bob's help, they started to make the holes to screw in the planks. This was also a difficult process. First they burrowed a hole in the plank with a drill, and then, with a large mallet, they pounded the huge spikes through the planks to hold them to the stringers.

The afternoon had grown late and the crew was tired. Terri, Mary and some of the other women volunteered to head back and start getting ready for the potluck.

"Hey, Cassie, are you coming with us?"

"Yeah, that's probably a good idea. It's going to take me a while to cook." Dusty didn't miss Roy's look of disappointment and he grinned broadly.

Terri chuckled, "Must be tough." She pulled her gloves off and headed to her horse. The other women followed.

Chapter Nine

The sky was just fading to indigo as the last of the work party volunteers straggled in, Val bringing up the rear. Dusty sighed. It had been a long day and it was a quiet ride back to camp. They had gotten a lot done; much more than they had anticipated. The prep work had really helped a lot. It was an all-day job just bringing in the gravel. Hauling gravel and caching it along with several of the planks last fall had made the job go much faster. Dusty was glad they had done it.

"We left the tools there," Val announced, "so we don't have to haul anything in tomorrow morning. Except ourselves," he added as an afterthought.

"And that there might be too much to ask," said Eddie.

The camp broke into an amiable laugh. "That's a fact," agreed Bob, rubbing his back.

Dusty noticed everyone was pretty tired and moved slowly around camp taking care of their horses and getting their dishes ready for the potluck. Seeing Roy's older dirty-white camper and light-green pickup truck pulled in not too far from Cassie's living quarters brought a spark of annoyance to Dusty. She'd parked next to Terri's truck and tent.

The campfire was roaring and tables were set up. Mary called out, "How is everyone doing? Would seven-thirty work out okay for dinner?"

Everyone agreed it would. With the aspiring Dutch-oven cooks in camp, a time to work toward completion was always important. They needed to get their coals just right. Dusty had his potluck dish ready to go—Kentucky Fried Chicken.

"Hey, Boss," Mike walked up, "You got the chicken ready?"

"Wow, how did you guess?"

"Well, you know, I am a private investigator. That, coupled with the fact it's what you always make." He laughed.

"Oh, yeah? And what has the Greek chef prepared this evening?"

Mike smiled sheepishly. "Oh, just a little something that has been passed down through the family for years."

"I can't wait." Dusty picked up his water bucket and carried it over to Muley, who plunged his furry head in and slurped greedily. Cheyenne watched attentively between mouthfuls of hay.

Mike smiled mysteriously and walked back to his tent.

It didn't take Dusty long to grab a bottle of water, bucket of chicken, his lawn chair and head down to the campfire. He handed the chicken off to the women buzzing around the food table and found a place by the fire.

Mary, who headed up the potluck, announced, "It's seven-thirty. If everyone wants to get their plates and start the potluck, let's go ahead."

Nobody wasted any time on getting in line. Roy was right behind Cassie.

Dusty held back and picked a spot at the end of the line. Somehow, miraculously, Shelley showed up right next to him. Mike walked in and set his bag down with the desserts. Moving to the fire area, he set up his chair and went over to the end of the line.

"That was a great work party today, Dusty. I'm so glad you and Mike could make it." Shelley smiled up at Dusty with big eyes and flushed cheeks.

"Yes, we sure got a lot done," agreed Dusty, quickly looking at the ground.

"It's really hard work too. I've never built a bridge before." Shelley continued to look directly at Dusty.

"Yeah, it really gives you a new respect for all those little bridges we see in the wilderness. Making things without the benefit of modern tools is a real eye-opener." Dusty looked over at Mike. At last he found somewhere to rest his eyes.

"It's nice to know that we still have to the ability to do it," said Mike. "With all the advancement of technology, we are still able to use our hands and work hard. Reading in my history books, this is a real small job compared to the pioneers' daily living."

"Yeah. I guess it's something that you just grow up doing, and then it probably doesn't seem like it's such a big deal," Shelley observed.

"I don't know. They didn't seem to live long back then," said Dusty.

As they reached the table, Dusty breathed easier seeing plenty of food left. "One thing about us Back Country Horsemen; we work hard but we always eat well." Several Dutch-oven pots held stew and fresh biscuits, homemade cornbread, salads and desserts. And at the far end of the table, on top of a bag, perched a pile of Oreo cookies.

"Wow, my favorite. Who brought the Oreos?" Dusty glanced at Mike.

Mike smiled and looked down at the ground. "I wonder."

"Well, do you think they might be kind of stale after all that handing down in your family?"

"Perhaps, Dusty, the handing down had to do with the thought, rather than the actual cookies themselves," said Mike evenly.

"That's good," said Dusty. They all laughed.

Everybody filled their plates and sat down by the fire. As more people came, they moved their chairs farther back to accommodate the larger group.

Cassie had pulled up a chair next to Terri and, much to Dusty's satisfaction, he saw that Roy had pulled his chair up by himself and sat on the outskirts of the group. Everyone was talking and laughing about the day's events. It sure wasn't every day they could single-handedly move a whole tree by themselves and they were pretty excited about it. More stories came out about work parties, past and future.

Soon after dinner the crowd began to thin out. The long day of hard work, the chill of the evening air, the warmth of the fire and camaraderie took its toll. People began heading back to their campers, leaving just a few people sitting in lawn chairs. Roy had managed to scoot to one side of Cassie as people turned in. If she noticed, she didn't act like it, Dusty thought. They all sat quietly staring transfixed into the flames.

There was something about the flames and gazing into the reddish-orange light that was hypnotizing. It was hard to look away and at the same time, Dusty thought, it felt so relaxing.

Mike turned to Cassie and Terri. "You girls have any more big pack trips planned?"

"I don't know about big—we kind of used that one up this year. But we're going to go on a couple smaller ones," said Cassie.

"Yeah. The more experience I can get, the better," added Terri. "I'm also thinking I'm going to take some shooting lessons and pick out a gun."

"Never a bad idea," said Dusty.

"Yup. Especially since we saw first-hand the hills are alive, and not just with four-legged animals," agreed Mike.

"You guys had quite the trip," said Mary. "Especially you, Terri, for your first pack trip."

"Yes. They say the first one's always a memorable one. I bet they didn't mean quite as memorable as mine was." Terri took a drink of her water. "You know what, though? I'd go back in a heartbeat. That was the most beautiful country I have ever seen in my life!"

"I've always wanted to go there." Mary looked pointedly at Val.

"Yes. Yes, we need to get in there too," he agreed. "I think we better go on our own pack trip, though. This crew is too wild for us!" Everyone laughed.

"I've always wanted to pack in with my horse. Anyone want to teach me?" Roy held still in expectation. It became quiet. The unspoken etiquette was that people were invited on trips; they didn't invite themselves.

"The different chapters have packing clinics you can attend and from there some of them have beginner pack trips," said Dusty.

"It's a whole different kind of riding than day riding." Mike looked at Roy, his eyebrows drawn.

"Boy, I'll say," said Terri. "There is a lot of work to get your animals ready."

Roy sat quietly. The one person he had hoped would invite him hadn't said anything. He could see this was not going to be easy. He also really didn't like the vibes he got from the big cowboy with the brown hair and the white teeth. Getting along with men wasn't real big on Roy's list, so he didn't pay a lot of attention to it. He was interrupted from his thoughts by Cassie.

"Well, I think I'm going to turn in. It was a long week." Cassie stood and folded her chair.

"Me too," said Terri.

The women walked back to their rigs side-by-side. Terri's voice faded into the dark as they walked away.

Roy didn't wait long and excused himself. Grabbing his chair, he walked back to his rig.

"You're doing a great job on the work party, Val." Dusty leaned toward the fire, warming his hands.

"Well, I really appreciate you and Mike showing up. I couldn't do it without you." Val leaned back in his chair.

"Thanks for heading it up." Mike took a drink from his cup.

"Well, I don't know about that. It kind of more boils down to—no one else wanted to do it," Val said truthfully.

"Still, that says all the more for the person that did." Dusty sat back in his chair.

"Well, thanks, you guys."

Mary beamed. "He always does such a great job."

Val looked embarrassed, and Mike and Dusty smiled.

Shelley, watching Dusty, added, "Mary, you did a great job with the potluck too."

"Thanks, Shelley. Me and everyone."

Dusty stood. "Well, all this thanking everybody has wore me out. Think I'll turn in too. Big day tomorrow, Val?"

"Yeah. I got a feeling we're going to lose half our crew, but we just have finish work to do now."

"Always happens." Mike crossed a booted leg.

"Count on me." Dusty walked off to his rig.

Mike stayed by the fire.

Shelley looked at Mike. "What am I doing wrong?"

"Nothing, Shelley."

"No, with Dusty. Is he just really shy, or something?"

"I don't think so. I haven't noticed."

Val and Mary laughed. "That's probably good, Mike," said Mary.

"No, seriously, Mike. Does Dusty not like me?" persisted Shelley.

"I think he likes you just fine. He's not a real expressive guy." Mike hated to be put into a position of trying to interpret his friend or his actions. He knew Dusty would hate it even more.

"Well, I guess o-dark-thirty comes early. I'm going to hit the hay." Mike hurriedly folded up his chair and headed back to his tent.

"It will be okay, Shelley," said Mary. "You'll get your cowboy yet—I did." She smiled at Val.

Val blushed. "Well, Shelley, you going to close down this campfire? I think I'm tired too."

"No, I'm going to hit the hay." She folded up her camp chair.

Val carefully banked the fire so it would burn out. The three of them walked through the quiet night back to their rigs. The only light was the foggy illumination of the three-quarter moon and a few visible twinkling stars above the darkened treetops.

Chapter Ten

Dusty awoke to low-throated, encouraging nickers filtering from the highline into his LQ, saying, *Feed me*, to the best of their ability. He got up and looked out the window at the gray day. If the sun was going to shine, it didn't look like it.

Putting the coffee on, he dressed quickly. As Dusty walked out the door, he saw his horses were already eating.

"Mike, you feed?" he called over to the tent.

"Yes. You want some coffee?"

"Remind me to never get rid of you, okay?" Dusty got his coffee cup out of the trailer.

"Hey, you went to bed too early last night," said Mike.

"I did?"

"Yeah, you missed out on Shelley wanting to find out your intentions."

"That must have been a short conversation."

"Not one I wanted to have," said Mike.

"I'm thinking I'll just saddle up once they're done eating and avoid the campfire this morning." Dusty took a drink of coffee.

"Sounds good to me."

Once on the trail again, Dusty felt alive. His head cleared. The sky was still overcast, but the fresh smell of the trees, the earth and the horses centered him. He and Mike took off by themselves down the trail pulling their empty packhorses. The ground was dry and the occasional click of a horseshoe off a rock in the dust was the only sound, except an occasional bird chirping.

Dusty gazed off into the trees and completely relaxed. Suddenly, Muley picked up his front feet and leaped about three feet in the air. Dusty kept his seat and flowed through the air with his horse. Cheyenne, without hesitation, followed right behind him.

"What the heck?"

"Will you look at that." Mike pulled Toby to a stop.

A fresh hole had been dug right in the middle of the trail, almost like a posthole, but large enough for a horse to put a whole leg down into it.

Dusty turned to see what had caused the ruckus. "That's pretty crazy, isn't it?"

"Yeah, I can't figure out what kind of animal that would be."

"Well, apparently he put the hole where he needed it. We'd better fill it in before somebody else steps into it and gets hurt." Dusty dismounted in one fluid motion and tied Muley to a tree. He dallied the lead rope of his packhorse over the saddle horn.

"You can just stay there. This won't take but a minute to get straightened out," Dusty called out. He crouched down and picked up some rocks along the side of the trail. Carrying them to the hole, he dropped them in and then added layers of dirt. Alternating layers of rock and dirt until it reached the top, he then stomped on it until it was level with the rest of the trail grade.

"Looks like you got it," said Mike, admiring the finished product.

"Yeah. That ought to take care of it. At least until we get some huge rains, anyway." Dusty turned and headed back to Muley. Untying him, he swung into the saddle and they headed back down the trail in minutes.

"We got a lot done yesterday," said Dusty, as they arrived at the bridge site.

"Yeah, today ought to go pretty quick."

Tying up their horses, they went back to the bridge and had just begun shoveling as more horsemen began to arrive.

Val and Mary rode in with Danny Conger right behind them. Cassie and Terri came a short time later, followed by Roy and Shelley bringing up the rear.

"Are you guys it for today?" asked Mike.

"Yeah," said Val. "Only us hard-cores left. I guess everyone else had something to do."

"Shouldn't take that long to finish up."

Dusty kept his head down and shoveled. The gravel had been hauled. They only had to spike on a few more planks and the bridge would be usable. The Forest Service trail crew would have to come back and complete the finishing touches, but at least the majority of the work was done.

Cassie and Terri dragged another plank down and placed it on the bridge next to the last one. Dusty and Mike helped hold the plank in place while Val drilled the holes for the spikes with a hand drill. Shelley shoveled gravel on the bridge approach and tried to work as close to Dusty as she could manage. They worked into early afternoon until, finally, Cassie and Terri decided they needed to get going.

"I've still got a lot of work to prepare for tomorrow," said Cassie, "so I better head back."

"I'll go with you. I think I heard my transcripts calling," added Terri.

"I'll ride out with you two," offered Roy, apparently happy to give up his position of standing around most of the day.

Cassie and Terri gave the man a slight smile as they walked by him. Dusty got the distinct impression they weren't impressed. That made him feel pretty good and he smiled as he pounded a spike in.

"Enjoying your work there, Boss?" asked Mike.

"Yeah, I am." Dusty grinned.

"'Bye, you guys," called Shelley, waving enthusiastically.

Dusty's smile faded. He put his head down and worked.

They finished up the last couple of planks, loaded up the Forest Service tools and got ready to head out.

"I appreciate all your help," said Danny. "We sure couldn't have done it without you."

"Our pleasure," said Val.

"Yeah. Just remember us when the eco people want those dirty equines off the trail. That's all we ask," said Mike.

"I will do that," Danny promised.

Dusty said, "Thanks a lot." He and Mike mounted up and rode back to the trailhead. The sun was just breaking through the clouds and hung low in the sky. Despite Shelley's efforts, she wasn't quick enough to ride out with them. Dusty exhaled deeply.

The ride back was quick. As they approached the rigs, Mike called to Dusty, "You still up to stop in at the Naches Tavern?"

"You bet. I'm hungry."

"Okay, then. I'll meet you there." Mike rode back to his rig and began to dismantle his camp.

Chapter Eleven

Dusty headed down the mountain pass on 410. The Naches Tavern at Greenwater wasn't too far from Buck Creek, a little town, which at one point in time had been a bustling logging community. The tavern was an older log building, and it had been around for a long time. Dusty liked that about it. He opened up the big log door and walked in. A massive stone fireplace stood in front of him; instead of firewood, it had whole logs burning. There were people seated at the small tables around the fire and a few on couches. All of them had the look of outdoor people: climbers coming down from a big day at Mt. Rainier, horsemen, hikers, motorcyclists, bikers, and people just out for a Sunday drive.

Dusty made his way to a table and waited for Mike. He didn't ordinarily go into establishments that served alcohol, unless he had a specific reason to be there. This time he did. He planned on ordering one of their double cheeseburgers and fries. And he couldn't wait to do it.

A young girl in a tight shirt and skinny jeans with an apron tied around her waist hurried up to his table. "What would you like to drink?"

"I'll take an iced tea."

"Well, here's a menu." She pulled one out of her apron pocket. "I'll be right back with your iced tea."

"I know exactly what I want, but my partner's coming."

She smiled at him and hurried off into the crowd.

Mike came in the door, sighted Dusty and pulled up a chair. "Have you ordered yet?" he asked.

"Just a drink. I've got a menu too, if you want to look at it," offered Dusty.

"Thanks. I pretty much know what I want."

"The double cheeseburger and fries?"

"How did you guess?"

"It was all over your face, Buddy!"

"Wow. I better work on that. I've got to get back on the job tomorrow," teased Mike.

"Yeah, good. Now that you bring it up, I need to talk to you. Julie Wolfe has an appointment with me tomorrow. Do you think you would be able to make it down?"

"I'm sure I can. What time?"

"One-thirty, right after lunch. Bring your full report and pictures, if you've got them."

"Okay. Will do."

The waitress returned and took their orders.

Dusty and Mike talked about the work party for a while. Dusty felt like someone was staring at him. He looked around and noticed Roy, sitting alone, with a full pitcher of beer in front of him. Dusty gave him a quick nod and kept talking to Mike.

Roy walked over with his beer. "Mind if I join you?"

"Not at all." Mike pulled out another chair for him. Dusty didn't say anything.

Roy set his pitcher on the table. "You guys can help yourself. Get a glass," he invited.

"No, thanks. I've already got a drink," said Dusty.

"Me too," said Mike.

If the fact that they weren't drinking beer seem to bother Roy, he didn't let on. "I was hoping you could give me some more information about the Back Country Horsemen group."

Dusty looked at him with no expression. "What kind of information do you need?"

"Well, where does it meet? When does it meet? Stuff like that."

"It meets at six-thirty the last Thursday of the month at the old grange hall. It's where the Eagleclaw Eagles used to meet before they got their own place," said Mike.

As Mike filled him in, the burgers arrived. Dusty was glad for that; it gave him something to do. Talking to Roy was not high on his list. As Mike and Roy talked, Dusty ate. He was enjoying the show. He figured Roy did not have near the interest in the Back Country Horsemen as he did in Cassie. The good part would be there were plenty of single women in the Eagleclaw Trail Riders. So if Cassie was unavailable, there were others that would be happy to take her place.

"Are you getting anything to eat?" asked Dusty.

Roy patted his beer glass. "No, I got all I need right here."

"That's what I was afraid of," Dusty said under his breath.

Mike didn't say anything else about it. He ate his cheeseburger and fries. Roy continued to ask questions about the group.

"You're going to probably really enjoy yourself. The women, as a rule of thumb, are about three-to-one to the men. And sometimes even more than that," said Dusty.

"That sounds better than dime night at the bar." Roy's eyes sparkled and he took a big gulp of beer.

"Oh, yeah," said Mike, "instant popularity."

"Way more than you probably want," added Dusty.

"Speak for yourself there," said Roy. "I never tire of female attention. This group sounds like a lot of fun."

Dusty was getting the uneasy feeling that they had just invited the wolf into the henhouse and he was really hoping that wasn't the case. Roy wasn't the kind of guy he hung out with, and he reminded him of those guys they used to call *greasers* in high school with Beatle boots and a pack of cigarettes rolled up in their sleeves. Roy smoked, but it didn't appear he had the pack rolled up in his sleeve. *Thank goodness.*

"Well, I better get my horses home. They've been doing a lot of standing around this weekend and they probably don't want to do a whole lot more of it. Have a good evening," he said to Mike, and nodded at Roy as he pushed his chair back and got up to leave.

Roy gave him an appraising look. "Good night, Dusty."

"See you tomorrow, Boss."

Dusty turned and walked out of the busy bar into the deepening twilight.

Chapter Twelve

Sitting at his desk and looking through his files, Dusty ran a hand through his hair. Julie Wolfe said she was ready to file for a divorce. Why she had to hire an investigator to see the proof of her husband's infidelity was beyond Dusty's comprehension. If you think someone is cheating, that probably would be a real good indicator of a breakdown in your relationship. Seeing it in a color photograph usually only added fuel to an already burning fire. Emotions ran rampant as it was in domestic law. He really hated doing divorces and TROs (temporary restraining orders), but work was work, and he needed to buy hay and pay his bills.

"Good morning, Mr. Dustin Rose," said Mrs. Phillips. She brought a steaming cup of coffee in and set it on the desk. "Did you have a good weekend?"

"Oh, absolutely. We put in a bridge up at Buck Creek," Dusty said.

"That's just wonderful that you do all that volunteer work with the Back Country Horsemen." She looked at him admiringly.

"Well, it works both ways. I really enjoy it too."

As Dusty perused the preliminary information in Julie Wolfe's file, he noticed that the Wolfes were pretty wealthy. It was old family money originating from Julie's side of the marriage. Julie was a long-time member of the Eagleclaw chapter, but Dusty could not ever remember seeing her husband at any of the events. It wasn't unusual, though. A good many of the women went to functions alone when their husbands were non-riders. Dusty took a drink of coffee. After that scene he'd witnessed in the street the other day, he was glad he hadn't seen him. It was hard to get the picture out of his mind—the man shouting and leaning over to intimidate the woman, then slamming his hand on the car next to her head. The car seat with the little kid in it crying as it drove away burned into his mind. He felt his neck get hot and his stomach tighten. He ran his hand through his hair. He was going to enjoy doing this divorce for Julie.

Turning back to the file, it looked to Dusty like Paul had married up. His financial wherewithal had taken a distinct leap when he married Julie. He'd seen it time and time again in his business—kind of a Cinderella thing. But often the guys couldn't take the strain of a successful marriage and they nuked it. *Guess we'll find out.*

Dusty called out through his office door, "Mrs. Phillips, would you mind putting together a summons and petition for dissolution of marriage for Julie Wolfe? Just use the standard bare-bones petition and we'll go over it and fill in the blanks this afternoon."

"Coming right up, Mr. Dustin Rose."

"Thank you."

Dusty perused the pile of mail on his desk. He saw a letter from Cassie's law office and immediately tore it open. It was a copy of a denial on the motion for reconsideration she had made before the court last Friday. That was probably what made her late to the work party. He was confident there were no grounds for reconsideration and had opted not to attend the hearing. Well, the court's denial was to be expected, but it probably didn't make her any happier when she lost again. Dusty put that in his *to be filed* basket.

He had a DUI client coming in at 10 o'clock, so he figured he better get ready for that one. The one-car crashers were not his favorite, either, but it was better than not working. And now that they had the new drug court, sometimes with plea bargaining there was a possibility of a good outcome. Dusty cleared off his desk and got ready to greet his next client.

The morning sped by and at noon Dusty grabbed his coat off the coatrack by the door.

"Have a nice lunch," he said, as he headed out the door to Maude's.

"Enjoy your lunch too, Mr. Dustin Rose," Mrs. Philips returned.

The weather was warm, in the mid-70s again; a beautiful August day in Eagleclaw. Dusty felt a little warm in his suitcoat as he walked over to the café. Making his way through the crowded restaurant, he took a seat at his usual spot at the end of the bar. Maude hurried over with a coffee pot and filled up his cup.

"How are you doing today, Dusty?" she asked.

"Oh, same old."

She smiled at him. "Back with your food shortly." She hurried over to the order window, greeting more customers as they came in. Since Dusty ate there pretty much every day, she didn't have to ask him what he wanted; it was always the special. She stuck the order on the swivel and turned to pour some more coffee for customers sitting down at the bar behind her.

Dusty drank his coffee and thought about next weekend. Another pack trip would be good, but where to go was the question. The high country was only open for a short time, so he had to get up there while he could. He was at Crystal Mountain just a couple weeks ago; it would be nice to head to Eastern Washington again. Maybe hit White Pass and ride along the PCT. As he mused about that ride, a voice came from behind him.

"Hey, Dusty." Mike slid onto the barstool next to him.

"Hi. Figured you'd show up. Did you get the file together?"

"Oh, yeah. Got it all right here." He laid a manila folder on the counter.

"Can't wait to see it."

"I didn't detect sarcasm, I hope."

"Oh, no, you would never get that from me."

"Good to know," said Mike. "So what are you doing next weekend? Or should I say, where are you planning on packing into?"

"Funny you should bring that up. I was thinking maybe Indian Creek Trailhead."

"Oh, that's a great one. I haven't been up there in a long time."

"You in then?"

"You bet!"

Dusty and Mike spent the rest of their lunch going over plans for the upcoming weekend.

Chapter Thirteen

Cassie was waiting to meet Terri for lunch and discuss plans for the next weekend. The sun was shining and it was warm—and it was supposed to hold for the foreseeable future. She sat in the quiet Chinese restaurant on the far end of the main street in Eagleclaw. Knowing that Dusty practically lived at Maude's place, she'd picked somewhere different. She didn't have a lot of hope for her appeal in the mill case, so she would rather not have to think about it every time she saw Dusty. She had a lot more cases going on than just that one. She knew she had to let it go.

"Hey, Cassie." Terri's voice broke into her thoughts.

Cassie looked up. "Hi. Glad you could make it."

"Yeah, it always gets a little dicey in depositions, as you know. At least these guys didn't want to work through the lunch hour."

"That's good."

"So have you ordered?"

"Nope. Waiting for you." Just then a waitress walked up with a teapot and filled Terri's cup.

Cassie and Terri placed their orders, then settled in with their tea to wait for their food.

"So how did you like the work party?" asked Terri.

"I thought it went pretty well. We got the bridge done, for the most part."

"Actually, I was wondering about Roy. How did that work out?"

"It didn't. At least not for me."

"Oh, did you end up going down to the Naches Tavern?"

"No, I didn't," Cassie shortly answered.

"Well, I guess that answers that," Terri said with finality.

"Terri, believe me, I told you before, I'm just not interested in meeting anybody. My law practice and riding keeps me busy. I don't have time for it."

"So what's going on next weekend?" Terri, eagerly asked.

Cassie smiled. "We should do a pack trip."

"Where to and what time do I need to be ready?"

"I was thinking we could head up to Fish Lake Way and maybe ride up to Tumac," said Cassie.

"Sounds great. What's Tumac?"

"It's an old Forest Service lookout, about 6,300 feet. It's a steep ascent, but from the top you have a 360-view of the entire area."

"Wow. Should I take Friday off?"

"I can't. I have to be in court in the morning, but let's leave early afternoon. That way we can pack in on Friday." Cassie took a drink of water. "There's so many places we can head after we get in there. I was thinking a good camp would be over at Frying Pan Lake. There is tons of graze for the horses and lots of room back off the lake."

"That sounds great. I'll be ready!" said Terri.

"There's fish in Frying Pan Lake too, if you're interested."

"Oh, really? Is that why they call it *Frying Pan*?"

"No, I think it's more because that's the shape of it topographically, although I've heard it's not bad for catching them, either."

Cassie thought about a trip a couple years back when a group of them packed in. It was so hot that year that they decided to cool off in the lake. Cassie put on her shorts and T-shirt. She and a couple of her friends waded into the lake.

An old-timer who came with them joined them in the water

looking very pleased. "I figured out how to get in the water and keep my clothes dry."

"How did you do that?" asked Cassie.

"I went around the bushes there and left them on the bank."

"Good idea, Dan."

"Yeah, years ago me and a buddy were fishing out here. We stripped down and waded out to the middle of the lake. We caught the biggest fish that way."

Sammy, Cassie's dog, had swam out with her. Sammy was starting to get tired. She was less than a year old. Cassie put her arms around her dog to support her. "I better get back out; Sammy's starting to run out of gas." Cassie had no sooner finished saying that then about fifty Boy Scouts came boiling over the hill and down to the edge of the lake.

Dan's face fell.

"So how did you say you get out again, Dan?" Cassie asked. The rest of the group roared with laughter and they got out, leaving Dan to his own devices.

Cassie grinned. Terri looked at her, eyebrows raised. "What's so funny?"

"Oh, just mountain memories. Let's get up there and make some more."

The women spent the rest of their lunch hour preparing for their trip on Friday.

Chapter Fourteen

Dusty hung his coat on the coatrack as he and Mike walked into the office. The worn mission furniture and log table made him feel at home.

Mrs. Phillips smiled up at them from the pile of paperwork on her desk. "Hello, Mike. Mr. Dustin Rose."

"Hello, Mrs. Phillips."

"I've got the coffee, water and glasses set up in your office for your one p.m. meeting."

"Thank you," said Dusty.

Dusty's office had a large mahogany desk and chair where he usually sat and worked. A Navajo rug covered the hardwood floor and pictures of horse packing in the mountains hung on the walls. Dusty and Mike pulled up a chair at the conference table by the window and sat down to go over Mike's file.

By staking out the *other woman's* house, Mike had been able to get pictures of Paul Wolfe coming and going. The really incriminating one was Paul on the front porch locked in an obviously passionate embrace with a woman. There were also a couple of pictures of Paul and the same women in a bar practically sitting on each other's laps.

"How in the heck did you get these pictures without being seen?"

"You'd be surprised how good cell phone cameras are

nowadays. It's actually a clearer picture than I can take with my regular camera."

They were still looking at the pictures when Mrs. Phillips came to the door. "Julie Wolfe is here."

"Send her in."

She stepped back out into the front office. "Mr. Dustin Rose will see you now," she announced.

"Hi, Dusty." An attractive blue-eyed, brunette woman walked into his office wearing jeans, boots and light T-shirt. She looked tired, but resigned.

"Hi, Julie. Have a seat. This is Mike. I take it you two have met."

"Yes, we have. Hi, Mike."

"Hi."

"Well, I guess we better get on with this. Mike has the pictures you wanted. I'm not sure whether you want to see them or not, but it's what you thought."

"Oh, no, I definitely want to see them," said Julie, her jaw set.

Mike opened the file and laid the pictures out. "I took these over a period of two weeks."

Julie silently studied the photos. When she saw the embrace on the front steps of the residence, Dusty saw a shadow of grief cross her face—quickly replaced by a stony determination. By the time Julie got to the bar pictures, she looked resolute.

"Who is this, anyway?" She turned to Mike.

"This is a new secretary he just hired. She is twenty-one," Mike said.

"Young and dumb. At least she has an excuse," Julie added wryly.

"Hey, don't get down on yourself. This can happen to anybody." Dusty patted her shoulder. "Believe me, I see it a lot—a lot more than I'd care to."

"Where's the paperwork? Let's get going with it," she said.

"I've got the preliminaries done. So let's just fill it in and get him served right away."

They spent the next hour going over what needed to be put in the petition. Dusty just needed a general idea of what she wanted. With her husband owning half of the business, they were going to have to put a hold on the community accounts and hope that he hadn't taken too much out. Getting the names of all the banks they did business with was a good start. Mike made a list of what he needed to run down.

"We are going to want to take him by surprise. The more notice he has, the more he is going to be able to move things around," said Dusty. "These things have a way of getting out before you want them to, so we'd better strike first. Mike, can you get him served tomorrow morning?"

"Piece of cake."

"Okay, Julie, we'll get this information rounded up and you be in here at nine a.m. to sign the petition. I have a court appearance in Seattle, but Mrs. Phillips will have it ready for you to sign. And not a word to anybody. We don't want Paul catching wind of it," Dusty cautioned.

"Okay." Julie said quietly.

"The only reason I'm telling you this is in an effort to save your assets. You have a lot. You sure don't want him to get more than he is entitled to. You guys weren't married that long. Three years is a short marriage. You're going to want to protect your daughter the most."

Julie nodded. At the mention of her eighteen-month-old daughter, tears formed at the corners of her eyes. Aside from that, she remained markedly stoic.

Dusty caught the emotion that crossed her face. His stomach tightened. He hated seeing her pain—it really brought out the protective instincts in him. Guys could be so utterly stupid and such lowlifes! Why didn't the idiot just leave? Why did he have to drag this woman and her young, innocent daughter through this kind of stuff?

"Don't worry," Dusty reassured her. "We're going to get this taken care of."

"Okay," she said in a small voice. "There is one other thing."

"What's that?" He perked up at the warning in her voice.

"I probably should have mentioned this in the beginning, but he has real anger issues. I'm afraid once he is served, he's going to lose it."

"Well, don't worry about that. We can get a temporary restraining order in place that will keep him from coming within a thousand feet of you. Do you think you need it?"

"Do those things really work?"

"Well, they may not save your life when it comes down to it, but at least you have a leg to stand on in court. If you've filed one and he ignores it, he's in big trouble."

"Okay. Well, I better get one of those too."

"That's going to require a court appearance. You go to the clerk's office at the courthouse, outline for them the situation, and they'll get you set up with the paperwork. Just make sure you have the facts that will support it."

She lifted up her shirt to show a big bruise on her stomach, "Will this do? He doesn't like to hit me where it shows."

Dusty clenched his teeth as a wave of heat coursed down his spine. *What a coward.* He was going to enjoy doing this dissolution a lot more than he thought he would. "Yes. I think that would more than take care of the requirements. You will need to swear that he did it and you are afraid for you and your minor child's well-being."

"No problem swearing to that."

"Okay, then. We'll get him served and get going on this," said Dusty.

She slowly got up and walked to the door. "Thanks a lot, you guys."

Dusty walked her out. "I know divorce is tough, but sometimes living in a bad situation is even tougher. You'll see when you get to the other side." He patted her on the shoulder.

Julie looked up at him gratefully. "I can't wait to get there. Thanks again."

Concern crossed over Dusty's face, "Are you and your daughter going to be okay at your home? You realize although a restraining order is legally binding, when push comes to shove, it is just a piece of paper?"

"I'm going to stay at my sister's for a while, just in case he tries to come back to the house." She paused in the doorway, her eyes were shining, "Thank you, Dusty."

"Okay. Be safe." Dusty opened the door and the bell jingled as it closed behind her.

"Tsk, tsk, tsk. Hate to see that happen to that nice young lady," said Mrs. Phillips.

"That's what we're here for, nice people like her." Dusty walked back into his office and sat down with Mike to lay out a plan for the next day.

"Mike, I'm going to need you to get into the records and find out if he has any accounts that Julie doesn't know about. Those are the ones we are going to need to list on the TRO. He's probably been taking money off the top of the business. Guys like this always like to have their own money hidden away."

"Yeah. Too bad their own money is always really somebody else's—or at least half somebody else's."

"Yeah. You'd wonder if they've had an original thought in their heads," agreed Dusty.

"So what do you think about him being violent?"

"I don't know. The way things are going these days, you can't be too sure. Best to be packing."

Mike smiled. "I always am."

"Yeah. Well, hopefully we don't end up with another Pasayten situation down here."

"That could be bad. Hope Cassie is close by," teased Mike.

"Yeah. Me too!" Dusty played along.

"Okay. I'll go work on the records and get back to you," said Mike.

"Thanks. I'll start on the paperwork."

"Later." Mike stood and walked out the door.

"We'll talk tomorrow." Dusty walked over and began to study the paperwork on his desk. He barely heard the jingle of the bell as Mike left the office.

Chapter Fifteen

The next morning Dusty had to make a court appearance downtown. He hated having to drive into Seattle in rush-hour traffic, but being the only guy in the office, he had no choice. It got to the point that what used to be less than an hour drive had now blossomed into two hours and more—if one of the other million or so people on the road made a mistake. As it was, Highway 167 was moving along at a snail's pace. He hadn't even been able to merge onto 405 yet, and that was his one hope things would get better. He had a nine-thirty hearing. If luck were
with him and he found somewhere to park—he might make it.

The traffic seemed like a long snake. It would flow, almost reaching fifty miles an hour, and then a sea of red brake lights would appear and they would come to a stop again. Meanwhile, the beautiful skyline of Seattle stretched out in front of him—the Space Needle, Columbia Center, Smith Tower—the buildings went on and on. The new Safeco Field stadium gleamed on his left as he finally drove by it. The sky was overcast, but since it was August, there was a good chance it would be blowing off soon. He hoped so. He was looking forward to the ride this weekend.

Dusty turned on Seneca Street, backtracked to 4th and James and the King County Courthouse. He lucked out and actually found a place to park—*Who would have thought?* Whistling, Dusty walked into the courthouse and went through security.

On the way home Dusty's mind was still on the hearing. It worked out okay for everyone involved, at least in his opinion. He loved it when that happened. His mind drifted to his case with Julie Wolfe. Her husband must have been served by now. Mike got the account numbers and they were able to get enough information to put together a summons and petition for dissolution of marriage.

Mike had said he was going to head over right before noon and serve Paul Wolfe. Dusty had not heard back from him yet. There was a warm breeze in the air and the early-afternoon sun sparkled like diamonds on Elliot Bay. The bay was filled with pleasure boats, and ferries glided back and forth across the waterfront. *This is why everyone wants to move here! They just don't know it rains almost continuously from January to May.*

His phone rang and he punched his ear piece. "Dusty."

"Hey, it's Mike. Figured you'd want an update on the service for Paul Wolfe."

"I'm listening."

"Well, to say it didn't go well would be an understatement. That guy has really got an anger problem. And that's putting it lightly."

"What happened?"

"His secretary was at the front desk—a cute little blonde. He could actually be her father by the age difference."

"Sounds typical."

"Yeah. So I asked to see Paul Wolfe. She said he was busy. I said I had something that he would definitely like to see and it would only take a minute. She hesitated and finally buzzed him and whispered into the phone.

"The office door opens and he comes out. I hand him the envelope and let him know he's been served. He looks at it for a minute and then rips it open. After that it went pretty fast. His face turned bright red and his veins stood out on his head. He started screaming at me to get out of his office. Basically went berserk. It was a pretty ugly scene."

Dusty twisted his mouth into a wry smile. "Hmmm…I wonder if he was heartbroken she was going to divorce him?"

"It looked more like loss of control."

"That's always ugly."

"It was a major production. He was yelling so loud I thought the windows were going to crack. He looked like he wanted to attack me. I'm not sure what stopped him." Mike paused for a second. "So I guess the good part is, he has been served. The bad part is, I'm not sure what he's going to do next."

"I better call Julie and let her know what's going on. I hope she picked up her restraining order yesterday. Unfortunately, it sounds like she might need it."

"He looked pretty capable of anything, the way he was carrying on."

"What was his girlfriend doing?" Dusty wondered.

"She was crying hysterically."

"That's weird. You'd think she'd be happy she could have a shot at the guy," said Dusty.

"I think there was a lot more drama than she had anticipated as a result of the service."

"Sounds like it. Okay. Well, good job, Mike. I'll get ahold of Julie and let her know to beware."

"Okay. Later."

Dusty disconnected the phone. Who would have known he would react like that? *I guess Julie had an idea. You don't get bruises like she had just by running into something.*

As Dusty merged back onto Highway 167, the traffic cleared out somewhat. It was still pretty early in the afternoon, and the congestion wasn't nearly what it was going to be. He took an exit and pulled over. Looking at his phone, he found Julie's number.

"Julie, this is Dusty Rose."

"Hi, Dusty."

"Were you able to get your restraining order yesterday?"

"Yes, I did. It was pretty easy."

"That's great. Mike served Paul and he got a pretty wild reaction. Is that normal for Paul?"

"I don't know. I've never sued Paul for divorce before."

"No, I'm just talking about his overall stability. Does he get pretty angry when his boat gets rocked?"

Julie was silent a few seconds. "Yes, that would be true. He does not like things changed unless it's his idea. I think he freaks out if it makes him feel like a victim."

"Okay. That makes sense. He wants to break through the chains that have fallen over him. He hates loss of control."

"Something like that," agreed Julie.

"I'm driving home from Seattle now. Make sure and keep your doors locked and have the sheriff's number handy, just in case you need it."

"Thank you. I will."

"If nothing else happens on the case, I will be updating you later this week."

"Okay. Wonderful. Thank you," said Julie, her voice brimming with gratitude.

"You're welcome. And no problem whatsoever. It's my job."

"Call you later. 'Bye."

The line went dead. Dusty looked at his phone for a minute, then threw it down in the console and turned back onto the freeway. He felt a gnawing uneasiness in the pit of his stomach. In his experience that kind of anger in the beginning of a divorce case was not a good sign. Things only get worse from here. He looked at the white peak of Mt. Rainier gleaming in the afternoon sun and felt a little better. Thoughts of horses and mountains always calmed him.

Chapter Sixteen

Dusty was in his office early Friday morning. He didn't beat Mrs. Phillips in, but it was 9 o'clock, which he considered early. He was hoping to get some paperwork done before he headed up to the mountains. It didn't really click in his head what was happening when he heard the explosive shouting from the front office.

"Where is Dusty Rose?" shouted an angry voice.

"Now, sir, you need to just settle down," commanded Mrs. Phillips.

"Like hell!" The angry voice seemed to bounce off the rafters and heavy footsteps headed for Dusty's office.

Dusty barely had time to look up when the office door flung open and bounced off the wall. A couple of pictures crashed to the floor, glass splintering. The man charged into his office with Mrs. Phillips in hot pursuit.

"Sir, people are not allowed just to barge into offices here. Remember your propriety!" Her cheeks were flushed and she was doing her best to rein the man in, but he was having none of it.

Dusty stood up and coolly stared at the intruder. "Can I help you?"

That seemed to add fuel to the fire. "Oh, I think you've helped enough. I got your little present in my office yesterday!" he shouted, holding up the summons and petition.

"And to whom do I owe this pleasure?" inquired Dusty sarcastically.

He turned to his secretary. "Mrs. Phillips, thank you for your assistance. I can take it from here."

"Should I call the police?"

"I'll let you know."

Mrs. Phillips whirled and walked out of the room, dusting off her hands as she walked and appearing for all the world to be happy to be rid of the man causing the scene.

"Paul Wolfe, is it?" Dusty inquired.

"Yes, it is," the large man answered. Still standing in front of Dusty's desk, he leaned forward menacingly, putting both hands on the desk. His shirt collar was open and his face was red and puffy. Dusty couldn't figure out if he had a wild night the night before or he'd slept in his clothes.

"Do you have a lawyer?"

Paul Wolfe's face darkened and his veins stood out on his forehead. "Not yet, but I'm going to get one. And he's going to be the best one in the Pacific Northwest. Not some two-bit, dime-store, country hick, lawyer like you."

"Good," said Dusty. "I can't wait to meet him. Until that time, I'm afraid I'm going to have to ask you to leave. I represent your wife and I can't represent you as well."

"Well, that's about the last thing I'm asking you to do," the large man bellowed.

"Well, I guess I don't know why else you stopped into my office."

"It's really easy, Mr. Dustin Rose, you weaselly little pipsqueak! I just wanted to stop in and let you know how unhappy your little note made me yesterday and to warn you not to do anything like that again!"

"No problem whatsoever," Dusty replied amicably. "Give me your attorney's name and I will be happy to keep all of my contact limited to him. Now, if you don't mind, I need to get back to work." He sat and picked up a file.

"There is also the matter of my money." Paul's eyes bulged and he appeared to become more agitated as he spoke. "All of my accounts are frozen. I need to be able to access my money."

"You need to calm down and have your lawyer call me. Until we can get an accounting of the community assets, they will remain frozen."

Paul's cheeks bulged and turned bright red. His eyes flashed; a crazy light washed over them. He struggled for a couple of minutes and, with a herculean effort, he managed to pull himself together. He hesitated for a minute, then seemed to arrive at a decision. "You'll be hearing from my lawyer!"

"Perfect."

The irate man turned and stormed out of the office, stopping only to slam the outer door as he went. A couple more pictures fell to the floor, frames shattering.

Mrs. Phillips hurried into his office and surveyed the broken glass on the floor. "What an ugly brute!"

Dusty stood surveying the broken glass. "Yeah, another perfect example of why I hate domestic law."

"Julie is certainly better off without that mannerless beast."

"And we'll make that happen for her. With pleasure."

"I'll go get the broom," said the practical Mrs. Phillips.

Dusty sat back down at his desk and stared out the window. To say that Paul Wolfe had an anger problem was putting it lightly. In all the divorce cases he'd had, this man definitely showed the most animosity he'd seen. It was always so strange. If they didn't want to be married, why did they get so mad when offered freedom? Dusty knew in the end it had a whole lot less to do with the loss of a person than it did with the loss of property and income. Obviously, Wolfe was the type of individual who wanted it all. Mike and he would probably need to do more digging into this guy's past. This kind of behavior didn't just come from nowhere. There was bound to be a history. If it wasn't criminal, then it just hadn't been reported. But there were going to be other individuals in his life who knew what he was capable of, and those were the people that they needed to talk to. Dusty jotted down notes and tucked them into the file. He shot Mike an e-mail outlining some more information he would need in the Wolfe case.

Dusty straightened up his desk and stacked the files in a tidy pile. There was plenty of time to take care of that when he got back. The mountains were calling him. He threw on his light suit coat and headed out of the office.

"Have a good weekend, Mrs. Phillips," he said.

She was standing by her desk with the broom in her hand. "I'm just going to clean up in your office and then I will be leaving as well. You have a wonderful weekend too, Mr. Dustin Rose, and don't let that vile man destroy your horseback riding."

"Thank you. Not a chance." Dusty flashed her a grin. "See you Monday." And he went out the door into the sunny afternoon.

Chapter Seventeen

Cassie slipped a halter over Prince's head. "There you go, boy. Time for a ride." She fastened the buckle on the side of the halter and lightly held the lead rope. She turned and called to her other horse, "Come on, Murphy. You don't want to be left behind." The second horse, a bay, waited quietly while she slipped the halter over his head. He was older and well broke. Cassie didn't know how many more years she was going to have him, but he was a great horse. That was the problem, she mused; as soon as they got really good, it was time to think about getting another one. With age came wisdom, and the age sometimes got in the way of hard, high mountain riding. Cassie took it easy with Murphy and just packed him lightly. Prince was another story, being her main riding horse, and he was always ready to go. Of course, he was only ten years old too, as opposed to Murphy's eighteen.

As Cassie walked to the pasture gate, Sam, her Australian Shepherd barked. "Calm down, Sammy. We're going as fast as we can." Cassie led both horses into the trailer, slipping their fly masks over their faces. Since she had drop-down windows, with the warm weather she had the windows wide open, and her horses' eyes were protected. It was also a good way not to forget the masks when she got to the trailhead. Going into Fish Lake Way you were usually guaranteed a good population of mosquitos. She had Frontline on Sammy, so ticks shouldn't be a problem. But Cassie always checked her out; the long fur made it possible for them to hide out in there.

She walked around to the cab of her truck and opened the door. "Load up," she said to her dog. Sammy didn't need to be told twice and enthusiastically bounced into the truck.

Terri only lived a few miles away and Cassie was there in minutes. As always, Terri was holding her horses, with all her gear packed in her driveway. She loaded the gear and put her horses in the trailer in no time.

"This is going to be a great weekend." Terri slid into the front seat of the truck. Sammy scooted over between them, panting. "There is no rain in sight!" She tossed her hair back and grinned at Cassie.

"Great," Cassie replied, putting the truck in gear.

The truck rumbled up Highway 410, the big Ford dually not even noticeably pulling the four-horse trailer behind it. The trees got thicker and greener and the two-lane highway wound its way into Mount Rainier National Park.

Terri looked out the window. "I always wondered if they shot that movie *Harry and the Hendersons* up here. You know, the one about the friendly Sasquatch?"

Cassie laughed. "Well, it sure looks like they could have, doesn't it?"

"That was one of my favorite movies."

"Yeah, it was okay, although I usually prefer westerns."

The afternoon sun dropped lower in the sky as they pulled down Bumping River Road on the east side of the Cascade Mountains. It wasn't the distance down the road, but more its rocky hollowed-out condition that made the going slow. After about forty-five minutes they pulled into the Fish Lake Way horse camp and trailhead. Cassie picked a pull-through camping area and rolled to a stop. They unloaded the horses and tied them to the hitch rails. The campsites were well kept. The pull-throughs were great for trucks and trailers, eliminating the need for backing up.

"I like the gravel in the pull-outs and metal fire rings," exclaimed Terri. "Even a vaulted toilet and a hand pump for stock water."

Cassie and Terri were a team now and knew their jobs. They brushed and saddled their riding horses, and put the packsaddles on their stock. Terri had weighed her gear by feel at home and thought it was pretty much equal. They quickly took the pack scale and, while one held the load up, the other read the scale.

"Whoa. A half a pound under, look at you!" teased Cassie.

"Yeah. Well, you know, I'm kind of a packer. I've been to the Pasayten."

"Oh, yeah. I guess you have."

Weighing Terri's other pack, Cassie said, "Well, a half a pound over this time. I'd say we call this good."

"Hot dog!" Terri grabbed her pannier and swung it up onto Moose's packsaddle, throwing the loops over the wooden crossbucks. The horse leaned to one side, steadying himself, while Terri walked around to the other side and threw the other pannier on. Once even, Moose stood quietly contemplating Terri as she went back and got her top packs.

Cassie busied herself loading her packhorse, Murphy. A brown horse with black mane and tail, known as a bay, he stood quietly waiting for his load. He'd done this for years and wasn't fazed by the packing at all. Cassie smiled. *Of course, this is a really light load for a couple of days compared to what we'd bring for a week.*

Terri held her packhorse's lead rope and swung into the saddle. Cassie locked up the truck and dropped the keys in her pommel bag.

"Let's do it!" She spurred her horse, who took off at a good clip toward the trailhead with Terri following right behind.

Neither noticed the light-green, older-model Ford pickup with the dirty-white camper and trailer parked in the far edge of the parking lot. They also missed the man staring intently at them through the soiled curtains in the camper window.

After stopping to fill out their tag at the Forest Service kiosk, they headed down the trail. Cassie took a deep breath. *Finally in the backcountry again!* The rhythmic beat of her horse's hooves as he walked down the trail and the smell of fir trees and earth in the late-afternoon sun was a balm to her soul. The sun was still shining as they broke through the trees and came upon a creek. The stream spread out and sluiced over a slab of rock, which took up the whole creek bed. The sun playing on the water and rock and made it shine like gold.

"This is my favorite part. Just watch so your horses don't slip." Cassie looked back to make sure her packhorse retained his footing on the slippery rocks.

"Wow. This is beautiful! You just never know what you're going to see next." Terri turned her head with her mouth open.

"Yeah. I guess that's what keeps us coming back. Maybe that or the fact we do know what we're going to see next and that's what keeps us coming."

Terri grinned. "Good point. Whatever it is, it works."

They splashed out of the creek on the other side and walked down the trail at a fast clip.

Terri was really enjoying herself being in the woods again. The trees filled her nostrils with the fresh scent of fir. She had gotten a funny feeling when they rode out of camp that made the hair stand up on the back of her neck. She shook it off, though, thinking it must have just been a leftover from her last big pack trip in the Pasayten. Her misgivings slipped away as they rode on through the thick green forest. It was alive with the chatter of birds, the buzzing of bees, and the occasional small creek babbling across the trail.

Chapter Eighteen

Dusty didn't waste time getting ready as soon as he got home from the office. He already had his clothes and food packed, so it was just a matter of putting in the perishables and loading his gear into the truck. Taking one last look around, Dusty locked up the house and went to catch his horses. Muley watched him coming, twitching his ears. Cheyenne stood silent, occasionally swatting his tail against his back, warding off flies. As Dusty unhooked the gate and walked into the pasture, Muley gave him a quick sideways look and walked off at a fast pace.

"Come on, boy. Don't do this now," coaxed Dusty.

Cheyenne watched for a minute and then slowly ambled after Muley. Neither horse was running, but they were removing themselves from the area. Dusty hated this. For the most part, his horses were good, but every once in a while they liked to test him. Dusty followed for a few steps and then stopped suddenly and turned his back. He had heard that confused the horses. Sure enough, after only a minute or two, Dusty felt hot breath in his ear. Muley was trying to figure out what had gone wrong. Cheyenne was still standing about ten paces away. Dusty let him smell him for a couple of minutes and then he reached out and began stroking the horse. Muley always wore his halter because he was hard to catch. Dusty scratched him and then deftly grabbed the halter before Muley had a chance to bolt away.

"Well, that was easy." Dusty snapped on the lead rope. Then he walked over, slipped the halter over Cheyenne's head and put his lead rope on. "Okay, let's go. We've got some ground to cover before nightfall." He led both horses over to his trailer, put the fly masks on and loaded. Scout followed him and jumped into the truck the minute Dusty opened the door.

Mike was packed and ready when Dusty pulled up, and it only took him a couple minutes to get his horses and gear loaded.

As he hopped in, Mike asked, "Indian Creek Meadows Trailhead?"

"That's it," said Dusty.

"Great. Probably see some through-hikers on the Pacific Crest Trail when we're riding out that way. Last time we saw Mother Goose up there handing out energy bars." Mike adjusted his seat belt and made himself comfortable.

"It's definitely the time of year for it." The through-hikers were people who started in California and hiked the PCT all the way to Canada. They went by the weather and usually started in early spring. By August, if they were on schedule, they were hiking in Washington to hit Canada before the snow fell. It was always an interesting group of people on the trail.

Dusty and Mike talked about their latest case and in no time at all they were on Cayuse Pass heading over to White Pass. Once they turned onto Highway 12, they went by the ski resort and continued over the mountains. They gazed at the large drop-off to their right with sparkling lakes below. Going by the old Indian Creek Outfitters sign, they turned left onto the twisting gravel road. Dusty drove slowly, taking care not to hit his horse trailer on any trees.

Once they arrived, it didn't take them long to unload their horses and pack up. As he rode though the dark forest, the pungent smell of pine needles and fresh earth filled his nostrils. Dusty looked around. He could see little of the bright sunlight they had enjoyed in the camp area. The trees were thick and the earth muffled their hoofbeats. A quiet stillness filled the air, and both men were lost in their thoughts as they wound down the trail.

Although a popular area, Dusty and Mike hadn't seen many hikers. The one or two they did see were pleasant and stepped far off the trail to allow the stock to go by. Dusty and Mike thanked them and continued on. There was only one steep spot on the trail. The Forest Service trail crew had worked on digging in the switchbacks a little deeper to the hillside, but it was still pretty steep. Mike pulled up while Dusty did the descent, then he followed. No sense in having one horse lose footing and fall on the person below. Once at the bottom, they watered their horses and contemplated the trail before them.

"To this day I'll never understand what they were thinking when they built those check dams into the switchbacks. They are way too short." Dusty gazed up at the steep dirt stairway out of the canyon.

"Well, one thing for sure, they weren't thinking about horses." Mike shook his head as he looked at the trail. The crew had taken logs and placed them as bulkheads to hold the dirt in place. The only problem was the stairs were so abrupt that the horses had to literally hop up to the next one. Once they got their back feet on, the step was too short. One enterprising person, no one knew who, had taken out every other stair in an effort to improve the situation. It hadn't helped very much and, of course, the resultant damage was blamed on the horsemen.

After climbing out of the canyon, the trail continued to gain altitude and finally they reached the beginning of a meadow. Grass and streams became more plentiful. Little log bridges lay across some of the streams. Fragrant bunches of lupine, white daisy-like plants with yellow centers, and Indian paintbrush grew interspersed in the grass.

"There's a really good hunting camp back there." Dusty gestured into a thicket of trees as they rode by.

"Is there any area that you don't know about?" Mike took a deeper look into the trees where Dusty had just pointed.

"Oh, maybe a couple of things. And I'm thinking most of them have to do with women."

"Well, I can't help you there, Boss. I'm still trying to learn about it by watching you."

"Then you're in a world of hurt. This is the blind leading the blind." Both laughed as they continued down the trail. The spotty patches of grass had opened up into a huge meadow with thick grass everywhere. A small stream ran through it, and off in the distance they could see the peak of Tumac jutting into the sky.

"Where's the best place to camp around here?" asked Mike.

"There's a great camp at the end of the meadow. It's got a little creek that runs in the back of it. It's pretty nice because when you hobble the horses, you can keep an eye on them."

"Great. I'll take it."

"Well, let's find out if someone's in it." Dusty led the way down the meadow with Scout on his heels. As they approached the dark trees at the head of the meadow, it was vacant.

"We're home sweet home," announced Dusty.

"Let's get the coffee on. That will make it official," said Mike.

They got the horses hobbled and the coffee ready in record time. The sun was just beginning to set as the fire crackled to life.

Dusty sat in his lawn chair by the fire. He watched his horses grazing on the sweet mountain grass. The only sound was their rip-and-munch and the jingle of the hobble chains as they shifted positions. Scout lay by his feet contentedly. Even though it had been a warm August day, the high mountain air was decidedly colder when the sun went down. The fire felt warm against his skin.

Mike had his cup of coffee and was walking back from the meadow, having checked on his horses. "You're lucky your horses stay right where you can see them. Mine keep wanting to drift right out the bottom of the meadow. If I don't keep an eye on them, I'll have to go get them back out of the trailer," he joked. "I just don't get what they have against this good mountain grass, anyway."

"Yeah, that's always baffled me too." Dusty rested his coffee cup on his knee. "I'd tell you the reason my horses never leave is because of excellent training, but I figure you'd never buy it. So to be perfectly honest, mine don't leave because they just don't want to."

Mike nodded. "Oh, I get it. So I just need to work on training my horses' attitude."

"Yes, try to get their attitudes worked around more like Muley's."

"Okay. This conversation has just dropped off the edge of any kind of believable. I'm going to grab my steak."

"Darn. I'll go get my steak too. But before I do that, I think I'll go bring Mr. Wonderful and his buddy back from the meadow before he maybe changes his mind and all the great training goes out the door."

"Good idea." Mike set his coffee down and followed Dusty out into the grass to catch his horses. Scout bounded out in front to help.

Chapter Nineteen

Once the horses were put up and dinner was made, Dusty was bone weary from the long day. It was so relaxing just staring into the fire, he thought he'd never want to stop. The sky was clear and the moon was full above them. The stars sparkled and the mountains surrounded them with dark shadows. Dusty caught himself nodding off. Abruptly, he stood up. "I think it's time to hit the hay. See you in the morning."

"G'night, Boss." Mike sat quietly looking into the fire.

Dusty didn't know how long he'd been asleep, but something woke him up. He looked next to him at Scout, always a good indicator he really heard something. His dog was wide awake and his ears were perked forward. Dusty lay still listening. It sounded like footsteps. He also knew there were a lot of animals that could be walking through the camp. They'd smell the residue of steaks and check it out. Dusty relaxed and waited. His Ruger Vaquero lay next to him, fully loaded. He didn't think a lot about his gun, but he made sure he had it, if he needed it. Dusty lay thinking about his last pack trip in the Pasayten. His firearm hadn't helped him a whole lot on that one, but Cassie's sure had. He thought of her long brown hair and straight posture in the saddle. As always, he felt a shift inside of him. *Man, she was some kind of woman.*

Scout issued a low-throated growl and Dusty froze. A shadow slowly moved along the tent wall illuminated by the moonlight.

Dusty reached over and picked up his gun. He wasn't sure what was going to happen next, but he needed to know who was there before he shot them.

"Hey, who's out there?"

The silhouette froze for a second and took off at a dead run. Dusty bolted through the tent door, gun in hand. Scout leapt in front of him. Brush crashed as the figure went through the trees. Dusty went full bore after him. Scout was making better time and barked viciously as he ran.

"What the heck's going on?" came a yell from Mike's tent.

Dusty ran as fast as he could, but with the darkness, the trees, and the intruder's lead, he soon lost sight of him. He heard Scout barking in the distance. Then a loud squeal. "Scout! Scout! Come here, boy." Dusty hurried toward the last sound from his dog. He felt sick to his stomach. *If anything happens to that dog, I just don't know what I'd do.* "Scout!" Dusty called again, trying to quell his rising panic at the thought of harm to his dog.

The salal bushes parted and Scout walked through. He was moving a little slower than usual and limping. Relief flooded through Dusty. He dropped to his knees and hugged his dog. "There you are, boy." Scout had a big smile on his face, but when Dusty hugged him, he whimpered. "What happened to you?" Dusty ran his hand along Scout's back end and Scout whimpered again. "The son of a bitch must have kicked you." Dusty felt anger flowing in the pit of his stomach. *What kind of an idiot is out here creeping around people's tents and kicking their dogs, anyway?*

Dusty and Scout slowly walked back to camp. When they got there, Mike was up and pacing.

"What's going on? One minute I'm asleep and the next thing I know, people are running, yelling, and Scout's barking his head off. Pretty sure I missed something."

"Yeah, you did. Someone was walking outside of my tent and Scout and I had a little chase. He got away, but not before he got a good kick into my dog."

Mike, concerned, turned to Scout. "Is he okay?"

"Yeah, just a little sore."

"This whole thing sounds a little messed up. I mean, aren't we quite a ways from the Canadian border now?" said Mike, referring to the recent pack trip to the Pasayten.

"Yeah, you'd think so." Dusty walked back to his tent. "I guess I'll try to get a little sleep, if that's possible."

"See you in the morning, Boss. Try not to cause any more ruckus, would you?"

Dusty gave him a rueful grin, "I'll try not to. Come on, Scout." The dog trotted into his tent and Dusty zipped up the door for the second time that night.

Sleep did not come quickly to him. He repeatedly checked Scout to make sure he was sleeping. Dusty kept hearing things and he had to use every bit of discipline he possessed to finally drift off to sleep. Dreams of the trapper cabin at Sheep Lake haunted him. He was finally able to replace it with a beautiful woman with long brown hair astride a gray horse. He smiled and drifted into a fitful sleep.

Dusty woke to the jangle of hobbles and the rip-rip-munch of horses grazing. The combined smell of damp canvas and wood smoke filled his nostrils. He slowly got up and pulled on his Romeos, jacket, and shoved on his hat as he pushed open the tent flap and stepped out. Mike was just pouring himself a cup of coffee. The snow on the distant peaks reflected the morning sun. The dark shadows of the night before seemed a long ways away.

"Good morning, Boss." Mike sat down with his steaming cup of coffee. This morning he was wearing a jean jacket and a red-and-black plaid shirt.

"Well, it will be after I get a cup of coffee. Where's Scout?" Dusty went over to the Roll-a-Table and picked up his coffee cup. Scout, on cue, came trotting back from the meadow, his tongue hanging out and a big dog smile on his face. Dusty bent down and petted him, running his hands down Scout's sides. The dog sat patiently, any touch from Dusty at all being a reward in itself. When Dusty hit the tender spot, Scout moved away ever so slightly.

"Looks like Scout is going to be okay," Dusty observed.

"Yeah, he's been running around this morning just fine. Thank goodness," said Mike. "I checked over by the tent. The grass was mashed down but no prints."

Dusty was relieved about Scout. He had planned a big ride today up Tumac, but he wasn't going to do it if his dog couldn't make it. He poured coffee in his cup and sat down in his chair. "I'm not surprised."

"Hey, I was thinking," began Mike.

"Always dangerous," broke in Dusty.

"Thanks." Mike gave him a pained look. "I was thinking about whoever that was last night and the chase with guns drawn, and stuff."

"Pretty wild, for sure," agreed Dusty.

"But the question came to me; what would you call us? I mean, we wear cowboy stuff. We have boots and spurs and western saddles. Instead of a lariat, we have a saw," Mike considered.

Dusty eyed him, finally taking note of what Mike was wearing. "Yeah, we do. What happened to your period-correct stuff?"

"That's what I'm talking about here," Mike said impatiently. "What we are."

"Oh, okay. Excuse me. Go on then. What are we?" Dusty said with mock politeness.

"Okay. So as I was saying, we have our western gear, but a saw instead of a lariat."

"Yeah, I always figured it was easier to saw down trees than to rope them," said Dusty.

Mike ignored Dusty's remark. Setting his coffee down, he picked up a stick and poked the fire. "Well, I figured it out."

"Oh, yeah?" Dusty studied Mike with some interest. "Okay. So what are we?"

Mike smiled broadly. "We're mountain cowboys."

"Mountain cowboys, huh? I like the sound of that." Dusty laughed. "And thank God, now I know what I am."

Mike looked at him defensively. "Well, people ask, you know, and they always seem to want to call us *cowboys* instead of *packers*. So, well, now they can. We're just mountain cowboys."

"Okay. If they don't call us *packers*, I guess they can call us that. Anything *cowboy* is always fine by me," said Dusty.

Mike stood up and looked out toward the horses in the meadow. "They've been eating for a while. Their heads are up. I'll go gather them. You still up for Tumac today?"

"Always." Dusty took a big slug of coffee. "Be right with you."

It didn't take the men long to get their horses saddled. Dusty threw a bottle of water and some trail snacks into his saddlebag. He tied on his rain slicker and was just swinging into the saddle as Mike rode up.

"Ready?" said Mike.

"Lead out."

Mike turned his horse and Dusty followed him down the trail.

Chapter Twenty

Cassie and Terri had found a great spot near Frying Pan Lake with plenty of graze. They took care to make their camp 200 feet from the lake, complying with Forest Service requirements for stock and water. Having the whole place to themselves, Cassie got a warm feeling in the pit of her stomach and felt relaxed. The horses were hobbled out and their tents set up just as twilight was falling.

"I can't believe no one else is here."

"Is it usually crowded, or something?" wondered Terri.

"Well, it can be. I've been here before where one night it was quiet like this, and the next day a huge swarm of Boy Scouts came pouring in."

Terri gazed around the campsite. "That's hard to imagine, looking at it now. It's so serene."

"Well, you do have to remember, the Pacific Crest Trail is pretty close, so you're going to have through-hikers too. Also, this is a popular pack trip coming from the other side at Soda Springs," said Cassie.

"Oh, I didn't even think about that," said Terri, "You know so much about the backcountry."

Cassie shrugged it off and tossed another piece of wood on their campfire. "Looks like we better get some more wood for tonight. I'll go grab my ax." She walked over to her pack gear.

Terri busied herself picking up branches and large pieces of wood and dragging them back to camp. In no time they had a large pile of firewood.

"Let's take a break and have some coffee," said Cassie.

"Great idea."

The women poured themselves a cup of coffee and sat down. The horses were still eating. A couple of deer had also come into the meadow, venturing down to the lake for a drink. The horses were of no concern to them, but they kept a wary eye on Cassie and Terri. Terri slowly picked up her camera and snapped a couple of pictures. Cassie felt herself relax, drinking in the pastoral beauty of her surroundings. A frog croaked by the lake. The water on the lake was calm. Tumac's peak turned golden by the final rays of the setting sun.

"Well, hello ladies. What a small wilderness we have," came a deep gravelly voice from behind them.

Terri let off a surprised squeak and Cassie stood up quickly. The deer scattered. Sammy, watching the deer, quickly turned and gave off a low warning growl.

"Roy, you caught us by surprise coming up quietly like that," Cassie said through tight lips. "That's not always a good idea." She stiffly faced him.

"Oh, sorry. I didn't mean to do nothing wrong." Roy stood back and smiled, showing his crooked yellow teeth. He held his hands up in mock surrender.

"You're fine. Next time call out when you come into a camp. It's backwoods etiquette," Cassie said through her clenched jaw. She felt heat in her cheeks.

"Will do." Roy stood belligerently with his back bowed and his arms crossed. He had on the same dirty western shirt from the other day, and the blue handkerchief looked limp. Cassie noticed he had dark rings underneath his armpits that were coated with dust. The unpleasant smell of armpit and stale cigarettes wafted to Cassie's nostrils.

It was all she could do to quell the annoyance she felt rising in her throat. *What is up with this guy? Why does he just keep showing up?* The giddy high of their solitude came crashing down in Cassie's stomach. Hard.

She stood, arms stiff by her sides. "What brings you up here?"

"Well, after all the talk last weekend about packing in, I thought I'd just try it out." Roy held his hands out, palms up. "It's a beautiful spot, for sure."

The backcountry was a different world. It wasn't like she could just shut the door in his face. Cassie sighed. Getting a person out of their camp, who obviously didn't have any manners in the first place, was going to be a challenge. Roy continued to smile at her, waiting. Cassie was conscious of her .38 revolver in the side holster under her light jacket. *Why does he just keep showing up?*

Terri was uncharacteristically quiet. Slowly putting away her camera, she walked back to her tent.

Cassie bent down to the fire to add another log.

"I can help with that." Roy picked up a log.

"Um, that's fine, Roy. I've got it. In fact, we were just going to get our dinner going, so this isn't the best time for a visit right now."

He stood, dropping the log. A red flush crept over his face. His eyes hardened as he stood planted by their campfire.

Cassie swallowed hard. *This is a scary guy. His emotions are all over the place. We better move our camp—soon.*

"Thanks for stopping by, Roy. Maybe we'll see you on the trail." Hoping he would get the hint, Cassie walked over to their Roll-a-Table to start working on dinner. She could feel his eyes burning into her back.

Roy just stood there and didn't move. As she turned around, she could see his hands clenching and unclenching at his sides. His eyes were expressionless. Finally, he spoke. "Well, I guess I'm not going to get a dinner invite here."

"We only brought enough food for the two of us. Sorry, Roy." Cassie wondered how long this was going to take. It was clear they didn't want him to stay.

"Okay, then," he said abruptly as he turned on his heel and walked stiffly off into the darkening evening.

Terri came out of her tent. "Boy, that is one weird guy. The hair was standing up on the back of my neck."

"Yeah, I know. Me too. Why does he keep showing up?"

"I wish I'd bought my gun," Terri said ruefully. "That's going on the top of my list for next time."

"I can't believe how much the wilderness has changed since I was a kid. We never had stuff like this happen then." Cassie pulled the collapsible grill out of her pack box.

"Figures." Terri's shoulders drooped. "As soon as I get here, everything goes down the drain."

"Oh, no. There's no drain here. We just have to be more proactive than we used to be," Cassie said with finality. "Let's get the steaks on."

Cassie was tired and she had fallen asleep the minute her head hit the pillow. It had been a long day driving up to the mountains, packing in and setting up camp.

Suddenly, she was wide awake. Uneasiness ground in the pit of her stomach. She looked down at Sammy. Her dog lay still with her head on the ground. The moon illuminated the canvas tent. As she lay on her back she could see the dark, irregular outline of the trees through the light cloth. There was something about Roy that was really bothering her. She couldn't put her finger on it exactly. His behavior was annoying. Always showing up and demonstrating very few manners. But it went beyond that—then it hit her suddenly. It was his eyes. She had learned as a young prosecuting attorney that people's eyes were a window to their soul. So many soulless people came through the criminal docket. The one thing they all had in common was the vacant eyes. Roy had the flat, emotionless black sockets of those people. Why hadn't she noticed that before?

Cassie checked her .38 right next to her bedroll on the tent floor. Easy reach. Sammy lay with her head down and eyes shut.

Cassie felt comforted. If there was anything to hear, her dog would let her know. She rolled over and fell into a restless sleep.

The sun was shining on her tent and the smell of fir trees and morning dew was in her nostrils. Sammy was looking at her expectantly. "Hang on. Just let me get my boots, girl." Cassie pulled on her boots, grabbed her jacket and they headed out of the tent. The meadow, although beautiful the night before, was spectacular in the morning light. The dew clung to the thick green grass. Frying Pan Lake lay flat and blue. The snowcapped mountain peaks gleamed around them. Prince and Cheyenne stood at the highline, their eyes riveted on Cassie, watching her progress. They offered an encouraging neigh and shuffled their feet, eager to get out to the meadow and eat.

Cassie left the hobbles on her horses during the night so they wouldn't paw at the delicate vegetation. It made it really easy in the morning to turn them loose. She untied their lead ropes and the horses immediately headed toward the meadow, gathering themselves and taking little hops. Horses adjusted quickly to hobbles. They had full movement of their back legs and could make pretty good time lifting up in the front and lunging forward. Cassie could remember one friend's horses that could even gallop in hobbles.

The old cowboys used to tie a bell around their lead horse's neck. The lead horse would be the one all the rest of the stock would follow. They could hear the bell chiming in the distance and easily locate their stock. For the present day it wasn't ideal. More people enjoyed the solitude of the backcountry, so a clanging bell was not popular with other campers. Terri's animals whinnied from their highline as the horses departed. Cassie walked over to turn them loose.

The fire crackled and the smell of coffee permeated the mountain air. Terri stuck her head out of her tent. Her long auburn hair tousled and curly. "Hey, is that coffee I smell?"

"Freshly brewed." Cassie poured herself a cup and set the pot on the rock next to the fire.

"On my way." Terri disappeared into her tent and came out a minute later, an empty coffee cup in hand. "Thanks for putting my horses out. I guess I pretty much passed out." She poured herself a cup of the steaming brew and sat back by the fire.

"No problem. They buddy up so quickly that you can't really put one set out without the others, anyway. Pretty sure the highline wouldn't last too long." Both women laughed.

"I never thought of that," said Terri. "So, where to today?"

"I've got a really good one for you. It's called Tumac Mountain."

"Tumac. What? Is that an Indian name, or what?"

"Well, it's actually a volcanic cinder cone rising some fifteen hundred feet above the general level of the area. The lore is that two sheepherders, McDuff and McAdam, used to race their bands to try to be the first to get the pasturage on the mountain. And from that came the name *Tumac*, for two Macs."

"Geez, Cassie, you never cease to amaze me."

"Well, I read a lot. What do you say we get those animals and go for a ride up Tumac?"

"Whoa. I thought you'd never ask. I can't wait to see exactly what fifteen hundred feet looks like."

"Pretty high. Did I tell you about the time I was up there by myself and a jet plane flew below me? I could actually look in the cockpit."

"Well, I hope that doesn't happen today. I don't know that Sugar is broke to jet planes yet."

"One way to find out." Cassie dumped the rest of her coffee and headed to her tent to get dressed.

Terri sipped her coffee sitting by the fire in the early-morning sun. "I'll get going in a minute."

The sun had fully broken over the surrounding peaks and it was just beginning to cast some warmth as they rode out. Cassie still felt a little uneasy, but Roy seemed to have gone back to wherever he had come from. She wasn't going to let it ruin her day. As they watered their horses in Frying Pan Lake, Cassie looked at the high peak of Tumac in front of them. Anxiety fluttered in the pit of her stomach, but she pushed it down and focused instead on the challenging ride that lay ahead of them. Sammy swam around the horses as they drank. Prince raised his head and water dripped back into the lake as he chomped on his bit. Cassie turned him, and they headed out. Shaking off excess water, her dog trotted along behind her horse.

Chapter Twenty-One

Dusty and Mike had been silent during most of their ride, lost in their own thoughts as they followed the trail past Blankenship Lakes. The early-morning sun hit the still water and it glistened with an occasional ripple when a trout hit the surface. The lake was transparent with sand and large stones around it. The early volcanic activity of the area was evidenced by the size of the rocks and their placement. Large rock outcroppings sat in the center of the lake. Only the horses' hooves made a muffled sound as they hit the dirt. The snowcapped peaks of the Cascades appeared in front of them from time to time. The fragrant smell of fir spiced the air. Bunches of wildly colored mountain flowers, looking as if planted in a garden—orange, yellow, blue and red—lined the trail. White flowers with yellow centers resembling mountain daisies were in clumps, adding even more color. Although they could see Tumac in front of them, the trail took a long detour down to the Sisters Lakes.

"I'll never understand why they didn't make a more direct trail here," said Mike. We could have just cut straight across and been there."

"Yeah, it does seem odd. But every time I think I know better where the trail should go, I end up on some rock face, or something."

"True. Sometimes it's fun trying."

"Yes, it is."

After about an hour they could see the shimmering waters of the Little Sisters Lake through the trees and backpacker tents erected at several points near the lake.

"Popular as ever," observed Dusty.

"Yeah, that short hike brings them in droves."

They turned with the trail and rode on. The fir trees broke into variable sizes, offering views of faraway glistening snowcapped mountain peaks. A wooden trail sign appeared indicating Tumac was one-half mile ahead.

As they rode, the trail began to pick up altitude. Dusty was in perfect rhythm with his horse. The trees began to drop away as the trail climbed. Muley put his head down and dug in. Dusty leaned forward to help the horse, and together they climbed up the switchbacks toward the top. Dusty loved this part of riding in the mountains. The trail dropped away to a gash in the steep mountainside. Muley, with his muscles bulging and head down, dug in harder as the trail got steeper. Dusty's nose filled with trail dust and horse sweat. The blue Blankenship Lakes looked like tiny ponds surrounded by green forests the higher they climbed. An adrenaline rush filled Dusty as blue sky surrounded him.

On the final steep switchback he could see the top of Tumac; a flat spot with large rocks around it. Muley was on the final pull. Suddenly, something was wrong. Dusty sensed it before he felt it. His saddle had a lot of play in it. Before he had time to react, he could feel himself sliding. Muley braced himself in mid-motion, feeling his rider out of balance. It was all the horse could do to stay on the steep, rocky trail. Once the saddle started its roll, everything went in slow motion. Dusty felt himself slide off his horse, trailside out, and he was airborne. He saw a quick snippet of blue sky and Muley's furry underside. He groaned as his shoulder hit the steep mountainside hard and he began his descent. As he rolled he could feel his gun grind into his leg. Dusty tried to put his hands down, but there was nothing to grab. He raked his hands into the dirt and dug in his heels, but it all gave way. Down he went, rolling and bouncing. He alternated between covering his head and reaching for anything to stop his fall as he plunged down the steep side of the mountain.

Scout, following at Muley's heels, watched the whole process. He gave a short warning bark of alarm. The minute Dusty hit the ground, his Aussie was in hot pursuit of his rolling master. In seconds all that was left of the two of them was a puff of powder.

Mike looked slack-jawed at his partner's body bouncing and turning down the hillside with Scout scampering behind. Muley stood still braced, four feet planted, the saddle under his belly, eyes riveted on the dog and man headed down. In a flash, Mike bailed off his horse on the narrow trail and ran after Dusty, stumbling and tripping down the steep incline.

Cassie and Terri rode toward Tumac. The trail became as big as a road and then slowly narrowed as they got closer to the mountain. The grass was deep green and lush, and the lupine was in fragrant bunches.

"Wow! This is so beautiful, Cassie. I could stay up here forever."

"I feel like that too, but I think it would get a little cold in the winter." Cassie pointed ahead. "The trail is going to get really steep in a little bit. It won't really allow for stopping, so just get ready to go full bore to the top."

"How does it not allow for stopping?" asked Terri.

"Well, in the fact that there is nothing for the horse's feet to hang on to. If you stop, you may just as well end up going backwards."

"Oh. I don't want to go backwards on the face of a steep mountain."

"Exactly."

They traveled about another half mile and came up to the foot of the steep aperture rising high before them.

Cassie turned to Terri. "Well, get ready to be thrilled."

"I'm always ready for that." Terri giggled.

Cassie gave Prince his head and started up the steep trail. They had barely gone five steps when Prince stopped dead and snorted. Cassie could hear a crashing above her on the hillside. Sammy began barking. As the noise got closer, they still couldn't really see what it was. A large object rolled, then hit a rock on the hill above them. There was a perceptible groan as the dirty form bounced and went airborne. It landed with a large whump right in front of Prince's feet on the trail in front of them.

Prince trembled beneath Cassie, ready to blow. She knew at times like this he was like a keg of dynamite. Her horse stood with his feet planted and his nostrils flared. There wasn't much room on the narrow trail. "Easy, Prince." Swinging down, she ran over to see if she could help the person who'd landed in front of her.

Dusty lay still. He was still conscious; thank goodness for that. That last rock had felt like it took his back out. Still, nothing felt like it was broken. He carefully moved his feet and his hands.

Scout barked from the top of the boulder. He jumped over it and slid the rest of the way down the hill, coming to a rest next to the man on the ground. The dog quickly nuzzled the mud-caked form. A dirty hand involuntarily came up and rested on the dog's head.

The realization hit Cassie like a ton of bricks. "Oh, my God," she yelled. "It's Dusty Rose!"

"Whaaat?" Terri peered around Cassie's horse.

Cassie knelt next to Dusty. He was covered in dirt and his face looked like it was going to bruise. His lips were dry and cracked. He groaned.

"Dusty, are you okay?" Cassie touched his face.

He slowly opened his eyes and tried to focus. It took a minute, "Caaa, Cassie?" he croaked out.

"Yes, it's me." As she looked at him, surprise and concern flooded through her. "Can I get you some water?"

"Ye...yes." A ghost of a smile pulled up the corners of his mouth.

Cassie walked back to Prince and pulled out a fresh water bottle. Just as she was kneeling down to give Dusty a drink, she heard the jingle of spurs. Mike came into view, jogging down the trail.

"How is he? Is he okay?" Mike ran up to them and knelt.

"I'm not sure yet. I was just going to give him a drink."

"Boss, are you okay?" Mike reached down to help Dusty into a sitting position.

"C-c-c-careful. I'm not broken, but for sure bruised."

"Oh, sorry. I'll try to be more gentle." Mike slowly assisted Dusty into a sitting position and leaned him against the dirt sidehill. Cassie handed the bottle of water to Dusty.

Dusty took a sip and winced. He hurt, but he felt like he was going to be all right. "Does anybody have any Advil on them? I think I'm gonna need about four."

"Right here," yelled Terri. She dug into her pommel bag and then bailed off her horse and hurried over to Dusty.

He swallowed the Advil, looked at Mike and croaked, "What in the hell happened? Is Muley okay?"

"I don't know what happened. One minute you were looking over the side in front of me and the next minute you were rolling down the hill. There didn't seem to be a whole lot in between," Mike said.

"What's with you guys, anyway? You always seem to be where I'm going," said Cassie.

Dusty studied her. She was beautiful as always, with a blue jacquard wild rag tied around her neck. The black vest went really well with the green-and-white plaid frontier shirt, silverbelly Stetson and blue jeans. Even out on the trail she didn't seem to have a lot of bad days. "Yeah," he said, looking at her, "I was kind of thinking the same thing. Maybe you're my rescuing angel, or something like that."

Cassie's cheeks reddened and she felt a warmth in the pit of her stomach, embarrassed and pleased at the same time. "Well, let's not get carried away. Besides, if that were true, I would think you'd treat an angel a little bit better in the courtroom."

Dusty laughed a low gravelly chuckle and winced. It even hurt to laugh. Sometimes he surprised himself with what he said—must have been the total beating he just took coming down the mountainside. "Well, I guess I'll have to think about it now. This is two times. Maybe after next time?" He winked at her.

Dusty's teeth looked even whiter than usual next to his dirty skin. Cassie stood up quickly, dusting off her jeans. "I think you're going to live." It was Dusty, as usual. She should have known.

"Hey, guys, if Dusty's going to be all right, do you think we could keep going up that mountain? I've heard so much about it. I would really still like to experience it." Terri pulled her brown-and-white Paint horse over to a big rock and, with a mighty lunge, she took her seat in the saddle.

"Geez. The only thing worse than a beginner is a pushy one," said Mike. They all laughed.

Dusty still felt pretty stiff and sore, but the Advil was starting to do its job. He was going to be aching tomorrow. He could probably make it back up the mountain. They talked for a couple more minutes, and then he carefully pushed himself to his feet.

"We gotta find your hat, Boss."

"Yeah. That is my favorite hat. It's taken me years to get it just right."

"We'll keep an eye out for it," offered Cassie, as she swung into the saddle.

"Keep an eye out for our horses too. Hopefully they're still there." Dusty stood and leaned against the hill.

Cassie and Terri rode past them, Sammy leading the way. Mike and Dusty followed on foot, with Scout covering the rear.

Chapter Twenty-Two

Huffing and puffing, Dusty and Mike finally topped the rise of Tumac Mountain. Cassie sat eating her sandwich and watching them walk in. Terri had an empty cylinder lying in front of her on a rock and was studying a scroll. The local hiking group had placed a rolled-up paper scroll in a plastic tube for hikers to sign in when they accomplished the steep climb up Tumac. Muley and Toby were tied to one of the few wind-blown fir trees on the mountaintop.

Dusty took a few steps and then sat down hard on a flat rock. "Boy, that hill is steeper than it looks. I'm going to have a lot more sympathy for Muley next time we decide to ride up."

Mike sat on the sandy ground beside him. "I've got a lot more sympathy for him right now."

Cassie put her sandwich down and stood. "I want to show you your cinch, Dusty. Something pretty weird is going on."

Stiffly, Dusty got to his feet. "Now what?" He followed Cassie over to where Muley stood and frowned. It seemed odd that his cinch wasn't tied. At first Dusty thought she had taken it off, for some reason. Maybe to take the stress off Muley? He wasn't sure what that was about.

As Cassie held the cinch in her hand, Dusty could see the clean cut right across the leather. "Looks like it was done with a knife."

"My thoughts exactly. Do you have any enemies?" She dropped the leather latigo.

"Well, it kind of comes with the territory in my line of work, but at this moment no worse than any other time." He ran his fingers through his dirty hair.

"It sure seems like someone wanted you to get hurt." Cassie's voice was heavy with concern.

"It sure looks that way." Dusty met her eyes and then looked away.

As they turned to walk back to their lunches, Dusty was lost in thought. It suddenly came to him. *What was the silhouette of a man doing outside of my tent last night? Did that have anything to do with this?* The saddles were lying out in their camp right underneath the mantie. It would have been simple for someone just to walk in and slice on his cinch. *One quick flick of a knife. But who? And why?* As Dusty sat down to finish his lunch, he had a sinking feeling this wasn't going to stop just yet. Paul Wolfe flittered through his mind, but that seemed pretty unlikely all the way out here. As far as Dusty knew, he wasn't a big outdoorsman.

Mike stood up. "Boss, I think I'll take a look at that cinch too."

"Yeah, help yourself. You think this has anything to do with our visitor last night?"

"It seems kind of coincidental." Mike walked over to Muley and picked up the leather. "No doubt, that's a clean cut."

"Yeah, they didn't cut it all the way through. Looks like they knew what they were doing. The horse was going to have to be really working to break that cinch, and that would mean steep and possibly dangerous terrain."

"Yup." Mike dropped it and walked back to the group.

"We've had kind of a weird visitor ourselves," said Terri.

"Who?" asked Mike.

"That Roy guy from the work party. He told us he's never packed before and then, all of a sudden, he walks up behind us in our camp last night. He didn't want to leave. I think he has a thing for Cassie. And he is a scary, weird guy." Terri finished in a rush.

Now Dusty's attention was piqued. "So how did you get rid of him, Cassie?"

"I just told him we didn't bring enough food. He was acting like he was going to eat dinner with us. And he got really angry and left."

Dusty thought about it. He knew something was off with Roy. It was the way he carried himself. He didn't seemed totally dialed in with what was going on around him. He just seemed focused on one thing. The more Dusty thought about it, the more it bothered him. That one thing was Cassie.

Everybody was silent while they finished their lunches. Even Terri was uncharacteristically quiet. She filled her name in on the scroll for climbing to the top of Tumac. After everyone signed it, she put it back into the cylinder for the next climbers.

"Where are you guys headed to now?" asked Mike.

"We've got our camp over at Frying Pan. We're staying there for one more night and then we're heading out tomorrow." Cassie stuffed her garbage back into her saddlebag.

"Yeah, it's right over there." She pointed at the blue patch of water between the swirling dark-green forest below.

"Oh, yeah. Is that your tent right there?" Mike looked intently over the edge.

"Where?" Terri tried to follow his gaze.

"He's pulling your leg, Terri," said Cassie. "No one can see that far."

"Oh, you!" Terri laughed and pushed Mike's arm.

Mike grinned. "What?"

"Well, we'd better head back. I think this time I'll ride down the mountain. It was a little rough going the other way." Dusty rubbed his arm ruefully.

"Yeah, Boss, and we still need to find your hat."

"I hope so. The vendor I bought it from at Rendezvous assured me that it held its shape, no matter what. I wonder if that includes rolling down a hill on it." Dusty stood up and brushed himself off.

Kind of a lost cause, considering the amount of dirt he already had on him.

"This should be a good test for you. Good luck finding the hat." Cassie turned to her horse.

"It was nice seeing you guys." Terri waved and followed Cassie.

Dusty watched them mount up. He kept thinking there was probably something he could say to Cassie, but he couldn't think of what it could be. "Hey, Cassie."

"Yeah?" She turned in the saddle and fixed her sky-blue eyes on him expectantly.

Why does that unnerve me so badly? For crying out loud, I can take on whole corporations. "If you're in the area, you guys should stop by our campfire tonight."

Her eyes lit up with merriment. "Why, thanks, Dusty. If we're up to a twelve-mile round-trip ride after we get back to camp, we'll head right over."

Dusty could feel himself redden. *Now, how stupid was that?* He smiled. "Well, you just never know. Have a good ride."

"You guys have a good ride too," said Cassie.

"Hey, Mike. I'll be waving to you from my tent, now that I know what good eyesight you have." Terri gathered up her reins.

"Great. I'll be waving back," Mike said, as he swung into the saddle.

After the women rode out, Dusty took some time to run baling twine through his cinch a few times until he could get it secured. Then he put his bridle on and swung into the saddle.

Mike watched him mount. "It looks like you're going to be okay. You don't even look stiff."

"That's good, because it sure doesn't feel that way from this side."

"Bummer," said Mike. "Well, the quicker we get at it, the sooner we'll be back to camp."

"True. Let's go." The two men headed off the mountain.

About halfway down, Mike suddenly stopped his horse. "Hold on a minute, Boss." He dismounted and walked up the hillside a little ways. Grabbing a brown thing that Dusty at first thought was a rock, Mike dusted it off repeatedly, hitting it on his leg. When he finished, he handed it to Dusty. "Your hat, sir."

"Now I feel normal again. Thank you." Dusty happily shoved the hat onto his head.

Mike looked at Dusty intently. "It almost looks normal. That's pretty good. I would have never thought it could take that kind of beating. I'm sold now."

"Yeah, me too." Dusty reined Muley and they headed out. "Holding the shape is good. It would be great if they could stay clean too."

"We gotta keep those hat cleaners in work." Mike kicked his horse and trotted after Dusty in the late-afternoon sun. Scout followed closely on Muley's heels.

Chapter Twenty-Three

Dusty and Mike made it back to their camp in good time. The sun was just getting low in the sky as they rode in. They stripped the saddles and had all four horses grazing in record time.

Sitting by the fire with a cup of coffee in hand, Mike asked, "So what's the game plan tomorrow, Boss?"

"We might as well get packed up and head out. I have some stuff to get ready for Monday."

"Is it on the Wolfe case?"

"You guessed it. That guy is really a piece of work." Dusty shook his head.

"Kind of gathered that from his reaction when I served him."

"I know we don't usually talk about this stuff, but that case has really got me concerned. I can't put my finger on it, but that guy is just a little bit different than your average guy."

"But not different than your average psychopath?"

"Unfortunately, that's what I'm worried about. Putting a hold on his bank accounts is going to put him under more pressure. We need to get an accounting ASAP of the money they have, or Julie is going to be out of luck. We'll need to do it on Monday."

"Right, Boss." Mike poked the fire with a stick.

The night sky was brightened by the full moon. The stars sparkled in the velvet sky. The moonlight threw shadows on the trees and in the distance they heard a coyote howl. After a couple of minutes, a few more howls joined in and soon a full chorus resounded off the hills.

Scout looked up and whined, ready to join the group.

"No, boy. You don't want to tell all of them where you are," Dusty cautioned.

Scout quieted down.

"So," said Mike, with mock sincerity, "do you think the girls will be stopping by tonight?"

"Don't even go there. I don't know what I was thinking." Dusty's face reddened again at the thought of it.

"Oh, I know what you were thinking. You were thinking you would like to see that woman," Mike said knowingly.

"Oh, well, thank you very much, Mr. Private Investigator. Hope you're not going to charge me for that pearl of wisdom."

Mike hesitated. "Well, considering the kind of day you've had so far, I'm willing to put that one on the house."

"Great. I think I'll go to bed now before I get awarded anymore free stuff." Dusty rose. "Come on, Scout. Let's see if we can find any other bad guys outside the tent tonight."

"See you in the morning, Boss. I'll just stay out here thinking."

"Well, please don't overdo it. See you in the morning."

Scout and Dusty disappeared in the tent. Mike stared into the fire under the moon and stars.

Dusty woke to the rattle of hobble chains and the pull-and-munch of the horses. The sun hit his tent and his nostrils filled with the scent of canvas and fresh grass. The pain from his tumble registered as soon as he moved. Slowly he got up and stiffly pulled his boots on and grabbed his coat. Fresh coffee joined the smells as he carefully walked.

"Any idea where the Advil is?"

"It's on the table. Figured you'd be kind of bunged up."

"I think it's a four-Advil day."

"That bad, huh?" Mike shook his head ruefully, "Well, I guess it could have been a lot worse." Sitting by the fire, he poured himself a cup of coffee. "You want a cup?"

"Oh, yeah. I'm not that bad off." Dusty took some Advil and picked up his cup off the Roll-a-Table. He threw out the old coffee from the night before. After filling it, he sat by the fire to wake up.

"Well, it was pretty quiet around here last night. How did you sleep?"

"If anyone was walking around my tent last night, I sure didn't hear them." Dusty took a drink. "It takes a lot out of you, rolling down a hill and then riding about ten miles. I slept like a rock. A beat-up rock, but a rock nonetheless."

Mike laughed. "That's what you get for trying to imitate a rock—you start sleeping like one."

"Bad one, Mike."

"Can't win them all. I actually didn't hear anything, either, last night. After the coyotes quit yelling, that was it." Mike looked out at the meadow to make sure all the horses were still grazing out there. He counted four and was satisfied.

"Guess they gave up after they couldn't talk Scout into joining them."

"Good thing too. I don't think a dog would want to go out that way, getting eaten by a ravenous pack of coyotes."

Dusty shuddered. "Don't even mention it." He stood up to grab some more coffee. "As soon as the horses get done eating, you want to break camp?"

"Sounds good to me. They've actually been out there about an hour, so as soon as they put their heads up, we can gather them."

"Okay. I'll get my gear ready." Dusty headed for his tent.

They were packed and ready to go in less than an hour. Practicing the principles of *leave no trace* as they rode out, the camp was left in the state they found it. Dusty was silent as he rode and tried to organize his thoughts on what he would do this week. His body was stiff, just as he figured. His head was still a little groggy from rolling down the hill, but he knew he'd be fine in the morning. Wolfe was going to be a handful and he was bracing himself for a busy week. He felt a sense of foreboding about that guy and he shook it off. That wasn't going to be the last nutcase he'd have in domestic law. He just needed to approach it carefully. Whether that cut cinch had anything to do with Wolfe remained to be seen. There sure were a lot of coincidences in a short period of time.

As Dusty rode, the late-summer sun warmed his back. The trail varied between open meadows and dark fir trees. At the end of the meadow a deep creek flowed through the grass. In his mind he could see himself and his wife Sarah, years ago. He was holding their little daughter, Katie, who was two at the time, on the saddle in front of him. As they crossed the creek, her binky had fallen out of her mouth. He'd never forget, as the clear water picked up the binky and it swirled out down the swiftly-moving creek, the look of panic and sadness on his little girl's face. She pointed excitedly at it and made alarmed noises. That was all a dad could take. He handed her over to Sarah and he and his horse plunged into the creek that abruptly dropped to about three feet deep where the binky sailed. He leaned over and scooped it up. As he rode back, his daughter's face broke into a huge smile of adoration and happiness.

Dusty shook his head. It was so easy being a daddy then. He looked around the forest and at the flowing creek. Even the grassy area of the creek with the deep end was still there. Why did life get so difficult? He knew he had let down his family, but he also had done his best to correct it. Now they all had their own lives. He and Sarah were friends. Not like real friends, but people who had shared a past and were still able to remember the good things about why they had. And he saw his kids occasionally, but they were busy too.

He looked down the trail lost in thought. He saw a woman, tall and strong on a gray horse. He looked again. It was just an old tree, bleached from winter and summer sun. Moss hung from a branch and blew in the slight summer breeze. He smiled to himself and thought maybe there was hope for him after all. After all the time since his marriage fell apart, he seriously thought he would never feel anything for another woman again. If nothing else, it was a good sign to find that he could.

He and Mike entered the trees and the sunlight filtered through. As they came to a creek crossing, Dusty could make out an unusually large fish swimming through the ripples. *Damn, I love it out here. There is no other life for me.*

Chapter Twenty-Four

A light summer shower pattered on the roof of his log cabin when Dusty woke up. It was about 6 a.m. and he could hear the rain slapping the leaves of the rhododendrons next to his house. There were no other noises to block it out—the beautiful silence of the country. Dusty never was able to sleep in the city—he hated it when he got stuck in town.

After feeding the horses and Scout, he grabbed a quick cup of coffee and sat on his front porch. He had a few more minutes before he needed to get in the shower. As he took a drink, the phone rang.

"Morning, Boss."

"Good morning, Mike. To what do I owe the pleasure of this early-morning call?"

"Well, first of all, I was wondering how you were doing after your, you know, um, mishap?"

"Very kind of you to inquire. I'm thinking I'm going to live. Actually, I'm just a little bit stiff."

"Great news. So did you want me to go ahead and do a check of all the Wolfe accounts and make sure they are frozen?"

"Absolutely. I think that better be the first order of business today. There is just no telling what's next with that guy."

"Will do. I'll check in with you after I do. And glad you're feeling better."

"Thanks, Mike." Dusty turned his phone off and smiled as he

took a drink of coffee. It was really nice to have someone who cared, even if it was just your buddy.

He got up and went in the house to take a shower. The old wooden screen door banged behind him.

"Good morning, Mr. Dustin Rose," greeted Mrs. Phillips as he walked in the door of his office.

"Good morning, Mrs. Phillips." Dusty walked by her desk and back to his office. He passed by the now empty spaces on the wall that had once contained the picture frames. It was

9 a.m. so the day was young yet. He hung his coat on the coatrack and sat down at his desk.

Just as Mrs. Phillips was bringing in his coffee, the phone rang. "Oh, drat. It happens every time." She plopped the coffee down on his desk in disgust and hurried out to answer the phone. "Rose Law Offices." She paused. "Just one moment, please." Mrs. Phillips hurried to his office door. "It's that nice Mrs. Wolfe, I believe. She sounds very distressed."

Dusty's stomach dropped. It sure didn't take long at all. "Well, put her through."

The phone on his desk beeped and he picked it up. "This is Dusty." A feminine voice sobbed on the other end, "Oh, Dusty, it was horrible." And a fresh torrent of sobs ensued.

"Just calm down and tell me exactly what was so horrible," said Dusty calmly.

"He came over to my house. I had locked the door and he c-a-a-a-m-m-e anyway." Her words shuddered with her sobs.

"I thought you were going to stay with your sister."

Another torrent of sobs. "Well, it was k—kind of crowded there, and I just wanted to be alone." She gasped for air and sobbed again. "I thought since he hadn't ca—alled, it would be okay to go ho—omme.

"Julie, you are going to have to calm down. I can't help you if we don't have all the facts."

"Okay. Okay." She took a deep breath and started again in a

shaky voice. "He, he kicked the door down when I told him to go away. And when he came in, I showed him the restraining order."

"So what did he do then?"

"He, he tore it in half. He said a little piece of paper wasn't going to keep him away from what was rightfully his."

"Did you call the police?"

"I, I tried. But he knocked the phone out of my hand and slapped me across the fa-a-a-c-c-e." Another rush of tears.

Dusty felt sick to his stomach. He had to tell his clients to pick up restraining orders, but personally he didn't have a lot of use for them. He knew of too many people who had been assaulted with one in their hand. The best combination he knew of was a restraining order and a sidearm until help could arrive. Usually if things were bad enough for a restraining order, then you needed a little extra help.

"After he left, did you file a police report?" persisted Dusty. "This is a criminal charge, assault and battery, and in violation of a restraining order makes him eligible for jail time."

"I haven't done anything. He said if I tried anything else, I would be a dead woman. I left the house and went with a girlfriend that he doesn't know. I've been in hiding all weekend."

"Give me your number and we'll get this taken care of," said Dusty. "You just sit tight until we can get him picked up."

"Okay. But I'm scared."

"It's going to be a whole lot scarier with him out there than if he's locked up. I can assure you of that," said Dusty.

"Okay," she said meekly.

As he hung up the phone Dusty's stomach tightened and his fingers curled into fists. He tried not to become personally invested in his clients, but he was a sucker and he knew it. Especially in cases like Julie Wolfe. She had clearly been taken advantage of by this moron and he just wasn't going to stop. The fact that he was physically abusive only made prosecuting him to the full extent of the law that much sweeter.

Dusty called the police and made a report on behalf of his

client. Then he called Mike and explained everything to that point.

"Hopefully they can pick him up at his office today. Just in case, could you call them with the address of his girlfriend and any other information for tracking him down that you might have?"

"Will do, Boss. And I called the bank and checked on the accounts. Apparently they had quite the scene at the Eagleclaw Bank late Friday afternoon. Paul Wolfe had to be escorted out by security."

"Why am I not surprised? That must have been right after he left here. Apparently he doesn't understand why he can't have his cake and eat it too."

"Yeah. Guys like this are a pleasure to take down, for sure," said Mike.

Dusty hung up the phone and stared down at his desk. Not a lot more he could do for Julie until they found Wolfe. He pulled out another file and started to work.

At noon Dusty walked into Maude's, nodding at the locals as he made his way to the end of the bar where Mike already sat.

"Did they pick him up yet?"

"Last I heard they were on their way," said Mike.

"That ought to be a good scene."

"Oh, yeah," agreed Mike.

Maude hurried up and set their drinks down.

As they discussed further plans with the Wolfe dissolution, Dusty felt a hand on his arm. The smell of perfume—a lot of it—filled his nostrils as a feminine voice spoke next to his ear. "Mind if I sit down?" Mike's face looked like he swallowed a canary, so Dusty had a pretty good idea who it would be.

"Sure, Shelley, have a seat." Dusty forced a smile.

That was more than enough for Shelley. She plopped on the seat next to him, bracelets jingling and her fingernails a shade of bright pink today. She was consistent in her low-cut top, with cleavage spilling over the blouse. Dusty tried not to notice. He was pretty sure that he failed because Shelley leaned closer to him and smiled welcomingly. He grimaced inwardly. *I wonder whoever told her that men would find clothes like that attractive, anyway?"*

"So what brings you out to the boondocks again?"

"Well, I was just wondering if you guys were going to be at the Eagleclaw Trailriders meeting tomorrow night."

"That time again?" said Mike.

"I hadn't given it much thought," Dusty added.

"It's Val's birthday. We're going to bring a cake and have a little birthday party for him after the meeting. I know you guys are friends, so I wanted to see if you're coming. It's a surprise."

"I guess it is. My private investigator here didn't know a thing about it."

Mike smirked. "That one got right by me."

"Good thing I came out here then to check," Shelley said in a bubbly voice.

"Yeah, I guess those phones just aren't what they used to be, huh?" said Dusty.

Shelley was ready for that one. "I know, Dusty. But with all the wiretapping and whatnot, I figured the most foolproof way to bring the message was in person. We for sure don't want Val getting wind of it. He's so shy, he maybe wouldn't come." She patted Dusty's hand. "We couldn't have that."

Mike had the big grin he always got when this stuff happened to Dusty. No amount of talking to him could seem to stop him from enjoying it, so Dusty had basically given up.

Dusty watched Shelley tolerantly. "Well, thank you for going to all the effort to see that Mike and I would be there. I'm sure Val would be very pleased."

"No problem at all. I didn't have to work today." She looked at him hopefully.

"Sure wish I didn't, but it's a busy day."

Maude hurried up with their food and looked at Shelley. "What can I get for you?"

"I'll have what Dusty's having."

"All right. Back in a few with it." Maude hurried off and Dusty heard her mutter, "Of course you will, honey."

They ate lunch and Dusty and Mike assured Shelley they would be at the meeting.

As they walked out of the restaurant, Shelley turned to Dusty. "Are you sure you have to work all afternoon?"

"Yes. Unfortunately, I've got a really busy schedule," Dusty assured her.

Shelley's lower lip stuck out. "You can't blame a girl for trying."

Dusty nodded at her and he and Mike turned to walk back to his office.

"Geez. At this rate I'm afraid I'm going to go home some day and find her waiting on the step."

Mike burst into laughter. "Oh, you gotta tell me about that one."

"What is with you, anyway? Why do you find this so funny?"

"Boss, I have no idea, but I sure do."

"Thanks," said Dusty glumly. They walked into his office.

Chapter Twenty-Five

Later that afternoon, after Mike had left and Dusty was working, Mrs. Philips buzzed him.

"There's a call on the line from the Barker Speilman law firm in Seattle."

"Really?" Dusty sat up straight. It was a prestigious Seattle law firm. They only handled seriously big cases, $400 an hour stuff. *I wonder why they're calling Eagleclaw.* He seemed to remember the Barker Speilman offices were in the top tier of the Columbia Center in downtown Seattle. He quickly went through his mind and couldn't come up with a case they were involved in. Maybe it's some backdoor EPA thing. "Thank you, Mrs. Phillips."

He punched the button. "Dustin Rose."

"Hello, Mr. Rose. My name is Kelly Barker, from the Barker Speilman firm downtown."

Oh, God. Dusty hated that. Seattle attorneys really enjoyed doing that—*downtown,* like downtown Eagleclaw wasn't a real downtown. In fact, there was no other downtown, but Seattle. Dusty bit back a retort. "To what do I owe the pleasure of this call, Mr. Barker?"

"I'm sending you a notice of appearance, but I wanted to personally introduce myself. I am representing Paul Wolfe in his divorce. It would appear that we have some issues to discuss—sooner rather than later."

"So it would appear." Dusty winced as he thought of the list.

"Let me know when the court date is, and I'll do my best to schedule it in."

"It will be as soon as possible. My client will need his money released."

"Yes. And my client needs hers protected."

"I'm sure a judge will help us with this dilemma."

"Nice talking with you," said Dusty curtly.

"Pleasure's all mine."

Dusty stared at the phone after he hung up. So Paul Wolfe was going big time. The *money was no object* approach. This case was getting more interesting by the minute. Apparently Wolfe had some reserves on hand to hire an attorney. And the *reserves on hand* part was what bothered Dusty. How much he took from the community funds was a big issue; one that hopefully Mike would be able to get to the bottom of soon.

Things stayed pretty quiet on the Wolfe divorce case for the next couple of days. Mike had been able to track down most of the money—at least the money that had a trail. Dusty's worst fear in a case like this was the money that might not have a trail.

On Wednesday he hurried home after work to feed his horses. Quickly changing out of his work clothes, he slipped on his packer boots, work shirt and blue jeans. He felt much more like himself. As he walked out to his truck, he looked out to the front pasture. Muley and Cheyenne had their heads down in their troughs eating hay. The crickets were chirping but it was otherwise quiet in the clearing of his log cabin.

He loved living in the country. There was something so grounding about horses munching on hay and the muted smell of flowers in the breeze that he couldn't put his finger on, but if he could, he'd be a rich man. The feeling of well-being was priceless. He stopped and looked back at his house. The logs were old and the cement caulking was intact. That was grounding too. The chopping block stood on his back porch with an ax embedded in it.

It didn't get a lot of use this time of year. He turned to get in his truck. Scout stood close to him and waited anxiously by the door. "Not this time, boy. I don't think you want to wait in the truck for the whole meeting." Scout looked at him anxiously, begging to differ. Dusty caved, "Well, okay. But if you get bored, don't blame me."

Scout barked happily. He bounded onto the bench seat of the pickup and assumed his position next to the passenger window. Dusty got in and started up the truck, rolling down Scout's window. Scout immediately stuck his head in the breeze, his tongue hanging out and a happy dog smile on his face.

Dusty headed to the Eagleclaw Grange Hall for the Back Country Horsemen meeting. He liked to get there a little early to catch up with friends on what they had been doing. Since it was summer, it was riding season. The meetings at this time of year were smaller and a lot of the members kept up on events through electronic means; Facebook, emails and whatever else they did. Dusty still preferred the old-fashioned kind of contact, face-to-face.

The lot was about half full when he pulled in. The usual cast of characters were all assembled in front of the grange. Loud guffaws washed all the way out to the parking lot.

Mike was already there, standing next to Val and Eddie.

"Hi, guys." Dusty greeted them as he walked up.

Val stuck out a big paw, and Eddie and Walt followed suit. Mike stood back and smiled.

They talked about the Buck Creek work party. Danny had said it was a huge success. "Way to go, Val," congratulated Dusty.

Val blushed. "Well, I didn't do it by myself."

"We needed a leader and organizer and you did a great job, Val." Mike slapped him on the back.

"That's a fact," agreed Walt.

"Hey, I hear you had quite the ride last weekend at Tumac," said Eddie.

"Oh, you did, huh?" Dusty looked at Mike.

Mike shrugged and held out his hands, palms up.

Eddie followed his gaze. "It wasn't your partner, so don't worry about that."

"Word sure passes quick on an interesting ride, doesn't it?

"You want to give us the inside, Dusty?" Walt encouraged him.

"Not much to add to it. My saddle cinch gave way and I took a header off of Tumac."

"That's what we heard, but no more details on the cinch letting loose part." Eddie raised his eyebrows.

"No, and that's the part I wish I knew."

The door to the grange hall opened and a medium-sized woman with permed strawberry-blonde hair called out, "Time for a meeting, everybody. Come on in."

Lydia McCorkle was a longtime member of the Eagleclaw Trail Riders. She was always available to support the club in any way she could.

Dusty and Mike followed the other men in the door. The hall was quickly filling up. Dusty nodded as he passed by friends and gave a quick handshake here and there. The women smiled at him. He hadn't seen Shelley yet, and that was unusual. He started toward the rear of the grange, where he preferred to sit. Just as he turned down an aisle, an enthusiastic female voice called, "Dusty, over here!"

Dusty looked up and saw the dyed-blonde woman with the dark root line down the middle of her head waving her arms frantically, bracelets clattering, and gesturing at the empty seat next to her about five rows up. Dusty sighed and waved back. He pointed at Mike and kept walking down the aisle. As he sat down he could see her lower lip began to stick out. Dusty turned his eyes to the front of the room. The chapter president in a tan cowboy hat stood before the podium.

"I want to welcome all of you to the regularly scheduled meeting of the Eagleclaw Trail Riders. Glad you could make it. We've got a lot to cover tonight and some really interesting rides coming up this month. So after we hear the secretary's report from the business meeting, we'll find out some of the latest things our chapter has been doing."

The business meeting recap went by fairly quickly. Dusty mostly listened as he scanned the room. There was quite a big turnout. Still, as he looked down the rows, there she was: Julie Wolfe had come to the meeting. She kept her head down, and when Dusty caught her eye, she gave a weak smile in return. He kept trying to figure out who she had come with, but it was difficult to see with all the people in the way.

The president concluded, "Well, that brings us to officers' reports. Let's start off first with Val Norman and the work party at Buck Creek. How did it go, Val?"

Val stood up at his seat. "We had a really big turnout for such short notice. And I want to thank each one of you who made it. Danny Conger couldn't say enough good things about the job we did. And the bridge is complete."

Somebody yelled out from the audience, "We couldn't have done it without you, Val." Applause started and Val blushed and quickly sat down.

The next events were outlined for chapter rides and work parties and the meeting drew to a close. Just as the president was asking for any other business, Shelley raised her hand. "May I say something?"

The president nodded at her. "Of course."

Shelley walked to the front of the audience. "Today is Val Norman's birthday. And I just wanted to invite any of you who would like to stay for some cake and ice cream to celebrate this event."

The group applauded and then someone stood up and started singing *Happy Birthday*. Within seconds everyone else joined in and the singing echoed off the rafters. A motion was made to adjourn the meeting and everyone slapped the red-faced Val on the back. The crowd headed over to the cake and ice cream already set out on the sideboard.

As Dusty walked over to the table, he noticed that one of the servers was none other than Julie Wolfe. She seemed subdued. He could see that she had quite a bit of makeup on, but it didn't quite hide the black-and-blue mark around her eye.

"How are things going?" asked Dusty.

She took a breath. "Well, they've been better."

"I'm sorry to hear that. You got the message about the meeting at my office tomorrow at two?" Dusty looked at her with concern.

"Yes. I don't really want to be there when he's there, but if you say I have to, I will."

"Mike and I will both be there, so you don't have to worry about your personal safety. But it would be really helpful for you to come, because if we start talking about any kind of proposed divisions of property, your input would be essential."

"Okay," Julie said in a small voice. People came up behind him, so Dusty moved out of the way.

Dusty was eating his cake and talking to Mike and Eddie when suddenly a hand fell on his shoulder and a familiar voice said, "How you doing, bro?"

God, he hated that word, *bro*. It sounded like they were brothers in some weird way. Dusty bit it back. "Well, hey, Roy. You made it to the meeting. How's it going?"

Roy took a bite of his ice cream and cake and replied with a full mouth, "Really good. I think I'm going to like this. Definitely a lot of women." He winked at Dusty, giving a full view of what was in his mouth. It wasn't a pretty picture and Dusty was hoping he could get out of there sooner, rather than later.

"Well, that's just great, Roy. I wish you all the best luck. Well, I'd like to stay and talk, but I have a lot to do at home. Enjoy yourself." Dusty turned and hurried toward the door, dumping his plate and spoon in the garbage on his way out.

The sun was just going down and groups of people were still milling around outside the old grange hall. Dusty saw Val in one group, so he rushed over to extend his wishes. "Hey, Val, just wanted to wish you a happy birthday! And many more years in the saddle to come!"

Val stuck out his hand again. "Thanks a lot, buddy. And thanks for all your help last weekend too."

"It was my pleasure. And we couldn't have done it without your stellar job of leading the work party. You do a great job, Val."

Val reddened once again. "Aw, thanks, Dusty. That means a lot to me, especially coming from a guy like you."

Dusty smiled and headed for the door. That was a little confusing. He wondered what Val meant by *a guy like you.* It always made him feel weird when people said that kind of stuff. If it was his occupation, it made no difference. Here he was a horseman, no different than anybody else at the meeting.

Dusty headed away from the crowd and toward his truck. Lost in thought, he didn't even see the woman walking towards him until he ran right into her. The woman squealed, "Dusty."

Dusty looked down to see Shelley sitting on her rear end on the ground in front of him. "Oh, I'm so sorry. Here, let me help you up." He grabbed her arm and helped her scramble to her feet.

"Geez. I just wanted to see how you liked the surprise. I didn't know I was going to get mowed down."

"My fault entirely. Please accept my apologies." Dusty looked at her in earnest, his deep-blue eyes imploring.

Shelley appeared to have difficulty breathing for a minute or two and then she regained her composure. "Accepted." She looked at him thoughtfully. "I was thinking, though, Dusty, you could make it up to me by taking me out for a drink." She gave him her most enticing grin.

Here we go again. "Well, that is certainly a wonderful idea, Shelley, but I have got a ton of work to go through before tomorrow. I'm going to have to take a rain check."

Shelley looked crestfallen. But then she perked up a little bit. "Really? A rain check?"

"Sure. Why not? I'll let you know when I have time. But you know, if you really wanted to have a drink tonight, I bet Mike would be happy to join you."

Dusty gestured over by the door where Mike, unaware, was talking to the old-timers.

Shelley looked over. "Well, I would rather go with you, but I guess if Mike wants to, I could probably go with him this one time."

"I think it's a great idea," encouraged Dusty.

That seemed to be all she needed. "Well, in that case, okay." And she headed off at a fast walk toward Mike's back.

Dusty hurried to his truck, swung in and slammed the door. Mike enjoyed Dusty's discomfort so much, it would be nice for him to get a little back. Dusty chuckled and pulled out of the parking lot.

He felt his hair stick up on the back of his neck, as if someone were staring at him, as he went out of the parking lot. The dog whined, and he looked down at Scout. "It's okay, boy." At the same time he wondered if it was.

A man stood by the far side of the grange hall and watched Dusty's truck leave. As the truck turned out onto the main street, the man took a final drag, dropped the cigarette and crushed it under his boot.

Chapter Twenty-Six

Dusty was lost in thought as he drove home. The meeting tomorrow with Paul Wolfe and Kelly Barker would be interesting. Usually he never saw other counsel until court, which was scheduled for Friday afternoon. The fact that Barker and his client wanted to meet ahead of time showed something. What it was, Dusty wasn't sure. They either wanted to find out what assets Julie had, or how much they figured they could keep. Either way, it was strange.

Dusk was just beginning to settle on the warm summer evening as Dusty pulled into the gravel turnaround. He got out of his truck and Scout bounded out behind him. An old mossy, weather-beaten fence surrounded his log cabin. The gate had long since fallen down. Dusty loved this place. His grandpa had really enjoyed building it, and it showed. A garage stood, well worn, with a cement floor and a rickety upstairs. It might have been planned to be an extra room at some point, because mossy stairs led to an outside door upstairs. Another small building sat right behind the cabin. Dusty had, more or less, converted it into an office. At one point his grandpa had used it for an extra bedroom. Dusty found it particularly entertaining that when the church people came to call and leave pamphlets, they couldn't figure out which door to knock on. He usually tried to make himself scarce for that, appreciating their good intentions, but he just didn't want to sit and talk. Heck, he did that all day at work.

Dusty went up the old cracked cement walk to his back porch.

A ready supply of wood was stacked by the back door. Actually, the upstairs wasn't heated at all, and there were three bedrooms up there. He sighed. He knew living in his log cabin wasn't for everyone. He had tried moving there with Sarah after the kids had moved out. What a mistake that had been. He'd never seen someone go through actual withdrawal for wall-to-wall carpeting. She finally packed up and moved back to their home in the suburbs—a tract home with a cul-de-sac and basketball hoop. She was happy there, and he was happy here with his horses and Scout. He stared out into the night, one hand on the back door. It was funny how things change as you get older.

Looking at the thick dark forest behind his house, Dusty heard a crashing. To call it the backyard would be an understatement. His property was fourteen acres in a narrow rectangle. Since his horses were pastured in the front, Dusty didn't have a lot of call to go in the back, which was choked with thick trees and salal everywhere. During the day the surrounding trees and isolation were reassuring, but at night it could be remote and eerie. There were rumors there was a bear den and cubs in the back of the property. It could be true. He had never checked it out. Once on a late Sunday afternoon, he had just gotten home from riding and was sitting in front of the television set. All of a sudden, he heard a huge ruckus in the side yard, Scout barking, and the biggest bear he had ever seen ambled by the house. Dusty checked on the horses in the front pasture. He had just fed them. They were calmly eating out of their troughs as if nothing had happened. *Must be downwind*, Dusty had thought at the time.

With his hand on the back door, Dusty hesitated, looking out at the thick woods behind his house. The only illumination was the old yard light. Moths flew in and around the light. Dusty's gaze was met by silence. The crash had sounded pretty large. He knew there were plenty of wildcats out in the area. People had reported more than one missing house cat or small dog in recent months. Since cougars bred like rabbits, Dusty knew the incidents of missing pets were only going to increase. He stood in the doorway uncertainly. He waited to see if the loud crash would be followed by something. But nothing. Dusty finally put the key in the lock and walked in his kitchen door.

Because the cabin was dark, his grandpa had compensated by making the downstairs all windows. Even the kitchen back door was glass. A break-in would be easy. So far Dusty had been pretty lucky and his only brush with crime had been a couple of teenagers who had kicked in his front door. Pretty funny really, he mused. The entire back was windows, but the front had only two windows and a big, heavy, four-inch-thick log door. They had kicked in the door and stolen the television and a couple of other things he had lying around. All told, they didn't get much. His guns had been locked in the gun safe and there was no way they were getting in there. All his camping stuff was locked in the horse trailer or the storage building.

The evening had taken on a chill. Dusty split a couple of logs and set about making a fire in his fireplace. He looked appreciatively at the river rock stones as they glowed in the firelight. He put on coffee. He knew it was strange that he drank coffee at night, but he had read somewhere that for some people coffee held the properties of relaxation, rather than making them wide awake. And he knew for him this was true. It didn't keep him up one bit, but in the morning it always helped him to wake up. He shook his head. *Strange but true.*

Sitting in front of his evening fire, he sipped his cup of coffee and opened Julie Wolfe's file. This was going to be an interesting case. He was going to need Mike to run down Paul Wolfe's credentials before he had become the next Mr. Julie Wolfe. Dusty had a feeling that the answers to Paul's behavior all lay in his past. They needed to know how to confront him and salvage as much of Julie's money as possible.

Scout slept at Dusty's feet. The fire began to burn low and Dusty closed up the file. He hit the bathroom and headed upstairs to his bedroom, Scout trotting along behind.

Dusty had no idea how long he'd been sleeping when he was

awakened by Scout's low-throated growl. Dusty slowly reached over to his bed stand and picked up his Vaquero. He scanned his room. Seeing nothing, he looked again at Scout. The dog seemed to be looking in the direction of the side yard parking area. Dusty listened and heard the low hum of an engine out in the driveway. He sat up, taking care to keep out of sight through the window. Peeking from the curtain on the side, Dusty could see a pair of headlights in the driveway. He couldn't see the driver, but the car sat idling for what seemed like an eternity.

Scout continued to growl, but he didn't try to move toward the bedroom door. It appeared that the visitor had not tried to access the house. *So far, anyway.* There was no way that Dusty was going to be able to go back to sleep. He slipped his shirt, jeans and Romeos on and walked down the hall and then downstairs. Gun in one hand, finger poised near the trigger, he pushed the door open with his free hand. He walked the length of the back porch, careful to keep hidden from the car. He yelled out, "Hey!" Running footsteps crossed the front porch. Whoever it was ran out to the car and slammed the door shut.

The car took off so fast it dug a big patch of gravel behind it.

Dusty's heart pounded in his chest. So they were trying to get in his house. The pit of his stomach tightened in a knot. He stifled the impulse to jump in his truck and chase the intruder. *Calm down. If he comes back, I'll be ready.* He needed to figure out who was doing this and what they were after. He walked up to the front porch and looked down the deck. Empty lawn chairs. He turned and went back to the back of the house and went inside.

Opening up the fridge, he quickly poured a mug of milk and put it in the microwave. A warm glass of milk at this point seemed the best idea. It usually helped him to sleep. Scout waited patiently on the kitchen floor, keeping an eye on Dusty.

They walked upstairs together and Dusty put his Vaquero on the bed stand next to him. He rolled over in bed. He couldn't seem to turn his mind off over who it could be and why. He tossed and turned most of the night.

Chapter Twenty-Seven

The sun streamed in Dusty's bedroom window as he woke up, and Scout was pushing his arm. Looking around groggily, he could tell he had overslept—exactly how long, he wasn't sure. Suddenly he remembered he was supposed to have a meeting with Paul Wolfe's lawyer today. He had to get into the office. In record time Dusty had showered, shaved and was on his way over to the office.

"Good morning, Mr. Dustin Rose." Mrs. Phillips greeted him as he came in the door. "Shall I bring you coffee?"

"Please." Dusty tossed his coat on the rack and hurried toward his office. He paused at the doorway. "Have you heard anything from Mr. Barker's office?"

"As a matter of fact, his assistant called to confirm your appointment with him this afternoon."

"Right. What time are they coming?"

"Well, she said it wasn't convenient for Mr. Barker to come to Eagleclaw. He wishes you to come to town for a two o'clock, if that will work for you."

Dusty's jaw felt still as annoyance pricked him. *And so the games begin.* "So what did you tell them?" He asked in a controlled voice.

"I said I couldn't confirm a change of location without consulting you."

"Thank you, Mrs. Phillips."

"Of course. Here is the phone number, and the assistant's name is Cindy."

Dusty picked up the message and thought about his next move. Already it was the big Seattle lawyer throwing his weight around against the small country lawyer and the *let's meet in town* thing, like Eagleclaw wasn't a town. Mulling it over, he picked up the phone. After one ring, Mike answered.

"So, anything new on the Wolfe case?"

"Pretty interesting stuff on the accounts. Some big transfers in the last couple of months. I need to look into it more. Julie isn't the first Mrs. Wolfe, either."

"Didn't think so. Any word on criminal history?"

"That's another thing I need a little more time on. Mr. Wolfe wasn't always Mr. Wolfe, and past charges are going to be under a different name. I have my source running the name, photo and social security number as we speak."

"Good. I have an appointment with Mr. Wolfe and his attorney this afternoon. They moved it to Seattle."

"Of course."

"Think you'll have anything by one?"

"I'll do my best. It's after ten now. Are you having a late morning?"

"Yeah, and that's a whole different problem. People seem to want to come to my house in the middle of the night and creep around my front porch. It's making it really difficult for me to get any sleep."

"That sounds interesting. Do you need any reinforcements?"

"I might. Maybe you can meet me at Maude's for lunch and we can talk about it?"

"It's a date."

"Thanks, Mike. It's the best one I've had in weeks."

"Yeah, and probably the only one, unless you can improve your style around Cassie."

Dusty sighed. "Yeah, you're probably right." He put the phone in the receiver.

He was going to call Barker's office, but he'd be darned if he was going to get right on it. He'd let them wonder a while. Setting the message aside, he thumbed through the mail.

Mrs. Phillips brought his coffee in. "I'd be happy to get some new frames for your pictures, Mr. Dustin Rose."

Dusty had forgotten about the blow-up in his office last week. He looked at the wall where the pictures had been. "That would be great, Mrs. Phillips."

At about ten minutes to twelve Mrs. Phillips buzzed him. "Mr. Barker is on the line."

"Thank you." Dusty had been so busy working, he'd forgotten to call back to confirm the afternoon appointment. *Just as well. Make them work for it.*

"Dusty Rose."

"Well, hello, Dusty. I had Cindy call your office this morning. I had a couple situations arise and I wondered if you'd be able to swing into town this afternoon for our meeting, rather than me having to travel out to the boondocks."

"Sorry about that, Kelly. I got busy. You know, disputes between the pig farmers and cattle ranchers out here. Just the usual."

"I see." Kelly Barker appeared to miss the joke completely.

Dusty moved on, "So what time were you thinking?"

"What about two o'clock?"

"I have a lunch meeting at noon, so as long as traffic doesn't hold me up, I could probably make it there by two-thirty."

Barker hesitated, "Well, if you can't make it any earlier…"

"Nope. That's it."

"Okay, then. Two-thirty. And thank you for making the accommodation."

"I don't mind this once," Dusty said pointedly, "but I do try to conserve my trips into Seattle."

"I understand completely. Pig farmers are probably quite time-consuming," Barker said with mock sincerity.

"Totally." Dusty hung up. He was going to enjoy winning this case twice as much as before. The lawyer was just as bad as the husband.

Grabbing his coat, he headed out the door.

Chapter Twenty-Eight

Cassie watched her horses as they ate. The pack trip last weekend had been eventful, as usual. It seemed that everywhere she and Terri went, Dusty seemed to be. He was an attractive man. The only thing that still bothered her was seeing him change in court. Putting facts in the order most advantageous to your client and putting on your best face was definitely a part of the practice of law. But at a personal level, seeing a person adopt a different persona so quickly and seamlessly made it difficult—difficult to trust him. And she knew that was her biggest problem—trust.

Roy was definitely a different sort of person. He seemed to have disappeared after she and Terri got back from the ride to Tumac. But his persistence and odd, almost possessiveness around her gave her the creeps. Terri had agreed that something was definitely off about him. Cassie wondered if he really wanted to ride horses and just happened to run into her up at Buck Creek, or if there was something more to it. Hard as she scoured her brain, she was unable to think of a reason why he would want to follow her. An old client perhaps? But she hadn't done criminal law in so long, it would seem like a pretty remote possibility.

She walked back toward the well-kept little farm house. Her flowers were blooming and everything was in order. She loved this place, always had. The house was a small bungalow, pale yellow with white-trimmed windows. The bright-red rhododendrons were in full bloom on one side of her house, and red-and-pink roses lined the porch.

She had a 10:30 appointment that morning and she needed to get to the office. As she put on her makeup, in her mind she could still see a groggy, dirt-encrusted face looking up at her. She stifled a giggle. If anything took Dusty out of the role of ruthless litigator, it would be rolling down a steep mountain and landing in a heap at her feet. Really kind of put the whole thing into perspective.

She picked out a dress that was summer casual, yet still professional—a sleeveless cream-colored sheath with a gold belt—and topped it off with a gold bracelet and earrings. She realized she had been pretty methodical about the whole process. It was time to go to Maude's Mountain Café and face her fears. Odds were Dusty and Mike where there, and she would just show up and see what happened.

She felt relieved. It was almost as if she had been holding her breath, waiting to see what kind of a decision she would make. And here it is. She was going to do it. She guessed it was better than waiting around and never knowing what would have happened. Cassie gathered up her files off the kitchen table and put them in her briefcase. She felt nervous, for some ridiculous reason. He could totally ignore her. She knew that wasn't going to happen.

Locking the door, she headed to her Ford Explorer and tossed her briefcase in. She had no sooner got in the driver's seat and was fastening her seat belt when the phone rang. "Cassie Martin."

"Hey, Cassie Martin," a low voice said with assumed familiarity.

"Hello," she replied stiffly.

"Well, I see you got back from the mountains safely."

Cassie felt a prick of alarm at the word *see,* what was that supposed to mean?

"Roy, why are you calling me?"

"Well, calm down, babe. I just wanted to make sure you got back all right."

Babe? This was getting to be over the top in a hurry. "Roy, I got back all right, just like I do every time I go anywhere. I'm not sure why you are calling me."

The voice dropped into an ugly snarl. "Because we're friends, right? Just calm down. It's not like I'm trying to sleep with you, or anything."

Cassie felt revulsion well up in the back of her throat. "Okay, Roy, that's it. I thought you were a nice guy, right up until a couple of seconds ago. But I'm past that. Listen carefully. You need to forget this phone number. If, for some reason, I've given you an idea that I was interested in being anything other than friends with you, I'm sorry. But now I realize that I am not interested in being your friend anymore, either. Good-bye, Roy."

She disconnected. Okay. Just when she is actually thinking about giving Dusty a chance, this nutcase decides to proclaim his lust for her. *Yuck. Well, never say die, unless you have to.* Cassie made up her mind. She was going to Maude's today and see what happened. Roy was going to have to figure out his own problems without her being involved.

Feeling energized, she pointed her car toward Puyallup, planning how she was going to meet with her clients in the opposite direction, get everything done, and just casually happen to show up at the restaurant at noon today. Cassie smiled. She'd done more difficult things before, that was for sure.

Chapter Twenty-Nine

Maude's place was buzzing with the lunch crowd and Mike sat at his usual place in the back. Dusty was so consumed with thoughts of his case, he almost missed the woman sitting in the booth with a cup of coffee in her hand.

"Hi, Dusty."

Dusty stopped in his tracks. Cassie's light-blue eyes looked up at him. Was that possibly a smile? The case completely dropped from his mind and he suddenly was in the back country again. "What brings you to this neck of the woods?" He smiled at her.

Cassie smiled back. "Well, I had a client over here. A different case than the mill," she qualified quickly. "I thought I'd stop in here and see if you'd recovered from your fall down Tumac."

Dusty reddened with embarrassment. "That's really thoughtful of you. Yes, I think I'm one hundred percent again." Dusty looked over at Mike, now torn as to what to do. He wanted to stay and talk to Cassie. Had she really stopped in to see him? It seemed hard to believe, but maybe so. He still really needed to have a game plan for the meeting this afternoon.

"Now that our case is over," Dusty said, "I was wondering if you might want to go riding?"

"I always want to go riding."

"Saturday?"

"Where?"

"How about Crystal Mountain?"

"That sounds really good, but should I bring my gun and my SPOT satellite?"

"Very funny again. How about, for something different, I bring my gun and see if I might be able to protect you?"

Cassie pursed her lips thoughtfully. "Well, are you sure? I mean, I don't mind rescuing you again."

Dusty laughed. "I'll bring mine. I really owe you one, anyway." He winked. "It's a man thing."

Cassie laughed. "If you're sure."

Looking over at Mike again, Dusty could see he hadn't missed a thing. "Oh, I'm sure. But tell you what; we can both bring them and have each other's backs."

"Deal."

"Meet you at Sand Flats at nine o'clock?"

"Sure."

"Great. That's just great. I've got to meet Mike now and go over some stuff for an afternoon meeting, but I'm really looking forward to it."

"Me too." She smiled.

He hurried over to the table where Mike sat. "Well, look at you."

"What?" Dusty could not stop smiling.

"Oh, come on. I saw the little exchange. Something just happened, I'm pretty sure."

"Okay. I asked her to go riding with me on Saturday and she agreed."

"Wow. That's progress. Who would have thought?"

"I know, right? Things happen when you least expect it."

"For sure. Speaking of that, what's with the people coming to your house in the middle of the night? I think that definitely needs looking into."

"Yeah, me too. Want to come over tonight?"

Mike grinned. "A sleepover?"

"Well, kind of, but I'll sleep and you and Scout stay awake."

"Sounds like a coon hunt. I'm in."

"Good. At least I can look forward to one night's sleep, anyway."

Maude rushed up and set their plates in front of them. "Two specials." She filled their waters. "More coffee?"

"In a little bit. Thanks, Maude."

"My pleasure. Let me know if you need anything else." The waitress turned on her heel in a flash of pink uniform and red hair.

Dusty picked up his Reuben sandwich and took a big bite. "What did you find out on Paul Wolfe?"

"The first thing has to do with his name. *Wolfe* sounded a little too common, so I checked and it turned out I was right. It was a little too common. In fact, that's not his name at all."

"Do tell." Dusty wiped his mouth. "I'm honestly not surprised."

"His real name is Richard Farengetti."

"Close, anyway," joked Dusty.

Mike smirked. "Yeah."

"So how did Mr. Farengetti stack up in the domestic violence field?" Dusty asked between bites.

"Not good. He has two prior marriages. Both of them ended with charges of DV. In the last one they added child endangerment."

"Must've blown up and used poor judgment with a child," speculated Dusty.

"Something like that." Mike started in on his sandwich and let that settle in as he continued. "His criminal record is not stellar, as you guessed. Along with the DV charges, he was charged with embezzlement after the last marriage and had to actually serve about eight months in jail."

"I wonder if Julie knows this." Dusty took another bite. "We also need to find out if he actually got a divorce and a legitimate name change, or this may not even be a marriage. It could all be a hoax with another embezzlement under the guise of community funds."

"I still have some records to check on that."

"All good points." Dusty pointed his finger at Mike.

"It would seem a waste of time to help divorce two people who were never legally married in the first place," added Mike.

"Thank you, Counsel. Nice to have backup."

"Anytime," answered Mike. "We aim to please."

Dusty threw his napkin down on the table and grabbed the check. "I appreciate all your effort, Mike. This is definitely going to come in handy at the meeting today. I better hit the road. No telling how long it's going to take to get to Seattle and park."

"Good luck, Dusty. Let me know what happens."

"Will do." Throwing a few bills down on the table, Dusty turned to walk out of the restaurant. He quickly glanced at Cassie's table but she had already left. He felt a small prick of disappointment and headed out the door.

Chapter Thirty

As Dusty drove down Highway 167 into Seattle, he thought for the umpteenth time how he really hated this drive. Since it was the middle of the day, a week day nonetheless, he knew it was much better than it would have been on Friday evening or the weekend. Why did he agree to go *downtown* for this meeting? He knew in his gut it was for bargaining power. Let the other side think he was easy—it would all play to his advantage later. Meanwhile, he had to pay for all the fuel, time and parking to get there. Dusty grinned. That's what made his job so much fun. You just never knew what would happen next. If he couldn't be in the mountains, he might as well make the best of it. Judy ended up not being able to make the meeting after all—her child care provider was sick. *It's probably just as well, I have no idea what I'm going to find there.* He had assured her he would call if any reasonable offer was presented.

Turning off on Seneca Street, Dusty took a few turns and ended up right in front of the Columbia Center, another favorite of his. Last time he checked it was *only* about $30 a day for parking—and that was probably for the early bird. He looked at the black hole looming in front of him, the entrance to underground parking. *Well, here goes nothing.* He turned his car and began his descent. The ceilings were low and the cars were parked very close together, and it took him four floors down to find a parking spot. Dusty tried to repress the feeling of suffocation as he got out and locked his car. The painted arrows led to the elevators and he began the trip up to the 72nd floor. Exiting the parking elevator, he made his way to the first bank of elevators for floors 1 to 40. Stepping on board, he punched the button and waited for the soothing elevator music. He was alone and the floor numbers reverted to a couple of Xs as he soared skyward. Dusty was certain he had left his stomach somewhere near the lobby. As his ears popped, a comforting voice announced, *40th Floor*.

Feeling a little dazed, Dusty stepped back onto solid ground, at least more solid than the elevator offered. Another bank of elevators presented themselves. The doors opened, he stepped in and punched in the button for the 72nd Floor. *This had better be good.* He again sped skyward. The Xs were back on the elevator readout, and then suddenly Floor 72 appeared. He usually liked to take a plane when he went this high. The doors peeled open and directly in front of him sat a receptionist at a desk, with the name "Barker & Speilman" in large metal letters on the wall behind her.

Dusty quickly gathered himself and, still clutching his briefcase, he stepped purposefully toward the desk.

"Dustin Rose here to see Mr. Barker."

The attractive brunette smiled at him. "Of course. I will let Mr. Barker know you are here. Please have a seat."

Dusty turned to sit. White leather couches faced floor-to-ceiling windows overlooking downtown Seattle. *It's a real good thing I'm not afraid of heights.* Having no choice, he studied the waterfront and ferries streaming back and forth across the sound. It was overcast in Seattle; not unusual. The gray sky looked like it could go either way today. The dampness was a way of life here, and no wonder.

Lost in thought, Dusty barely heard Kelly Barker come up behind him.

"Dusty, thank you for coming downtown today. I really appreciate it. I owe you one."

Kelly held out a hand.

Dusty took his hand in a firm handshake. "My pleasure," he said, giving Kelly Barker his best grin. "Nice office."

"Oh, thanks," said Kelly with false modesty. "We had to find a space with a little more room as the firm kept growing. Come on back." Dusty followed him past the receptionist down the hallway to the conference room. They passed two or three open office doors and finally turned a corner. The conference room was on a corner of the building, sporting floor-to-ceiling windows on both sides with an impressive show of Seattle. Dusty wondered just how strong those windows were. It seemed like a reasonable question at 72 floors above the ground.

Sitting at the conference table was none other than Paul Wolfe, or Richard Farengetti; whatever name you wanted to use. Dusty smiled at him.

"Good afternoon, Mr. Wolfe."

He smiled back at Dusty. "Have a good drive?"

"Just great. Never mind it at all," Dusty lied.

"Well, have a seat and let's get to this," said Kelly.

Since Paul and Kelly were already seated with their backs to the window, Dusty took the seat directly across from them with his back to the door. Not his preference, but with windows like that, just as well. You never knew when you might develop your first case of vertigo. He pulled out his yellow pad, placed it in front of him and looked across the table.

"What it really boils down to at this point are four bank accounts," Kelly stated. "There are the house accounts with joint checking and savings, the corporate account and the trust. Our proposal is that Julie release the hold on the corporate account and the trust so that Paul can continue to do business. He would be agreeable to signing off on the house checking account, after a full accounting, of course, and the joint savings account can remain frozen until an agreement for distribution of funds has been reached."

Dusty listened without reacting. Kelly looked across the table expectantly.

Finally, Dusty said, "That's it?"

Puzzled, Kelly replied, "Yes, that's it. What else would there be?"

"From Julie's standpoint, quite a bit. Without the joint savings account, what would she be putting into her checking account? And without a complete accounting of the business account, how would she know whether she is getting an appropriate share?"

Dusty began to pack up his briefcase. "This is a five-year marriage, Kelly, with my client putting the lion's share of money into it. She is entitled to a full accounting of that business before any monies go to anyone—except for the necessities for running the business and the home."

"Hey, wait a minute. How about a counteroffer?" said Kelly, his face a mask of concern. "I'm sure we can come up with something today."

Dusty stood for a moment looking at Paul Wolfe. "How can I make a counteroffer—or even have a discussion when I don't know who I am talking to here? Is it Paul Wolfe, Richard Farengetti, or exactly who are you?"

Wolfe turned white. He froze in his chair. Kelly Barker looked at his client and back to Dusty. "What are you talking about?"

"I'll let your client explain it to you. But since we're all together, I might remind your client that there is a restraining order in place and he'd better respect it. If he chooses not to, I'm sure you can fill him in on the consequences. Good afternoon, gentlemen." Dusty walked out of the conference room and back to the elevators. Paul Wolfe was going to hesitate before he pushed anything else, that's for sure. Julie had enough money to carry on. Paul was another story. They were going to have to figure out what to do with the business, but Dusty bet Paul or Richard, whoever he was, wasn't going to be playing a major role in it.

The elevator doors opened and the receptionist called out, "Have a good afternoon."

Dusty grinned. "You too." The doors closed and he glided earthward.

Chapter Thirty-One

Mike pulled his blue Ford pickup truck into the driveway. Toby and Duke were waiting at the pasture fence and began neighing almost simultaneously as the door of the Ford creaked open.

"Be right there. Just hang on," Mike called out.

His house was a small two-bedroom farmhouse. He bought it as a fixer-upper and had put a lot of work into it. It was something he had always dreamed of when he was a kid in the Midwest. He wanted to move to the Pacific Northwest and be in the mountains. He knew that was a draw to a lot of people, or at least he found that out later. But as a kid, he just knew it was his dream. Growing up just outside of Chicago, they had had cornfields and farmland. That had been okay—it wasn't mountains, but at least it was outside. He had spent winters skiing in what they called *hills* in Northern Wisconsin, cross-country skiing, snowshoeing and winter camping. In the summer he had backpacked, canoed and dreamed of mountains.

After graduating from high school, he finally got his chance. After a slight bump in the road—a marriage to his high-school sweetheart that ended in nineteen months—he headed Out West. He grinned thinking back to when he first saw Mount Rainier. He was with some friends and he said, "Hey, let's run up to the top of that mountain." They laughed at him and told him it would take a lot of time and preparation to go up there, a mere 14,000 feet. It was all so different than the flatlands Back East.

Mike had quickly found a home in the Pacific Northwest. He spent the weeks managing a roofing company, and the weekends were completely devoted to the mountains. At first he backpacked. Always alone. He liked it that way. The peace and serenity of the hills were a balm to his spirit. He was at home. Horses were always in the back of his mind. His little sister had gotten one in Illinois and he had ridden it a couple of times. He even took riding lessons. While backpacking he would see riders and packhorses go by, and he knew one day that was going to be him.

Toby was his first horse. Mike had decided to ease into horses again, and the girl he took riding lessons from found Toby, an energetic two-year-old quarter horse. Mike and Toby had developed a bond that had spanned a good ten years at this point. His horse would do anything he asked; a rare quality that Mike had seen in very few horses. Dusty and Muley were another example of that. More neighing sounded and Mike set his mail, briefcase and keys in the house and came back outside.

He walked to the barn, grabbed a couple flakes of hay and threw them into the troughs. Toby and Duke eagerly tore into the hay. Mike watched them and thought about his life.

Toby had been a great horse, and with that too there had been a slight bump. With roofing there had been drinking after work. He had gotten so into partying that for a while he had forgotten what his priorities were. Selling Toby had not been one of his brighter moves. He bought a sports car, and in his early thirties he was living the dream, or so he thought. The mountains faded out, and he drove his sports car around and drank. An empty life.

Since alcohol can lead to sudden changes, he decided to find himself again and applied for a job at a dude ranch in Colorado—at least back to the mountains. So he worked there for a season. When it came to spending the winter working at a ski resort on the lifts, he thought about his bad knee and decided to come back to the Pacific Northwest. He called his old boss, who promptly wired him the money, and he came back. Back to his old job. Fortunately for him, the person he had sold Toby to needed to sell him, so

Mike got his horse back. He had vowed that never again would he get out of horses.

After that he spent every weekend in the mountains and worked at the roofing company during the week. He decided to take some night classes on investigation. He never wanted to be a cop, but learning how to find information out about people had always fascinated him.

He walked back into the house and put on some coffee. Alcohol had also become a thing of the past for him. After working in Colorado and coming back, he decided he wanted things to be different. It was a decision that he was very thankful he made. It had been about ten years ago. Now coffee was as strong as it got.

Meeting Dusty at Back Country Horsemen had been another life-changing event. He was able to actually start doing private investigation work full time. He bought the house in Eagleclaw, right at the foot of the Cascade Mountains, like he'd always dreamed.

As Mike poured his coffee, the phone rang.

"Hey, Mike."

"Hi, Dusty."

"So what did you find out about the names and domestic violence?"

"Well, it gets a lot better than just Richard Farengetti. I'm not really sure who this guy is. My friend didn't find DV offenses for Richard/Paul in all other states, but he did locate a few more aliases in Washington. How did it go in Seattle?"

"I just got back. That traffic never ceases to amaze me. How much I hate it also never ceases to amaze me. The meeting was brief. They had it all laid out where this deadbeat would continue to run the company, have full access to the accounts and they would just agree to freeze the joint savings account. Great deal. Just leave the wolf in the henhouse."

"That's very imaginative."

"Yeah, I thought so. I think he was trying to baffle me with stupid. Unfortunately, it didn't work. Took him about five minutes to lay out his little plan. I stood up. Called Mr. Wolfe, or whoever he is, *Richard Farengetti*. He turned a very stark shade of white, and I walked out the door."

"What did his lawyer do?"

"He was really puzzled. I'm sure it was a big imposition to have something like that thrown on him in his own palace. But hey, what could I do?"

Mike laughed. "Yeah, what could you do?"

"If you could drop what information you have off for me tomorrow, we can go over it."

"Will do, Boss." Mike took a drink of coffee. "So are you getting excited about your big ride this Saturday?"

"Yeah, Mike, it's going to be a big relief for me. I know if I fall off and roll down a hill, I'm going to be saved. And if somebody tries to kill me, they're going to get shot."

"You're a lucky man." Mike switched gears. "Oh, yeah. Speaking of rescuing, do you want me to come over tonight and sleep on your couch?"

"I'd totally forgotten about that."

"I don't mind at all. In fact, I think it would be kind of exciting if someone did show up. I never get anyone over here."

"Yeah, okay. I guess so."

"I'll load up and be over after I take care of a few things here."

"Sounds good."

Mike walked upstairs to pack.

Chapter Thirty-Two

Paul Wolfe left his lawyer's office in a burning rage. *Who did that two-bit country lawyer think he was dealing with? This isn't my first rodeo.* He'd been married twice before in this state alone. *Those women got what they deserved.* His only problem with Julie was that she had a lot more money than the others did. *I'm sure not going to miss all her whining for me to go riding and camping with her, or doing things with that stupid horse group.*

He thought about his daughter. He thought she was okay, but he didn't feel any real attachment towards her. He couldn't really explain why. Kids just didn't do anything for him. Women, in general, didn't do a lot for him. He thought about it as he walked to his car. He liked being married just fine. But women always wanted more and he got tired of them. Every time he got out of a marriage, he figured he was done, but there was always another one. Started out with no commitment necessary and then it always came around to a commitment. Well, he was done for sure this time.

Growing up in Tacoma, their family never had any money. His dad worked at the Costco warehouse. And when he came home it was to drink beer and sit in front of the television set. Their house was a dump. The walls were once green, but they were covered with dirt from years of neglect. The house had an upstairs, but the banister was completely torn off and remained that way. The house had piles and piles of junk lying around and no one ever bothered to clean it up. It was an embarrassing place to live. His mom was always in her own little world. Sometimes she would sing. He hated that—it was scary. If they had not had a close-knit neighborhood of boys, he didn't know what he would have done. He learned everything he knew from them. They were his parents and his family.

He noticed at a young age that he didn't really care about other people. He didn't care about animals, either. Maybe because no one had cared about him. He didn't know what it was, but he knew he had to fake it a lot. He had to act like he was friends with people, when he wasn't. He had to act like he was in love with women, when he wasn't. It was just something that he had to do to get what he wanted. It wasn't particularly pleasant for him.

He remembered in grade school they had sent him to a counselor. He had slammed another boy's head against the blacktop in the playground. The boy had gotten a concussion. He told the teacher it was an accident. He actually liked doing it and it was really the first time he realized he didn't care about the other kid. They put him through a barrage of tests before he could come back to school. They told him he was a sociopath. He thought it was kind of a cool word, but he didn't know what it meant back then. Because he was so young, they couldn't really prove anything. It wasn't really anything he'd ever had to deal with, because his dad got mad and transferred him to another school. But Paul had learned about himself for sure then. He smiled.

He put his key into the Mercedes ignition and the engine purred. Now, this was the life he had quickly grown accustomed to. *If that bitch thinks she's going to take it all away from me, she's got another thing coming. I'm going to have to teach her a lesson. She's definitely a slow learner.*

But first things first—her lawyer. That idiot really needs a lesson. He doesn't take hints very well, so he's going to have to have it laid out more clearly. We're going to have to step it up. Scaring was one thing, but we need to take more action. It's pretty simple—the divorce has to be stopped. Julie just needs to be a whole lot more understanding. We need to have a little talk about it. As he thought about it, Paul felt himself relax. He felt light and happy. *That's what needed to happen.*

Paul punched his cell phone. "Hey."

"Yeah," a sullen voice answered.

"How's it going with your surveillance?"

"It's okay. I drove over to his house last night. Woke him up. I was going to break into the front door, but he just about caught me. It's the damn dog—I need to put him down." An evil laugh coughed over the phone.

"I don't care about the dog. But I do want you to step it up. He needs to back off this divorce case and he obviously is not getting the hints."

"Okay. But it's gonna cost ya. This guy does not stay in one place very long. I'm having to hike into the mountains. Creep around remote farms. It really ain't cool and it's not gonna be cheap."

"Quit whining. Name your price and just get it done," Paul snarled.

"Five thousand should ought to cover expenses. And that's just for the warning," the sullen voice added quickly.

"Fine. Hurry up." Paul turned the phone off and threw it to the floor. He signaled and merged into I-5 traffic.

Chapter Thirty-Three

Mike pulled into Dusty's driveway at about 9 p.m. It was just getting dark. The trees were thick and dark in the back and the yard light was clicked on. Mike looked at the horses in the front pasture still munching their hay. The cabin stood silent in the clearing.

As Mike got out of his truck, a voice called from the front porch.

"Hey, you want to move your truck?"

"That's probably a good idea. Where?"

"I'll open the garage door and you can park it inside." Dusty got up and walked to the barn, Scout following behind.

"Might as well. If we're going to do this professionally, let's do it." Mike got back in and put his truck in the garage.

In the house Dusty turned on the kitchen light. "I've actually got three rooms upstairs, so you can stay in the one at the top of the stairs."

"Sounds good."

"I'll make sure the doors are locked, and then I think I'll turn in. I didn't get much sleep last night and it was a big day."

"I don't blame you at all, Boss. Well, don't worry. Reinforcements are here."

"Thanks a lot. I really do appreciate you coming, Mike." Dusty shook his hand.

"No, problem. And I'll check the doors."

"Thanks again." Dusty and Scout walked down the hall to his room.

Dusty wasn't sure what time it was, but he heard the low noise of an engine idling. He looked down at Scout and, sure enough, his ears were perked up and he was alert.

"Oh, damn it. Not again," mumbled Dusty. He looked out the window. The yard light shown off the hood of a car. The fog lights were on, but the rest of the car was dark.

Dusty grabbed his Vaquero and carefully opened his door and started down the hall. Mike's door was closed. Dusty did his best not to step on creaky boards in the hallway. With the cabin being so old, it was hard to do. He slowly turned the knob on Mike's door and pushed it open. The barrel of a gun was pointing from behind the door.

"Mike, it's me," Dusty whispered. "Someone's trying to get in downstairs."

Mike opened the door the rest of the way. "Thank God. I thought I was going to have to shoot someone." He stood in his white T-shirt and undershorts, gun in hand.

"It's not over yet. Let's go."

"Right behind you, Boss."

Dusty turned to go down the stairs. This was the tricky part. He had a stairway that was closed and had a turn in it. So once he went down the first half of the stairs, he made a right turn and would be totally exposed. Dusty inched down to the turn, then quickly went around, both hands on his gun and ready to shoot. Mike fell in behind him. They hot-footed it down the last few stairs and then dropped to the floor. The kitchen windows and back door completely exposed them to whatever may be outside, so they stayed down. Scout had followed and crouched on the floor next to Dusty. It was the first time Dusty noticed that Scout was with them. It wasn't where he wanted him to be, but now there wasn't much he could do about it. Scout felt his job was to protect Dusty and he wasn't going to be talked out of it.

The men and Scout remained silent. The dark car was still out in the driveway, but they couldn't hear the engine. It seemed they sat there for hours. The handle on Dusty's heavy log door moved quietly. Scout emitted a low growl and Dusty quickly silenced him. On hands and knees they crawled into the living room and waited behind the door. The robber must have had a lock pick. It didn't take him very long. Dusty cursed himself for not getting a deadbolt in there. In his grandfather's days he had never even locked it, so deadbolts were not a priority. Obviously, he underestimated the future of his home.

Dusty crouched behind the door with Mike and Scout next to him as it creaked open. Both had their guns drawn. The intruder took a couple of tentative steps into the house, flashing a small penlight around. Dusty waited for him to completely enter and then, in one swift motion, he kicked the door shut and tackled the intruder. They both went down with a thud. The intruder on the bottom let out a rush of breath. The penlight shot across the floor. Suddenly recovering, the man rose up and jabbed a knifelike elbow into Dusty's side. He seemed to be reaching for something while he pushed off Dusty. Mike wasn't waiting for him to find it. He jumped in and kicked the man's hand. The intruder let out a yelp and then cursed.

Dusty was larger, but the man was obviously a professional. He used every dirty move. He slammed a knee hard into Dusty's crotch. As he doubled over, the intruder was up. Scout growled viciously and latched onto the man's leg and was biting it for all he was worth. The intruder, having located his gun, took aim at Scout. Mike launched himself at the man and knocked the gun out of his hand before he could get a shot off. Together, the two men and the dog fell hard into the front door. Mike was trying to get him in a headlock. The intruder got a lucky punch into Mike's face. Blood squirted out Mike's nose and he brought his hands to his face, trying to clear the blood out of his eyes. The man jabbed his elbow hard into Dusty and savagely kicked Scout in the ribs and dislodged him. A loud yelp resounded. Staggering to his feet, the intruder tore the front door open. Then running across the front wooden porch and gravel drive, he leapt in his car with Mike, Scout and Dusty limping behind.

The car door slammed and for the second time in as many nights, with gravel flying, he burned out of Dusty's driveway.

"Did you see the plates?" Dusty panted.

"No. Well, there wasn't one on the front of the car. And I couldn't see the back; the light was out."

"What kind of car? Did you get a look at that?"

"Yeah. It's a guess, but I'd say a blue Mercury Montego."

"That's a pretty good guess."

"My old man used to have one."

"Okay, then. I guess now you have kind of an idea why I am having a hard time sleeping."

"Yes, I can see it might be a problem."

"I'm hoping we can get to the bottom of this pretty soon. Last night he just got to the front door. Tonight he got in the house. I really don't want to find out what happens tomorrow night."

"Well, now that he knows what he's up against, I'm sure he wouldn't even consider coming back," Mike quipped.

"Yeah, that's what I'm afraid of," said Dusty ruefully.

"I bet he didn't realize there would be two of us here." Mike walked toward the house.

"And Scout," Dusty added.

"And most importantly, Scout," agreed Mike. "But where was Cassie this time?"

"Good point. That would have probably gotten rid of him for good. I'll ask her next time I see her." Dusty chuckled. "In the meantime, we'd better get some ice for your nose. Looks like you're going to have a couple of black eyes."

Mike's nose was clearly beginning to swell and his eyes were darkening. "Would that be for me or you?"

"Aren't we the dream team? Call us for your first line of home defense. Not!" Dusty laughed painfully.

"I hope this doesn't interfere with your ride on Saturday," Mike wondered nasally.

"No way. That's why they made Advil!" Dusty felt a pang of doubt. Boy, he hoped after all this that he would be able to ride with Cassie on Saturday. He found himself worrying more about missing the ride than wondering who was breaking into his house. He thought about that for a minute—a break-in while he was home. That was definitely a bad sign. It was a well-known fact that robbers broke in when no one was home. Whoever did this knew that Dusty was home and assumed he was alone.

"Atta boy." Mike feebly slapped Dusty on the back, and they stiffly walked back to the house. Scout trotted behind them. The trees stood in tall silent shadows against the blue-black night sky.

Chapter Thirty-Four

Dusty slowly limped into the office, the bell jingling behind him. Mrs. Phillips was busily typing on her computer.

"Good morning, Mr. Dustin Rose." Lifting her eyes from the keyboard, she noticed for the first time his gait. "Is everything okay? Did you hurt yourself?"

Dusty's cheeks reddened. This wasn't really a conversation he wanted to have with

Mrs. Phillips.

"I, um, had an intruder at my house last night," he finally managed.

"Oh, my land. Did you call the police?" All thoughts of the computer abandoned, Dusty had her full attention now.

"There wasn't really anything to report, other than it happened. Mike was staying at my house to help me out. And, well, I guess we need a little more training on apprehending intruders."

"That's horrible, Mr. Dustin Rose. Is there anything I can do?"

"No, thank you, Mrs. Phillips. Mike will probably stay over again. After he gets his broken nose taken care of, anyway," Dusty threw in casually, hoping to draw attention away from his own somewhat embarrassing injuries.

"Mike has a broken nose?" Mrs. Phillips had a horrified look.

"I haven't gotten the final word from him on it yet, but I believe that was the direction it was going."

"Land sakes." Mrs. Phillips shook her head.

Dusty grabbed his messages and turned to go into his office. If he walked kind of bow-legged and slow, the pain wasn't too great. Since it was Friday morning, this injury had exactly one day to go away.

Easing into his chair, Dusty flipped through the telephone messages. Kelly Barker caught his eye immediately. It was only 9:30. *Did that guy ever rest?* Dusty figured he better return this call right away.

"Kelly Barker, please." Dusty waited for the elevator music while the call was transferred. It was so much nicer to listen to the elevator music in the safety of his own office, rather than catapulting skyward in a metal box. His thoughts were interrupted when Barker picked up.

"Dusty, is that you?"

"Yes, it is. What's left of me, anyway."

"Oh, yeah? Tough night?"

"You could say that. I had an intruder at my home two nights in a row. The first night he prowled and left when I yelled at him. Last night he broke in."

"You're kidding?" Kelly sounded incredulous.

"Not at all. The really scary part is my car was right there, so he knew I was home."

"Boy, I sure don't like hearing that. I hope you figure out who's doing it and get it taken care of," Kelly said sincerely.

"Me too. Why did you call?" Dusty asked. Having relayed the information, he wanted to move on. Listening to Kelly's voice, he was satisfied that Kelly didn't know anything about it. He sounded too shocked to have been involved. Or have prior knowledge of it, for that matter, at least as far as Dusty could tell.

"I wanted to let you know that after last night I am officially withdrawing as counsel for Paul Wolfe."

"What brought that on? Or I guess maybe I should ask, which particular thing?"

"I guess at the end of the day, I can't represent someone who lies to me. That's it. I am in the position, after all these years, to be able to pick my clients. And if they are not going to level with me, I'm not going to represent them. You will get my notice of withdrawal in the mail."

Dusty was surprised. This was not what he thought the phone call would be about. He had expected some kind of an offer, but not a withdrawal. Recovering, he asked, "So how did that go down when you told Paul you weren't going to be his lawyer?"

Kelly laughed nervously. "That was another thing. He didn't take it very well, and that's an understatement. He went ballistic and started swearing and threatening me. I had to call security to have him escorted out of the building."

"Wonderful."

"Yeah, that was really the main reason I called you." His voice dropped into a confidential tone. "You should be careful when you're dealing with him. I mean, from a personal safety standpoint."

Dusty tried to shift to a more comfortable position in his chair. "You know, I've kind of got that impression from Mr. Wolfe myself. He already paid me a visit and rearranged the glass and picture frames in my office before he hired you."

"Really?" Kelly said. "Well, then you know what I mean." He shifted into his professional voice. "Well, good luck with the case. I guess I'll see you in court."

"One of these days," said Dusty. "Thanks for the call."

As Dusty hung the phone up he heard Mrs. Phillips in the front office. "Mike, your poor nose. Are you okay?"

"Yes, thank you, Mrs. Phillips. You should have seen the other guy."

"Oh my," she exclaimed.

Mike beamed as he walked into Dusty's office. His nose was swollen and looked even more so with the big white bandages on it. His eyes weren't particularly large in the first place, but between the big white bandage and the swelling, they now looked like little slits.

"You should have seen the other guy?" Dusty repeated.

Mike smiled sheepishly. "Well, you know, it's a guy thing."

"I guess," Dusty said. "It would have been way better if we had actually gotten him."

"Yeah. Another day."

"Hopefully."

"By the way, how are you this morning?"

"Never been better," Dusty was quick to reply.

"That's just great. Great," Mike mumbled. *Just keep telling yourself that.*

"So did you bring the reports with you today?"

"Yes, I did."

"Great. Things have changed a bit since Paul no longer has a lawyer. Kelly Barker called me this a.m. He let Paul know that he wasn't going to be able to represent him any longer."

"Really. Why?"

"Because apparently when I dropped the Richard Farengetti name, an issue of Paul's truthfulness came up, so Kelly terminated their agreement."

"How did that go over?"

"The usual. They had to call security to escort him out of the building."

"At least he is consistently out of control."

"He is that."

"So let's go over the reports. We'll try to get on the motion docket for next Friday and see if we can get a temporary order, at least. See what Paul does between now and then."

"Sounds good." Dusty and Mike laid the reports on the conference table and started the review.

Chapter Thirty-Five

Cassie pulled into her driveway. Sammy, her Aussie, barked in welcome alongside the car. She got out and her dog bounded around her. Prince and Murphy raised their heads and looked at her from the back pasture. It was good to be home after a long day, preceded by a long week.

Tomorrow she was going riding. That made it all worthwhile. And she was going riding with Dusty Rose. That was something she had not quite figured out yet. She was pretty excited about it, but not sure why. He seemed like such a different person up in the mountains. She really hoped that was the real Dusty. She thought of the last case they had worked on together with the Goldsby's Mill case. She would definitely not dream of riding with that person.

Then again, anybody who could pack into the Pasayten couldn't be that bad a guy, at least not to her way of thinking. And she really liked his Uncle Bob. With thoughts of the Pasayten, Cassie changed her clothes and walked out into the front room as the phone rang.

Cassie picked it up. "Hello."

"Hey, Cassie," a perky voice said.

"Hi, Terri. What's up?"

"Just wondered if you wanted to go riding tomorrow?"

"Well, I do, but I'm already going with someone."

"Oh, okay." The hurt was apparent in Terri's voice.

Cassie recognized it. "Terri, it's kind of a…um…well, it's like a…"

Terri piped up, "A date?"

Cassie froze. Yes, that's what it was. That's exactly what it was. She was quiet for a minute. "Yes, I guess that's what you would call it."

"Cassie!" Terri screamed. "With who? No, wait. Let me guess. Dusty Rose?"

Cassie was surprised. "Well, yes. But how did you know that?"

"Oh, Cassie. That was sooooo obvious. I'm so happy for you!"

"Geez, Terri. Calm down. We're not getting married, or anything. We're just going riding tomorrow."

"Oh, yeah," said Terri knowingly. "You know how that goes. Well, I hope not, at least right away. I really like having you as a riding partner."

"Me too," agreed Cassie.

"You haven't run into that weirdo Roy anymore, have you?"

"Not lately. I'm thinking that guy has issues."

"For sure. I think his main issue is you, though, so please be careful."

"Will do."

"Maybe we can ride on Sunday, if it works out," said Terri. "I have a bunch of transcripts due, and I could work on them tomorrow and ride on Sunday. I was going to work one day, anyway."

"That sounds great."

"Okay. I'll talk to you tomorrow night. Can't wait to hear how it went."

"Talk to you later." As Cassie walked out of the house to feed her horses, she thought about what Terri had said about Roy. He did give her the creeps. He seemed to always turn up wherever she went. She seriously was beginning to think he was following her. It was like a stalker. She wanted to think it was her imagination, but she felt like she was being watched. Not all the time, but too often. As she grabbed a couple of flakes of hay from the barn, even then she felt eyes following her every move. Cassie glanced down at Sammy, but her dog just smiled up at her. Certainly if someone was stalking her, her dog would notice. She tossed the hay to the horses and watched them for a few minutes. The day had been hot. The dusk air was cool and refreshing without being cold. Cassie heard the bees still buzzing and the birds were chirping their evening before-bed songs. The air was sweet with summer. She sighed and her shoulders relaxed. She absolutely loved this time of year.

Feeling good, Cassie walked back in the house. She still had bagged salad in the refrigerator. Seemed that was what she lived off of these days. It was so easy. As she opened the door, the phone rang.

Thinking it would be Dusty to make final plans for tomorrow, she picked it up.

A deep gravelly voice said, "Hello, Cassie."

Her heart dropped.

"Hello, Roy. What can I do for you?" She was getting really tired of this. Enough was enough.

"Well, that's pretty forward of you, but I accept," he said with a nasty undertone.

Revulsion hit Cassie. "Very funny. We both know that's not what I meant."

"Oh. Are you sure about that?" Roy said in a low, suggestive voice.

Anger flashed through Cassie. "Roy, I've tried to be nice to you, but you are really pushing it to the end. Please stop calling me. Stop following me. Just stop," she said firmly with an edge in her voice.

Instead of being angry, Roy became very patient. "Babe, you just need to relax. Nobody is doing anything to you. In fact, I just called to see if you would like to go riding with me tomorrow."

Cassie was finding it hard to speak. "Okay," she said in a tight voice. "My name is not *Babe*. I am not interested in riding with you. I am also not interested in speaking with you on the phone. So please just leave me alone. I'm going to be forced to file a restraining order if you don't stop."

Roy's voice and demeanor changed abruptly. He said in a cold voice, "Well, if it isn't Miss High and Mighty Lawyer now. I tried being nice. I guess you don't like it that way. No problem."

Cassie felt her stomach clench. Before she could say anything more, Cassie was listening to a dead line.

She stared at the phone stunned. She had had guys want to go out with her before, but this really took the cake. Why would someone want to be around her that she obviously didn't want around her? He definitely had mental issues. That was scary. She knew something was off with him when they ran into him on the pack trip, but it just seemed to get worse all the time.

She headed back into the kitchen to check on the bag of salad. After that last phone call, she wasn't even sure if she was hungry anymore. Just as she put her hand on the refrigerator door, the phone rang again. *Geez! Isn't this getting like an Alfred Hitchcock movie, or something? What now?*

Walking back into the living room, she picked up the phone.

"Hello?"

"Hey, Cassie, it's Dusty." Relief flooded through her. She hadn't realized how uptight she was getting from Roy's call until she heard Dusty's voice.

His voice sounded warm and friendly—self-assured, without being cocky. Cassie flashed again on the courtroom. *Who was this man on the phone, anyway?* "Hey, Dusty."

"Is everything okay? You sound a little stressed."

"Kind of an understatement. I'll have to fill you in tomorrow."

"I know what you mean. My week has been a little tough too."

"What time should I meet you at Crystal?" asked Cassie.

"Is nine too early?"

"Not at all. If it's hot, it's always nice to get an early start."

"My thoughts as well," agreed Dusty.

"Great. See you up there at nine."

Cassie hung the phone up thoughtfully. Boy, talk about a roller coaster night on the phone. She'd switched from revulsion to happiness in the span of just a couple of minutes. It would probably be a good idea just to get away from the phone for a while and read. She opened her salad and dumped it in a bowl. Pouring herself a glass of ice water, she opened the latest issue of the *Back Country Horsemen's Trailhead News* and thumbed through it.

Sammy lay contentedly at her feet and Cassie finally began to relax. She was probably just blowing the whole thing out of proportion with Roy. He was definitely a different sort of person and that was all it was. Cassie got up to pack her lunch for the next day.

Chapter Thirty-Six

The sun was just breaking over the mountaintops as Cassie pulled into Sand Flats horse camp about 8:30. The snow glistened on top in the bright light and reduced to dark shadows at the bottom. It had been a beautiful summer. The crisp alpine air reached her nostrils, even though the window was only open a small crack. It smelled wonderful. Cassie always felt lucky living on the west side of the state when the days were long and warm and the rain just about nonexistent. In the Pacific Northwest winter the days were short and gray, and most of the time it seemed unimaginable that it would ever stop raining. The country station played *Rocky Mountain High* and she hummed along as she looked around the horse camp.

The area was about half full with overnight campers, but it wasn't hard to see Dusty's truck and trailer in the day parking area. Cassie pulled in next to his rig. Dusty's horse was saddled and stood tied by the side of the trailer. She got out and Sammy bounded out behind her. Cassie unloaded Prince, tying him to her trailer. She was glad she saddled at home; it always made it easier when she was getting ready to ride. It also greatly reduced the chances of forgetting a piece of important tack at home. She prided herself on being ready on time. Now not only was she early, but she was ready.

Walking around to the front of her truck, she saw Dusty sitting by a small campfire, and his dog Scout lay on the ground next to him. A second lawn chair sat by the fire. A pot of coffee steamed on a rock. He was wearing his silverbelly cowboy hat and a red wild rag around his neck. The light blue of the work shirt enhanced his tan and the deep blue of his eyes as he turned and focused on her.

"Good morning." Dusty's face lit up as he smiled at her.

"Good morning." She smiled back at him.

"Sit down and have a cup of coffee," he invited.

"Boy, that sounds really good." She took the blue metal cup he offered her. He picked up the pot with his leather glove and poured the coffee. *This is just really incredibly cool. How many dates have I ever been on that started out like this? On second thought, how many dates have I ever been on where they even rode?* Her first sip of the hot coffee burned as it went down. Coupled with the smell of fresh pines, mountain air and campfire smoke, Cassie felt like this was as close to heaven as a person could get. She and Dusty stared into the fire drinking their coffee for a while.

Dusty had arrived early. Amazingly, it was quiet around his house last night, so he was finally able to sleep. Sitting next to Cassie at the campfire felt like they had done this forever. He also couldn't think of a lot to say, which was really unusual for him. Cassie sat comfortably in her chair, her cup of coffee steaming in the chilly mountain air. She stared into the fire and looked very relaxed.

"So where would you like to ride today?" Dusty asked.

"Anywhere would be fine."

"Well, I guess I won't be showing you anything new up here."

"Well," she smiled at him, "it's new every time I come—at least that's what it feels like."

"I can relate."

Finishing their coffee, they sat by the fire for a few more minutes, neither one wanting to break the moment. Finally, Dusty stood up. "Well, we're burning daylight."

"We don't want to do that." Cassie laughed.

The fire had burned down to coals. Dusty banked it. They each got their horses ready to ride.

The sun was above the peaks as they approached the switchbacks of Norse Peak. A few cars headed up to the Crystal Mountain parking lot as they crossed the road and disappeared onto the trail. The forest was thick at the bottom but thinned out as the trail rose. It was a steep climb and Cassie was glad Prince was in shape. Dusty set a good pace, and although her horse was gaited, he had to concentrate on keeping up. Cassie stared at Dusty's back as he rode. It was unfathomable that this was the same person she had seen at the King County Courthouse. How did the mountains change a person that much? Even as she thought about it, Cassie knew it was true, though. The actions required of people in the city completely fell away in the backcountry. Looking at the worn Schaefer slicker on the back of his saddle and the faded jean jacket, she just didn't see it. Dusty sat loose and relaxed in the saddle. His Vaquero was holstered on his left leg; its brown holster faded into his chinks and was almost unrecognizable.

As they rode higher, Cassie was amazed that Dusty did not seem fazed at all by the heights. Wasn't it just a week ago he had fallen off the top of Tumac?

"How are you doing since your fall?" she heard herself ask. Funny, she knew it wouldn't embarrass him.

Dusty gave a low-throated chuckle. "Good as new, as far as I can tell."

"You're really fortunate. That was quite the tumble."

"Yeah. In all the years I've been on the trail, that's the first cinch I've had go out on me."

"Especially in probably one of the worst places you could ride."

That brought a full laugh. "Well, I don't know that I would give it that much credit."

Cassie blushed. "Oh, sorry. I forgot about you and Mike and your high-adrenaline rides."

"One ride is as good as the next. We just end up with those kind of rides more often than not," Dusty quickly added.

"Well, that's one way to run into people, I guess." She smiled, thinking of him landing in the middle of the trail in front of her.

"Guess so. Although I've never used it but that one time. And I don't think I'd like to do it again."

"Probably not a good idea." Cassie was silent after that, lost in thought.

The horses methodically climbed the trail. The only sound was the occasional rock on steel as the hooves struck a stone. Sammy usually followed along right behind Prince's heels. Today she was running side-by-side with Scout. That was amazing. Usually her dog didn't take to other dogs. The two dogs ran side-by-side, and when the trail got narrow, they actually were glued to each other momentarily, their four legs pumping in unison. *I guess a lot of records are being broken today.* She smiled and shook her head.

As they intersected a user trail on top, they looked down into Big Crow Basin. The old shelter was still sitting on the bottom. The roof had long since fallen away and disappeared. Only a few logs lay on top of each other, giving the vague idea that a three-sided cabin had once sat there. They began to descend the gravel trail, the echo of their hooves louder in the bare expanse of the basin.

At the bottom Dusty turned in his saddle. "Do you want to have lunch at the Tin Shack?"

"That sounds great."

They rode on in silence, oblivious to anything but the mountains, fir trees and horse sweat.

Chapter Thirty-Seven

Roy pulled into the parking area of Crystal Mountain and swore. Cassie was there. He knew it. And he bet anything she was riding with that lawyer fella. No doubt in his mind. *Well, we'll see how well that works out for them.* His mouth fell into a grim line as he unloaded his horse.

"Come on, Blaze. We got stuff to do." Roy jerked the lead line and pulled his huge black horse out of the trailer. He began brushing his horse in quick short strokes. He hadn't formulated a plan yet for when he caught up with Dusty and Cassie—all he knew was he was going to do it.

As he pulled his saddle out of the trailer, his thoughts were interrupted. "Hey, Roy, is that you?"

A chubby woman ran up to him. She was wearing a sparkling jean jacket, tight jeans and pointy cowboy boots. Her low-cut T-shirt left nothing to the imagination. It took him a minute to realize who she was.

"Hello, Shelley." Roy flashed a phony smile at her. He stopped, slicked his hair back and put his cowboy hat on.

Shelley gave her biggest smile and looked around. "Who are you riding with?"

"Just up for a little ride by myself. Good place to do some thinking." Roy hoped that would give her the hint he wanted to be alone. It didn't.

"Well, isn't that just the craziest thing? Me too! You want some company?"

Roy let out a big breath. *Figures. Now what to do? I don't want to make this lady mad at me. Who knows? His mouth twisted into a cruel grin. Hell, I could have plans for her down the road—at least maybe for a night. The main thing right now is Cassie. I cannot abide those snotty, too-good-for-everyone bitches like her. She'll soon learn who's in charge. I would have showed her how to obey me up at Frying Pan Lake—but there were too many people around. And that little nonstop talker she rode with was there to;, that would have just caused more problems. What I need is to get her alone. Not with Dusty. Not with Shelley, just all alone. Then we can have a meaningful conversation.* His upper lip twitched in anticipation.

"Hey, Roy, are you there?"

Shelley was peering into his face waiting for an answer. She was standing too close. Roy took a step back and smiled at her with what he hoped was a sheepish grin. "Yeah, that would be fine, Shelley."

"Okay. I'll be ready in about ten minutes." Shelley trotted back to her horse trailer.

Roy never questioned the way he was. He had grown up in a little house by the Tacoma smelter. He heard now that arsenic was a big health problem. *Funny how they always come up with stuff like that years down the road, when it was too late to do anything about it. Now the lawyers come swooping in and want to sue everyone. For the families, they said—yeah, right. The only ones making money off it was the lawyers.*

Roy's dad worked at the smelter. When he was home, he sat in front of the TV set with a beer in his hand and wore a T-shirt with holes in it. The only time his dad talked to his mom, if you want to call it that, was to shout at her to get him another beer. He couldn't remember them ever having a conversation. His mother's name was Gladys, but to listen to his dad, he would have thought it was, *Hey Bitch*. Roy thought it was funny. He and his older brother, George, called their mom that too. She would laugh.

She laughed a lot, he thought—when she wasn't crying, anyway. When his dad got too drunk he would backhand their mom and then she would cry. That's how he grew up. Roy didn't see what was wrong with it. He found out later, though, after spending time in jail for first degree and second degree assault. *Gee, it was a good thing no one had told his mother about charging for assaults. His dad would have never seen the light of day. He was so glad too, that his dad never had any time for him and his brother.* That kind of attention he could do without.

If his dad cared whether he and his brother went to school, he never showed it. Some of Roy's best childhood memories were when all the other kids were in school and him and a couple friends were taking the day off. Getting people to buy them beer and sitting down in the deep woods of the gulch by his house drinking and getting high. Great times.

"You ready?" Shelley rode up on her sorrel mare.

"Ah, yeah," Roy said, jolted out of his thoughts. He locked his truck, put the keys in his saddlebag and swung into the saddle.

"You ride up here very often?" Shelley asked.

"No. Actually, this is my first time."

"You new into horses?"

"Yeah, I am." Roy thought he was going to be out of horses as soon as his cousin came back from serving overseas and realized he was missing one, and a trailer. But until that time he intended to enjoy himself.

"Okay. Well, I'll lead out then."

"Yeah, that'd be great."

They rode out of the parking lot and paused at the pavement to make sure no one was coming. They took the same trail Dusty and Cassie had only a little while earlier.

Roy looked carefully at the trail as he rode behind Shelley. He could see two sets of fresh hoofprints besides the prints that Shelley's horse was making. She chattered on and on, and he made a grunt here and there in reply. He was busy planning on what he wanted to do when they found Dusty and Cassie.

As they crested the top of the Norse Peak trail, Shelley asked, "Which way do you want to go?"

"Let's go down." Roy pointed, as he looked at all the hoofprints going that way.

It was silent, except for Shelley's voice, as they descended into Big Crow Basin. The sun rose well into the sky, and the morning dew shimmered off the grass as they rode. Bunches of lupine adorned the sides of the trail, with an occasional splash of Indian paintbrush and clumps of mountain daisies. Approaching the old shelter, Shelley turned in her saddle. "Would you like to go to Basin Lake or over to the Tin Shack and Airplane Meadows?"

"What's that way?" Roy pointed at the trail past the shelter, taking in the newly-disturbed dirt in the trail.

"That would lead to the Tin Shack over Martinson Gap."

"Let's do it."

"Okay. That's a great place to have lunch in the meadow. It's lush green grass and a real spring bubbles out of the ground," Shelley agreed. She always loved to share the high country with a person who hadn't yet experienced it.

As Shelley rode she stared at Roy. He was kind of handsome in a street-tough kind of way. His clothes could, for sure, use an upgrade. It was funny how some people dressed in clothing they thought was cowboy. *In Roy's case, the fake denim jean jacket and cowboy boots—definitely cheap.* But taste wasn't always something people were born with and it could be acquired, she knew.

The horses plodded down the trail and Shelley's thoughts drifted to Dusty. Now, there was a guy who couldn't look bad. She'd run into him out on the trail a couple of different days and he looked like he just stepped out of the cover of *Cowboy Magazine*. His sidekick Mike was pretty handsome himself; he definitely nailed his style. If he wasn't born a buckaroo, he sure looked like he was. Shelley smiled, adjusting her light-pink cowboy hat with jeweled hatband, and kicked her horse to speed up as they rode into the thick, dark fir trees.

Chapter Thirty-Eight

The late morning was warm and the flowers were pungent as Dusty turned his horse off the Pacific Crest Trail. A faint trail in the mountain meadow at Martinson Gap cut down into the trees. It didn't stay in one path, but split off around the trees, all branches heading down the mountain slope.

"This trail always cracks me up. It's like the cabin at Sheep Lake. Nobody is supposed to know about it and everybody knows about it," Cassie reflected.

"You still at least need to know where it is before you can find it." Dusty reined Muley between the thick fir trees on what appeared to be a narrow game trail. After riding for less than a mile down dried creek beds and fallen trees, the hillside opened up into a lush green meadow. An old log cabin sat in the middle of the clearing, its tin roof gleaming in the sunshine. The only sound besides their horses' hooves was the gurgle of the spring next to the cabin bubbling out of the earth and down the hillside.

Cassie couldn't help but admire the way he sat on his horse. Dusty and his horse rode in one fluid motion. Ducking under tree limbs and over logs, he and Muley didn't miss a beat. Looking at the faded jean jacket and the worn silverbelly Stetson, it was hard for her to equate the man in front of her to the lawyer she had opposed in the Goldsby Mill hearing. It seemed so long ago now. He was well-turned-out then too, in his suit and tie. He was at ease in a courtroom as he was in the saddle. *A man comfortable in his own skin. Such a rarity these days.* Cassie tossed her head. That day in court still had a bite to it. *Pulling out evidence at the last minute. Who does that? And was it on purpose?* The loss of that case still burned. She shook her head slightly and continued into the beautiful meadow. She rode to get away from her work—she wasn't going to think about that now.

"Looks like we have it to ourselves." Dusty rode up to the hitch rails next to the cabin and dismounted, slipping Muley's bridle off and tying him up.

Cassie got off and took care of Prince. Sammy stood close by waiting.

Dusty walked to the front of the cabin. The huge stump that served as a splitting block sat with an ax embedded in it. The cabin had a crosscut saw hanging on the wall. He stepped up on the porch and opened the screen door. The cabin smelled of old logs and pungent wood smoke. The interior was remarkably roomy. It was much longer than it appeared from the outside. Against the far wall were bunk beds. Sealed 55-gallon drums next to the beds contained mattresses. In the center of the room sat two huge Franklin stoves; one for cooking and one for heat. Dusty chuckled. You never could doubt the ingenuity of a packer. There was nothing too big that couldn't be pieced out and packed in on a horse or a mule. He could only imagine the old-timers' faces as they packed the stove, brought it in and lit it up.

He looked around and noted that on the far wall the food stocks were still in place. A sign declared: *You can take it, but replace it next time.* The shelves were lined with canned goods. He noticed half a gallon of unopened wine sat on the shelf. Dusty turned back to the table behind him. A silverware box held flatware for at least 20 people, and plates were stacked neatly underneath on shelves. A guest book with pen lay on the table and Dusty opened it up.

Cassie walked in the door. "Are you signing in?"

"Yes, thought I would."

"I should check and see if my sign-in is still there. This is where I stayed on my first pack trip. We got totally snow-and-rained out in July—this place was sure a sight for sore eyes."

"I'll bet. So what year was that?"

Cassie reflected. "It's been about 15 years ago. I went with my grandpa. It was pretty much a dream come true."

Dusty watched Cassie's face come alive with the memory. It touched him again that this woman could operate at such different levels. The corners of his mouth turned up.

"What?"

"Oh, nothing. Let's have a look here." He flipped back through the pages. The lined paper curled up on the edges from years of being in the cold and damp. In some places the words were smudged from water drops. The comments were all pretty similar. People expressing gratitude for shelter in an unexpected storm. *It just doesn't get much better than this.* Then he saw a long, almost illegible scrawl, *James Olsen.* Underneath that in round girlish print, *Cassandra Martin, my first pack trip.*

"Well, it's official. You really were here."

"What?" Cassie grabbed the book. "You're kidding!" Looking at the page her face glowed. "I've got to have this."

Reaching into her jacket pocket, she pulled out her iPhone.

"An iPhone in here?" Dusty stood back with mock appall.

"Means to an end." She clicked off a picture of the page. "Grandpa died a few years after that trip. It was a huge deal for me. Changed my life. Or maybe better put, affirmed to me who I was."

"Wow," said Dusty with admiration in his voice. "Well, what do you say we grab our lunches and sit down by the creek. I need to hear more about that pack trip."

Cassie followed him out of the shack, and the screen door creaked and slammed behind her.

Chapter Thirty-Nine

Sitting by the creek in the warm August sun, Dusty could not remember feeling more relaxed. Scout lay down next to him. Cassie's voice sounded a lot like the mountain creek as she spoke—sweet and flowing.

Unaware of his thoughts, she continued with her story of the pack trip. "I started riding horses at five, and by the time I was twelve, I knew I wanted to pack into the mountains. Getting there from my urban home in Tacoma was another story. I finally got my grandpa talked into taking me, and my parents agreed. We stayed at the parking lot at Crystal Mountain. It was a beautiful sunny morning in mid-July. It had been a warm year, so we were pretty sure that it was going to be clear. Besides, Cassie laughed, Grandpa couldn't have stopped me, even if it were a monsoon."

She took a bite of sandwich and continued. "As we climbed the Norse Peak trail, the weather began to change. We put our slickers on and a slight rain hit us, which eventually turned into a full-blown snowstorm. I remember to this day crossing over the top into Big Crow Basin and we were in a complete winter wonderland—in the middle of July."

"So did you wonder how you were going to get out again?"

"Never crossed my mind," Cassie answered, her eyes sparkling.

"A woman after my own heart." The words were out of his mouth before he even realized he said them. *Way to go. Scare her off before you even get to know her.*

Two pink splashes appeared on Cassie's cheeks and she continued. "The ride in the snow down into Big Crow was fun. Grandpa said to just go with the slide and turn your horse's head uphill so you don't go down. It was like riding a toboggan. I'll never forget, he tells me how to do it, then as much as he turned his horse's head uphill, his packhorse behind him kept going downhill. I don't know if he noticed or not, but we made it down just fine, anyway."

Cassie tossed Sammy a piece of her sandwich. "Once we got to the bottom and started toward Martinson Gap, we ran into the biggest herd of elk I have ever seen. They came off a hill and funneled into a trail crossing right in front of us."

"How did your horses like that?"

"Well, Grandpa's stock were fine with it. Mine had never seen elk before. I was riding an old steady horse and pulling my POA. The herd was so enormous that it took them about a half hour to all go by. My horses were fine for a while, but then they couldn't take it anymore. My riding horse turned and ran into my packhorse and I almost had a wreck."

"What did you do?" Dusty was interested. "A twelve-year-old pulling a packhorse in an almost wreck? You don't hear of that very often."

"I got her pulled around, and the elk finally finished crossing shortly after." Cassie pulled out her grapes. "We made it the rest of the way uneventfully and it was the coolest trip in my whole life. My grandpa died a few years later. I'll never forget that pack trip."

Dusty stared into the creek and thought about a little light-brown-haired girl and her grandpa packing into a snowstorm.

"What about you?"

"I worked at Uncle Bob's outfit every summer. I was going to be a packer when I grew up."

"And?" she prompted.

"And the family business got in the way. My dad and my grandpa were both lawyers. They wanted me to carry it on. My dad's brother is my Uncle Bob. He was the rogue in the family—

just wasn't going to do it. Dad and Uncle Bob are polar opposites. But at the end of the day, once I got into college, law school was just right around the corner waiting for me. It seemed like before I knew it, I was graduating from law school and getting married."

Cassie had figured he had been married before. It was no shock. Usually men didn't reach their late 40s without having been married.

"Did your wife like to pack?"

"Oh, no way. She couldn't even stand horses. She was a good person. Besides the kids, neither one of us got what we wanted out of that marriage, and after twenty years we decided to call it a day."

Dusty looked at her. "So what about you?" He found himself really wanting to know. It was crazy. He made it a rule to stay away from women. They always wanted something more from him than he was willing to give. He'd been through it once and he wasn't going to do it again. In his business he met women all the time, and he made it clear from the beginning that he was not interested. Living in Eagleclaw word got around pretty fast about who was on the market and who was not. Some women found that even more challenging, though, thinking they would be the one to change his mind. Between college, law school and marriage, not only did he not squeeze in much dating, he never really got the hang of it, either. Right after his divorce Dusty tried noncommittal dating. It didn't take him long to find out that didn't work. He came home from the office one day to find a woman he'd been seeing for only a couple of months had moved all of her stuff into his house. At that point it became obvious to him, he did not understand women at all.

Dusty abruptly stood up and walked over to the stream. Tiny fish darted through the clear water, almost transparent as they blended into the sandy bottom. He felt an attraction to Cassie that he could not explain, and he hoped putting a little space between them would help. The minute she started talking again—it didn't.

Cassie watched him curiously. "Something I said?"

"Oh, no. Just thought I'd stretch my legs a little from sitting." His cheeks flushed and he cleared his throat.

The edges of her mouth turned up. "I guess I've always been pretty independent, and compromising hasn't been one of my strong suits."

"Oh, do tell." Dusty grinned.

Cassie flushed. "That obvious, huh?" Sammy lay on the ground next to her, and she absent-mindedly scratched her head.

"It seems hard to believe that you haven't ever had, if not a marriage, at least a serious almost-married relationship," pushed Dusty. He didn't know why it was important to him to even know, but something inside pushed him to ask.

"Well, okay, one."

"I knew it."

"Yeah," she acquiesced. "He was a guy I met in law school. We were in the same study group. It was a great time of discovery in my life and a lot of hard work. He was my parents' dream of the perfect guy for me. Came from a good family; lawyers, of course. He had a position waiting for him in a large, prestigious law firm in downtown Seattle—room for me. He showered me with gifts. There was nothing he wouldn't do for me—almost."

"He didn't ride," finished Dusty.

"How did you guess?" Cassie looked at Dusty and saw his deep-blue eyes watching her intently. She felt an electricity so strong, she gasped inwardly. Losing her thoughts, she paused a moment. "That was when I learned that I couldn't compromise. Life's too short." Cassie wondered if he felt that too, or if it was just her.

Dusty walked over to Cassie and held out his hand to help her up. As she stood up, he wrapped his arms around and held her. Her hair smelled faintly like strawberry shampoo and mountain fir. He didn't think he had ever smelled anything better. He laid his cheek against her head. A warm feeling filled the pit of his stomach. The sun, the cabin, the horses and Cassie. For the first time in his life he felt complete.

Cassie knew the minute Dusty walked over to her, he had felt the same thing. As she stood and put her arms around Dusty, she could feel shocks of electricity all the way down to her toes. The smell of aftershave and wood smoke intoxicated her. Dusty was tall, over six feet. Cassie, at 5'9", felt small in his arms. Time seemed to stand still in the small alpine clearing. Dusty bent his head down to kiss her. Cassie raised her head to meet his lips and the feeling washed over her that they had known each other for a very, very long time. The electricity and heat poured between them and Dusty pulled her closer. Cassie felt like she never wanted it to stop.

"Well, hey. Didn't mean to interrupt anything." A sullen voice penetrated the still mountain air.

Chapter Forty

Dusty and Cassie jolted apart and looked up.

Roy rode his big black horse into the meadow with Shelley following close behind.

"Roy," she pleaded. "I think we're interrupting something." Shelley pulled her horse to a stop. "There's lots of places to go b'sides here."

Roy ignored her and kept his horse at a fast walk right at Dusty and Cassie. Just when he looked like he was going to ride right over the top of them, he hopped out of the saddle, landing next to them. Shelley pulled up behind him. She smiled uncertainly and waited.

Dusty didn't want to let go of Cassie, even more now, but he did. He took a step in front of her to talk to Roy. This guy definitely appeared to have a screw loose and Dusty wasn't sure what was going to happen next. His mind flashed to his Vaquero, and he was glad he wore it.

Roy was vibrating as he stiffly walked up to Dusty. "I'm thinking we need to have a little talk."

"Talk," the larger man replied.

"Yeah. If you'll remember the work party, I have a prior claim on Cassie."

"Is that so?" This truly amused Dusty. *What does this guy think it is, 1890?*

"That is absolutely ridiculous," Cassie chimed in from behind Dusty. "No one has a claim on anybody around here."

Roy's vacant eyes shifted from Dusty to Cassie and he turned bright red, a vein pulsing in his neck.

"Come on, Roy, let's go," tried Shelley one more time.

Dusty firmly stood his ground. "You heard the lady, Ro"— He never got the last syllable out. Roy punched him so hard in the mouth, it knocked him off his feet. He was dazed for a couple seconds, as if a camera flashbulb had gone off in his eyes. Dusty scrambled back to his feet and went after Roy full force. He headbutted him in the stomach. Throwing his full 6'2", 200-pound frame into Roy, he heard a hard exhale as Roy flew over backwards. Dusty was no longer seeing a flash—he was seeing bright red. Roy went down hard on his back. His horse snorted and jumped back. Shelley tried to reach for his reins as he bolted away.

Roy was oblivious to the horse. The only thing his black vacant eyes focused on was Dusty. As they wrestled on the ground, Roy pulled a knife out of his belt. Roy lunged forward toward Dusty's chest. Dusty forced his wrist back. Roy was strong, but Dusty was stronger. He slammed Roy's hand into the ground hard and slammed it a couple more times until he dropped the knife. "You crazy son of a bitch!" Dusty panted in disbelief. Cassie ran around and picked up the knife. The next time he looked, she had her .38 out and pointed at Roy. Dusty got off him, still trying to catch his breath.

Both men were pretty beat up, but Roy had the worst of it. His nose was bleeding and his shirt was torn. He looked at Cassie and smiled at her. "It's all for you, Babe."

"Ugh, don't call me that," she said. "Better yet, don't talk to me at all."

Dusty looked at Shelley. "Hey, Shelley, you better ride out with us."

"Yeah, come with us, Shelley," Cassie added.

Shelley looked at them both uncertainly. "Guess I better."

"Sorry, Roy," Shelley said meekly, "but I think you're going to be looking for your horse for a while." She rode around him and over to Cassie and Dusty.

Roy stood up and brushed himself off angrily. "This ain't done. Not by a long shot. So don't be getting any ideas it is."

"That's just fine, Roy. We'll get the restraining order ready first thing in the morning on Monday. So you can expect to be no more than one thousand feet away from either Cassie or me after that time."

Roy flipped them off and stormed into the woods after his horse.

All three watched him stomp into the trees. Dusty tucked in his shirt and picked his hat off the ground. Shelley looked dazed. They picked up what was left of their lunches and packed up the saddlebags. It was early afternoon and the alpine meadow once again buzzed with the gurgle of the creek and the buzzing of crickets.

"Shelley, you can do whatever you like, of course, but I think that guy is dangerous. You can probably find safer people to ride with," said Dusty.

"He really seems to fixate on people," added Cassie.

"Oh, you guys don't have to worry about me. I didn't meet up with him to ride, or anything. We both just ended up here at the same time and same place." Shelley straightened out her saddlebags behind her on her horse. "I'm the one who asked him if he'd like to ride together today. He didn't ask me."

"Well, that's good," said Cassie. "Less chance of him putting you in his sights that way."

"Cassie, I think he's already got that covered with you."

Cassie felt a knot in her stomach tighten in dread. "Yeah, that's what I'm afraid of."

Dusty swung into the saddle. "Well, you don't need to worry. We'll get that taken care of."

The three of them rode down the trail. Dusty in front, then Cassie and Shelley. Cassie was silent as she thought about today. It had been a lot of fun, right up to the end, anyway. Dusty was a different person in the mountains than in the city, for sure. She couldn't even begin to imagine what his legal colleagues would think of him rolling down mountains, getting in fistfights with people in the dirt, and anything else that was sure to come up that hadn't happened yet. That was it—anything could happen. The mountains felt more and more like the Old West the more she rode them. They weren't that far from Seattle, but there were fistfights, old cabins, good guys and bad guys.

Watching Dusty sit effortlessly on the big blue roan, Cassie was impressed. His saddle and boots were quality. She liked seeing a guy that actually knew what was good equipment in riding and packing gear. No drugstore cowboys. She winced when she thought about how Roy dressed—a cheap imitation of what he thought a cowboy should look like. Pretty bad.

Now what? Cassie wondered about Dusty. She hoped they'd ride again. He hadn't really said anything, but she doubted he ran around kissing women—at least she didn't think he did. So he probably would get ahold of her again—she hoped.

They got down to their rigs about 5 o'clock. "Thanks a lot, you guys, for letting me ride back with you." Shelley headed back to her trailer.

Cassie rode to hers, right next to Dusty's, and began untacking. Dusty did the same at his trailer and they both finished about the same time. Cassie opened the trailer door and loaded Prince. She started her truck and left the door open so Sammy could load up. Then she walked over to Dusty's rig. He was just shutting the trailer door behind his horse.

"Interesting ride, Dusty." She smiled at him.

"Yes, it was. Not exactly what I had planned." He smiled ruefully.

Cassie thought he looked even more ruggedly handsome now. He had one eye swollen and his suntanned skin was dirty from the fight. "Well, take care." She turned to walk back to her trailer.

"Just a second." Dusty walked up to her, turned her around and wrapped her in a big bear hug. Cassie hugged him back. They stood there for a couple minutes. The electricity hummed through her again. It was the strangest feeling, but she liked it. Dusty leaned down and kissed her.

Cassie's heart soared, as if the mountains, the horses, everything whooshed by in Technicolor. For a minute she forgot where she was, but then a voice whispered in her ear, "Let's try it again. I'll give you a call."

"Sounds good," she said. Her lips tingled and her ear felt warm from his touch, Cassie floated back to her truck. Sammy looked at her expectantly from the passenger's seat. "Let's go home, girl." She sat for a minute regaining her composure, then put the truck in gear and they headed down the mountain.

Dusty stood by his trailer and watched her drive away.

Chapter Forty-One

Dusty walked through the door of his office and set his briefcase down. He managed to make it by the front desk without Mrs. Phillips seeing his eye. He didn't feel like explaining what happened at the moment.

The phone rang on his desk and he picked it up.

"Mr. Dustin Rose, Line 1."

"Thank you, Mrs. Phillips." Regardless of the fact that Mrs. Phillips was sitting at her desk only fifteen feet away in the front office, Dusty would do things her way. It always seemed to work best for everyone if he did.

"Dusty Rose."

"Dusty, this is Julie. He was here last night."

"Did you call the police?"

"I didn't have a chance. I went back to our house because I got tired of putting my sister out. I figured he was over it by now..." She began sobbing. "He kicked the door down, came in and...and...it was awful."

Dusty's heart sank. Battered women never seemed to get it—men don't change. Second chances often turn out to be last chances.

"You need to call the police. Have them come out and make a report. Do you need to go to the doctor?" He dreaded the answer.

"I don't know," she said quietly. "A couple of my teeth are loose, but other than that, I don't think anything is broken."

"Well, get the police report and we can get a warrant to have him picked up. I'm sorry this had to happen—again." He ran his hand through his hair, "I take it your daughter wasn't right there when it happened."

"She was already in bed."

Thank God. "Okay. Get the police out there and let me know when you have the report."

"Thanks, Dusty."

"Take care." He carefully hung the phone up. *What a week! And it's only started.*

The sky had been gray and overcast as he drove to work. Sitting at his desk he watched the torrential downpour stream across his windows. He stared morosely outside. What a weekend. It had been the best weekend in some ways. His thoughts once again strayed to Cassie. He thought about the kiss. That was some woman, he thought, for about the hundredth time. He wanted to see her again, that was for sure. But he needed to figure out what to do about Roy. Was he the guy who kept trying to break into his house at night? Or the person who had been lurking around his tent? It seemed kind of far-fetched, but he wasn't about to put anything past him.

Dusty's thoughts were interrupted when he heard the bell jingle at his front door. Normally he didn't hear the bell at all, but now he thought, *What next?*

Mike walked into his office—actually, he seemed to almost dance into the room—and sat down. A huge smile on his face, he looked a lot like the cat that just ate the canary. Dusty examined him. "To what do I owe the privilege of this visit?"

Mike looked at him. "Lunch. I thought you might want to have lunch."

"Okay. So what happened this weekend?"

"Oh, nothing. Went riding. *We* had a great time."

Dusty was catching on now. "Oh, *we* had a great time. Who would be the *we* and why am I getting the distinct feeling it's a woman?"

"Huh. Maybe you should have been the detective."

"Maybe. So who was the lucky lady?"

Mike smiled coyly. "Terri."

Dusty shook his head. "You sly dog. I would have never guessed."

"Yeah, well, I was probably as surprised as anybody else."

Mike seemed to see Dusty's face for the first time since he walked in. "Hey, what happened to your eye?"

Dusty stood up and slapped Mike on the back. "Let's go to lunch, I've got a story to tell you about my ride."

Dusty and Mike hurried through the downpour to Maude's place. Eagleclaw had side-by-side storefronts on the main street, but not a lot of awnings. Fortunately for them, the café was only a few doors down from Dusty's office. They hurried into the door of the restaurant. It was steamy and warm inside with a combination of the late-summer warmth and the moisture from the rainstorm. The lunch crowd was starting to flow in and Mike and Dusty grabbed their usual seats at the end of the long bar.

Maude bustled up, coffee pot in hand. "Good afternoon, Dusty and Mike. How are you boys today?"

Mike grinned his Cheshire cat grin. "Couldn't be finer."

"Well, that is good news to an old woman's ears. What's her name, Mike?"

Mike's confused look caused Dusty to double up laughing. He managed to get out, "Maude, you are sharp."

The waitress self-consciously smoothed her apron. "Shucks, Dusty, when you've been around as long as I have, you just figure stuff out. You both want the special today?"

Mike, still speechless, nodded.

Dusty pulled himself together and took a drink of coffee. "I was feeling kind of down today, Mike. Glad you stopped by."

"No problem, Boss. Always glad to help."

"Hey, Dusty, you mind if I sit down?" Shelley stepped up next to Dusty. "Hi, Mike." Her usually flamboyant, glittery look was quieter today. She wore big earrings and lots of makeup, but she wasn't pouring out of her shirt nearly as much as she usually did.

"Help yourself." Dusty gestured to the barstool next to him.

Shelley dropped her purse on the counter and climbed onto the barstool. "I'm so sorry about what happened this weekend."

"What exactly did happen this weekend? That guy is a real piece of work."

"I just invited him to ride with me. I came up by myself and ran into him at the trailhead. Running into you guys up at the Tin Shack was a total surprise." Shelley held her coffee cup out as Maude bustled up to pour. Before she could ask, Shelley volunteered, "I'll take the special."

The red-haired waitress nodded and hurried off.

"Well, it might've been a surprise for you, but I don't think it was any surprise to him," Dusty said.

Mike sat forward in his chair, listening intently.

"Well, I never knew he was so angry at you, Dusty. Had I known, I would have never invited him to ride with me." Tears glistened in Shelley's eyes.

Instantly Dusty felt bad. "Don't worry about it. There was no way you could have known."

"So what exactly happened up there, Dusty?" Mike asked.

"Cassie and I went up to the old Tin Shack. We had just finished lunch when Roy and Shelley showed up. We ended up in a fistfight in pretty short order."

Mike whistled. "Boy, I wish I could have seen that. Who won?"

"Dusty did," Shelley said without hesitation.

"I got a couple good hits in." Dusty took a drink of coffee, hoping to move the conversation along. "There is definitely something wrong with that guy, though, Shelley. You should stay away from him."

"You don't need to say that twice. I got hit enough by my ex. I'm sure not taking it from somebody I just met," she said emphatically.

"Good for you." Dusty smiled at her.

Shelley soaked up his approval, her tear-filled eyes sparkling.

"So how did it end up, anyway?" Mike was still trying to put it together.

"Well, we just rode in, and Dusty and Cassie was in the middle of a big old kiss and—"

"Waaaaht? This is getting better all the time. Go on," Mike prompted with enthusiasm.

"Oh, come on." Dusty reddened.

"Anyhow, Roy and I rode in and interrupted them two, and Roy just went off like a crazy man."

"That basically sums it up," said Dusty.

Mike shook his head. "I always miss the good ones."

"I rode out with Dusty and Cassie and that was about it." She took a sip of coffee and frowned. "Except he said that it wasn't over."

"Oh, great," groaned Mike.

"Yeah, well, it was kind of stating the obvious. Cassie said he had been calling her. And he keeps showing up wherever she goes. She and Terri packed into Frying Pan Lake, and there he was. Wanted to hook up with them then, but he was rebuked. It didn't seem to stop him from calling her again on Friday to ride with him on Saturday," said Dusty.

"That's scary." Shelley shuddered.

"Yeah, that pretty much falls in line with a stalker, all right." Mike nodded.

Dusty stared into his coffee cup.

"What's the deep thoughts, Boss?"

"I was just wondering if I'm included in the stalking. I've had my little visitor too."

Mike considered it. "That's the confusing part. That guy wasn't Roy. So is there more than one stalker, or what?"

"It is a puzzle. I thought those guys usually worked alone."

"Have you had anything else happen?" Mike looked at him questioningly. "I've been kind of busy. I forgot to ask."

"Everything looked in place last night. I was a little tired."

"Well, you would have known if he came in, anyway. And I guess you've been kind of busy too," Mike said with a sly smile.

Shelley watched the exchange. "You guys are too funny."

Maude bustled up with their food, "Three specials for the cowboys. Oh, and cowgirl." She smiled at Shelley.

"Thanks, Maude. You're the best chuckwagon cook in this town," said Dusty.

"Oh, you silver-tongued devil." She blushed in appreciation.

"That's the truth," agreed Mike.

"Well, eat up. You don't want it to get cold!" She was gone in a flash of red hair and pink uniform.

Chapter Forty-Two

Cassie went through the motions at work. Luckily, she didn't have to go to court today; just a few appointments for will signings and some files to go through in preparing for depositions. Her mind kept returning to the weekend.

It had started out so perfectly. She could see she had misjudged Dusty. He was more complex than she had given him credit for. Usually people that were as eloquent and agile in the courtroom weren't able to be as unguarded and down-to-earth as the person she had ridden with yesterday. She was drawn to him—there wasn't really any point in denying it. He shared her love of horses and the outdoors. You could always tell that about a person, how they carried themselves out in the wilderness. They were either completely natural, or they were all stiff and in a hurry to get back to their comfort zone. He was the former. She could see him just as easily throwing a saddle blanket down and spending the night outdoors as riding back out. In fact, it seemed like he was more reluctant to leave.

Cassie had learned a lot about people over the years. Guys would talk up a big storm about what great woodsmen they were, but at the end of the day they always found a way to shorten their trip and get out of the backcountry. Funny, too. He found his love for horses and packing them through an uncle instead of his immediate family. *Guess that's just how it works. When it clicks with you, you know it. And no matter what anybody may think, you couldn't fake the love of that kind of lifestyle. It's hard work for one. And it only takes a select few who choose to ride fifteen to twenty miles and call it a good day's ride.*

The afternoon rain was pouring down the window panes of her office. Amazing how in the Pacific Northwest it could be beautiful one minute and torrential downpour the next. Cassie sighed and shut her file. She really wasn't getting much done here; nothing that she couldn't do at home, anyway. It was almost 4 o'clock and the bulk of the day was over. Her legal assistant hadn't made it into work today, so she was alone in the office. The only sound was the rain drumming on the windows.

She grabbed her coat and briefcase and left, locking the door behind her. Driving home she had her wipers on full blast. These kind of rainstorms in late August were an unwelcome visitor. It was bad enough having the amount of rain they did in the winter, but geez, it would be nice just to have a dry August for once. Of course, she mused, every time it stopped raining for any period of time, all she heard on the radio was the fact that they were in for a drought and all kinds of bad things were going to happen because of it. *How much water could we possibly need?*

As she pulled into her driveway, Sammy ran out barking. Her lights flashed off the old garage next to her house. She grabbed her briefcase and hurried up to the back door, her feet getting soaked by the newly-formed puddles in her driveway. She caught the scent of roses as she ran by the flower garden, bringing up visions of her aunt digging away in the flowers. When Cassie was a little girl and came to visit, she would take her plastic shovel and help her. Prince and Murphy nickered from the back fence.

"Hang on, you guys. Let me get changed first," Cassie told them. Quickly entering in the code for her alarm, she let herself into the mud room and Sammy followed. Even though it was August, her thick Aussie coat was beginning to grow back in from her summer haircut in preparation for winter. Cassie tried to get through the second door before her dog shook off the rain, and just about made it. As she slipped through the back door, the water splashed her legs. "You can stay back there for a while and dry off." She dropped her briefcase on the table, hung up her raincoat and hurried upstairs to change.

Cassie buttoned the plaid shirt as she walked downstairs. She was going to go out to feed her horses, but noticed the red light blinking on her answering machine. *Four calls. Boy, that's unusual.* Nowadays people called her on her cell phone. She listened to the first call. It clicked, and then it just sat there. She thought she could hear breathing and then a hang-up. The hair on the back of Cassie's neck stood up. *Oh, no. What now?* She played the next one—same thing. Call three. Cassie stiffened herself for the next hang-up, but instead Dusty's deep voice came on. "Hey, just thought I'd check and see how you were doing. I'll try and call you later. Oh, this is Dusty."

Cassie smiled. Like she wouldn't know that. Still smiling. She punched the fourth call. A rough, gravelly voice came on. "Cassie, this is Roy." She felt her stomach contract in revulsion. "I just wanted to talk to you about yesterday." He lowered his voice in a confidential tone. "I just wanted to apologize. I'll call back later." She didn't want him to apologize. She didn't want him to do anything but go away. She was just going to have to make that more clear to him. Meanwhile, she reached into her drawer and pulled out her handgun and her holster. She liked the way her .38 Firestorm revolver fit in the concealed side holster. Better safe than sorry. And after watching Roy's attack on Dusty yesterday, there was no doubt that he could erupt without warning.

Cassie pulled on her Muck boots, raincoat and hat. She and Sammy headed out to the horses. Although they had an old barn, Prince and Murphy preferred to stand in the open. At least when they were hungry, anyway. She grabbed a couple of flakes of hay for each and threw it into the troughs. The horses tore into them like they hadn't eaten in days. She and Sammy watched for a few minutes and then turned and headed for the house. It was still raining hard and she wanted to get out of it as soon as possible.

As Cassie poured water into her coffee maker, she noticed the light was blinking again on her answering machine. It was getting to feel more like Russian roulette than phone answering lately. Who was it going to be this time? She punched the button. Terri's little voice chirped over the line, "Hey, Cassie, I wanted to catch up with you and see how your weekend was." And then she added mysteriously, "Mine was pretty good." Cassie grinned at the answering machine. "Call me back and I'll fill you in."

Curiosity got the best of Cassie. She picked up the phone and punched in the number. Terri answered on the first ring.

"Hi, Terri. So how was your weekend?"

"Not so bad—" Terri was really poor at keeping things back. "It was great! Mike and I went riding."

"You're kidding. I wondered what happened to you on Sunday."

"Yeah, he called me out of the blue, and I thought I just couldn't pass this up. So I couldn't go with you, sorry." Terri said.

"No problem at all, Terri. Don't think another thing about it. I got a lot of stuff done around here. But where did you guys go?"

"We just went up to the Mill Pond riding." She added quickly, "It was no big deal."

"Oh, really? Well, it sounds like kind of a big deal."

"Yeah?" Terri lowered her voice, "Cassie, I really like him."

"Oh, Terri, that's so great. He seems like a really nice guy."

"Oh, he is," her friend gushed. "You know, he's from Back East and he came on purpose to the Pacific Northwest because he wanted to ride horses in the mountains."

"I guess it just doesn't get much better than that, Terri."

"No, it doesn't."

"I'm really happy for you," Cassie said, her eyes shining.

"Yeah." A pause. "Cassie, how was your ride with Dusty? Gee, look at me. I forgot to even ask about you."

"It was great. I had a really good time…almost."

"Almost?"

"Yeah, right up until Roy and Shelley showed up."

"What happened?"

Cassie filled her in on the events of the weekend.

"There definitely is something wrong with that guy. I just knew it when we were at Frying Pan Lake. I mean, I don't hide in my tent from very many people, that's for sure."

"Yeah, I have never see you do that."

Terri sounded embarrassed. "Well, Mike is going to help me pick out a firearm, so I won't have to be hiding anywhere anymore."

"Uh-oh, Terri Oakley."

"You got it."

"Well, I'll let you go. I need to get some dinner," said Cassie.

"Have a good night, and stay armed," warned Terri.

"Will do." Cassie hung up the phone and headed over to start her dinner.

Cassie sat at her kitchen table when the phone rang. She was starting to get a little apprehensive about answering. She walked over and looked at the caller ID: *Dustin Rose.* She quickly picked it up. "Hi, Dusty."

"Hi. Just thought I'd call and see how things are going."

"Pretty good, I guess, except for a few hang-ups and messages here and there."

Dusty went on alert. "He's still at it then? You want me to come over?"

Cassie's heart warmed at the concern in his voice. "I think I'll be okay."

"Are you sure? That guy is pretty persistent. And he's a nutcase on top of it."

"I guess the more I hang out with you guys, the more I'm getting used to it." She tried to joke.

"Well, that is kind of true here lately—sad but true." He laughed. "I'm hoping that will change."

"Yes. It's not every first date I go out with a guy and he ends up in a fistfight over me."

Dusty laughed shortly. "I'm sorry. That sure wasn't part of the plan."

"Oh, I get that. And under the circumstances, I really appreciate it. I'm not a real good fighter and I don't want to keep shooting people."

"I think you should be about at your quota," Dusty agreed.

She was joking about the incident in the Pasayten where Cassie had to shoot and kill a man to save a little girl a couple months ago. Cassie had done it and she had come to some kind of acceptance of it, but it was still difficult for her. Sometimes she thought if she just joked about it, it would become normal.

Dusty seemed to understand her intent. She could hear it in his voice.

"Well, feel free to call me anytime if he shows up. Maybe we could try a repeat ride next weekend, without Roy?"

"Now, that sounds like a plan." Cassie felt warm inside just at the thought of riding with Dusty again.

"You're on. I'll call you later. Have a good night." Dusty hung up.

Cassie looked at the phone for a long time before she disconnected. She felt really, really content. She couldn't remember ever feeling that way before. Maybe around Christmas or her birthday, but not because she got a phone call from someone. She shook her head.

Just as she got ready to stand, the phone rang again. Assuming it was Dusty again, she picked it up.

"What did you forget?"

"I didn't ferget nothin'. I tried to call you a bunch of times today. Are you ignoring me?" a deep smoker's voice snarled.

Cassie's voice was stone cold. "Would you please stop calling me."

Roy quickly changed tacks. "Listen, Babe, we just got off on the wrong foot on this phone call. I wasn't trying to get you all riled up."

Her stomach recoiled at the endearment from him. Ignoring that, she tried to talk sensibly to him. "Roy, you and I don't have anything else to say to each other. Would you please stop calling me."

He continued on like she hadn't spoken, "I was thinking we just needed to start all over again. I can come and pick you up and we could go out to dinner. How about Friday night?"

"Roy," Cassie tried again, "I am not going out to dinner with you."

"Cassie." He began to sob, completely switching tactics. "Come on, give me another chance. I'll make you happy, you'll see."

The call was just getting weirder and weirder. "Roy, I am hanging up now." She doubted he heard her over the raucous sobs. Carefully replacing the phone in the receiver, she stared at it like it was a snake. Now what? She knew well enough there was nothing to call the police about—he wasn't on her property. If he had been earlier, she couldn't prove it. He hadn't directly threatened her—this time, anyway. *What can I do? Call Dusty? I would love to, but that seems ridiculous. I've taken care of herself this long and I'm going to continue to do so. It's not like I haven't spent many, many nights in the wilderness alone in my tent. Tonight is no different.* Almost—she corrected herself. *Except this time there is some crazy lunatic who seems like he has to have me. He isn't going to succeed.* She put her dinner dishes in the sink.

Chapter Forty-Three

Sleep was elusive. Cassie tossed and turned. She had lived in this old farmhouse for so many years and visited there often growing up. She felt she knew every little creak and groan of the house. But tonight there seemed to be some new ones. Even Sammy would lift her head from time to time. And just when Cassie thought she should pick up her gun, her dog would lay her head down again.

Cassie wasn't sure what time it was, but she sat up wide awake. The alarm downstairs was going off. *Oh, my God! He's in the house*! She grabbed her .38 and rolled off the bed. It flashed through her mind that he may have been in the house before and knew the layout—she had to move quickly. Sammy growled deeply and ran out the door. "Sammy," she whispered loudly, but it did no good. The dog was focused.

She looked around her room and slipped behind a small dresser. Being an older house, it had two small closets. She wasn't going to risk either one of those, because that was the first place people looked. Downstairs she could hear the agitated barking of her dog interspersed with the alarm. The alarm went right to the sheriff's office, even if he tore it out of the wall—which, by the sounds of it, he did.

There was a big yelp as Sammy was kicked and then more snarling and growling. Cassie prayed nothing would happen to her dog. Another big thud and then silence. She felt sick in the pit of her stomach. What had that vicious animal done to her dog? Cassie felt steely resolve replacing her panic and anxiety. The minute she picked up her weapon, she was there to do a job. She was not going to let anything cloud her judgment. If she shot, she was shooting to kill. She'd proven that in the Paysaten and she'd do it again, if she had to.

Heavy steps began to ascend the stairs. They creaked as they received the weight. Cassie knew the steps well enough to know when he reached the top. And she was right—he did know her house. He was walking right to her bedroom door.

She made herself as small as possible behind the dresser. The old style of it with the large mirror made it big enough that she fit easily behind it without it appearing to have moved. It looked like it was still flush against the wall. *Thank goodness my cousins and I played hide-and-seek in this house when we were kids.*

"Come on now, pretty lady," Roy said cajolingly. "Daddy's home."

Hurry up, Sheriff. Cassie willed herself to be calm. She held the gun in both hands and kept herself in as much of a shooter stance as possible behind the dresser.

Roy, gun drawn, walked over to the bed and felt it. "Still warm. Come on, Baby, I know you're close by. Daddy's got a big surprise for you." He cackled, dropping down on one knee and checking underneath the bed. "Not there."

"Looks like the closet." He walked to the closet nearest to the bed, grabbed the door handle and flung it open, stepping to one side. When nothing emitted from inside the closet, he carefully stepped in. Using his gun, he moved the clothes aside and looked behind them.

"Nothing in there. It looks like we have one more closet to check, and then it's time for the present." As he walked across the room, Cassie measured the distance with her eyes. She could make a clean shot from here. She held back. It wasn't because she couldn't make the shot—it was because she didn't want to. If there was another way to resolve this, she would rather do that. He was armed, she reasoned. He was dangerous. Cassie took some deep breaths to steady herself. Her hands were sweating. It made it difficult to hold the gun. She willed herself to be calm. She'd give him a few more minutes to see what happened.

He approached the second closet door in much the same fashion as the first. He stood to one side and kicked the door open. Then using his gun, he moved the clothes aside. "What the fuck? Where are you, you little bitch?" He began to unravel again. Cassie was hard-pressed to remember seeing so many mood swings in so few minutes. He grabbed the side tables by the bed and smashed them on the floor in a rage. She was going to have to do something in a hurry because she knew he was going to trash the dresser next.

As he turned to grab another side table, Cassie slowly stepped out of her hiding place. Grabbing the muzzle of her gun, she took two steps and hit him as hard as she could on the back of the head. He froze in mid-air, turned and looked at her with a puzzled look on his face. He tried to raise his gun hand and then toppled over in mid-action. The minute he hit the ground, Cassie jumped over the broken furniture and grabbed the gun away from him.

She heard sirens in the distance. She remembered what the alarm installer had told her. *The alarm will get you help, but you will need your personal defense weapon handy until they get here.* Turns out he was absolutely right. Taking the gun, she hurried down the stairs to look for her dog.

Sammy laid sprawled out in the kitchen with her eyes shut. Cassie threw her arms around the inert furry form. She could hear breathing. Looking at the dog's head, she saw a bloody spot where Roy must have hit her. Cassie whispered, "Hang on, girl. Help is coming. You're going to be just fine." She stroked the dog soothingly and waited, sitting on the kitchen floor.

Two Eagleclaw County Deputy Sheriffs walked in. They looked around the kitchen and saw the broken alarm box on the floor and the dog with her head being cradled by a beautiful light-brown-haired woman.

"He's upstairs and he's not armed." Cassie pointed to the stairway.

The deputies quickly drew their guns and hurried up the stairs.

As Cassie sat holding Sammy, she felt tears slide down her cheeks. The stress of the night had finally taken its toll and Sammy was hurt. As she buried her head into her dog's fluffy ruff, she felt a warm tongue lick her arm. She looked down and saw Sammy's beautiful brown eyes looking up at her. "Oh, Sammy." It was too much. Cassie sobbed.

That was how Dusty and Mike found her when they walked in the back door a couple minutes later. Dusty quickly bent down and enveloped her and her dog in his arms. "Are you guys okay?" he asked, his voice thick with emotion.

"I am, but Sammy's been hurt," Cassie managed to rasp out. "How did you guys get here?"

"I've got a buddy who is a private investigator. He has a habit of listening to police band radios. He heard the call, knew the address and came and got me. I'm so glad you're okay, Cassie." Dusty held her tighter, careful not to squeeze Sammy.

The two deputies clomped down the stairs. Cassie, Dusty and Mike looked up expectantly. The first deputy, an older man with gray hair and a medium build, said, "There was nobody up there."

"What?" said Cassie in disbelief.

"We looked in all the rooms and closets," said the younger man with brown hair.

The older deputy added, "It looked like a big commotion in the first bedroom, some broken tables, but no sign of anyone up there."

Mike said, "I'm going to go take a look."

"I think I will too. Be right back, Cassie." Dusty hurried after Mike up the stairs.

Cassie continued to hold Sammy and stroke her. She felt hollow inside. This maniac had violated her home and hurt her dog. And now he was gone. This was too much. The deputies began making out their report. "Ma'am, you're going to have to repair your alarm system. It looks like the wires have been cut and it's been torn out of the wall," the older man said. Cassie dumbly looked at the hole where the former security system box had been mounted.

A few minutes later Mike and Dusty came back into the kitchen. "Looks like he got out your bedroom window."

"I'm going to check outside," said Mike.

Dusty looked again at Cassie. "I'll help you get Sammy to the vet. I want to look around outside too. Be right back."

Cassie remained on the floor cradling her dog. The deputies finished up and left. Mike and Dusty came back a few minutes later, out of breath, and their boots dirty.

"We found where he stashed his truck. There's an old driveway around in the back. He seemed to know his way around here, so he must have surveilled the place at some point," Mike said.

"Wonderful," replied Cassie.

"There was some blood upstairs on the window ledge. He didn't get away unscathed," Dusty added.

He bent down to Cassie, hugging her. "Don't worry. The sheriff's office is putting out an all-points bulletin on him now. Breaking and entering with a deadly weapon and attempted assault. There's quite a bit of time involved with that, although criminal law isn't my specialty."

"Mine, either," said Cassie. "But I seem to be getting involved in more and more of it as we go along. I liked it better when I didn't know as much."

Cassie gently stroked Sammy's head. "I need to get her into the vet as soon as possible." She pulled out her cell phone and hit the button, "I'm calling the Eagleclaw 24 hour emergency vet line," she said, her eyes shining with tears. The service came on and Cassie described her dog's symptoms in a calm voice, belying the anxiety that was etched across her face. She nodded at the phone and then punched off.

Dusty looked at her questioningly, "What's the verdict?"

"They said because she is responsive and licking my hand,

she'll be okay to wait until the regular office hours. I just need to keep an eye on her. Make sure there is no bleeding from her ears or nostrils. Her pupils remain equal. And that she doesn't display any seizure activity."

Sammy's gaze remained intently on Cassie as she talked.

"Well, it's just about daylight. What do you say we go get some breakfast and by then the vet ought to be open to see Sammy." Dusty started to stand up.

"I don't want to leave her." Cassie clutched his arm.

"I didn't mean that—I mean bring her with us." Dusty stood up and held has hand out to help Cassie get up holding Sammy.

Cassie relaxed. "Sounds like a plan. I'm kind of burned out on this place right now."

Dusty put his arm around her and they all walked out to the car.

Chapter Forty-Four

They pulled into the parking lot of a vintage restaurant midway between Cassie's ranch and Dusty's. It was actually one of Cassie's favorite places to eat. They made Sammy comfortable in the truck laying out a thick blanket. The dog was perkier on the drive, even sitting up and looking out the window, so Cassie felt okay about leaving her. The three of them walked into the restaurant. The walls were knotty pine and the smell of dark coffee and bacon permeated the air. Several locals sat with coffee cups in hand and a newspaper laid out on the table.

The waitress took them to a booth and Cassie slid in next to the window. Dusty slid in next to her and Mike sat down on the other side. Although he must have literally run out of his house, Dusty looked good, as always. He had a green-and-black plaid shirt and lined jean jacket on. His hair looked slightly ruffled, but outdoorsy. He caught her glance. "What? That bad, huh?" He ran his hand through his hair.

Cassie laughed, embarrassed he'd seen her looking at him. "No, not at all." She picked up the menu and studied it. The waitress came up with a coffee pot and they all put their cups up. "I'll be back in a few minutes." She turned and walked back to the kitchen.

Mike put his menu down decisively. "I know what I want."

"Me too," said Dusty.

"I'm not all that hungry," said Cassie.

"Don't worry, Cassie. We'll get to the bottom of this." Dusty said, reaching down and squeezing her hand.

"We're going to find him," said Mike. "My next stop after breakfast is to hit the sheriff's office. I want to talk to a friend of mine down there and check a few things out."

Cassie rubbed her eyes. "I don't know if you have noticed, but Roy has got a real issue with mood swings. I mean, real big mood swings. He goes from happy to violent in a real short time, with no warning. When I was hiding behind the dresser he kept saying weird stuff from *Honey, Daddy's home with a present* to *Where are you, you little bitch*. It was pretty crazy."

"You're one brave lady," Mike said with admiration.

"Yes, she is." Dusty was having a hard time keeping his eyes off her. He kept wanting to touch her, put his arm around her—something. *Roy's not the only crazy one around here.* He shook his head and took a drink of coffee.

By the time they finished breakfast, early-morning gray sky had thinned out to daylight. The big clock above the bar showed 8:30. "I think we should be able to take Sammy in now," said Dusty. "We can take her to my vet; he's pretty close by. And he lives right next-door to the clinic. I thought I'd give him a little more sleep. He gets pretty cranky and expensive if you wake him up too early in the morning."

"Really?" Said Cassie. Relief flooded her face. "My regular vet is gone on vacation. I wasn't sure where to take her. I don't care about the bill—I just care that Sammy's okay."

"Sounds like he's going to be there one way or the other," said Mike.

Dusty flushed, "That is the important thing." Then he brightened, "What are friends for?"

Sammy ended up with a mild concussion, but she was going to be okay. Cassie still held her as Mike drove her back home. "What a relief. Having her take it easy for a while is something I can handle. I'm so glad she wasn't seriously injured."

"That was definitely a lucky break," agreed Dusty. "I just can't stand the thought of a dog getting hurt. It's such a cowardly act." He remembered back a couple of weeks ago at Indian Creek Meadows when someone in the night kicked Scout. Strange coincidence. *Lots of strange coincidences lately.*

They pulled up in Cassie's driveway. "You know, Cassie, that guy is still out there and he could come back. Do you have another place to stay for a while? I really don't think it's a good idea for you to be here again alone." Dusty looked at her in earnest, hoping she wouldn't insist on staying there.

Cassie thought about it. "I'll give Terri a call and see if I can stay over there for a couple nights."

Dusty exhaled. He hadn't realized he'd been holding his breath waiting for her to answer. "Great."

"I think I'll stay here, if you don't mind," said Mike. "If he comes back, I want to be waiting for him. Cassie, do you think you could leave your car out front and we could drive you to Terri's? The more convinced he is you're there, the better our chances are of nabbing him."

"Our?" Dusty raised his eyebrows. "Are we having a sleepover?"

Mike laughed. "If you'd like to participate."

"Why not? I'll make sure and leave Scout at home."

"Wow. If you guys are going to have all the fun, maybe I should stay here too."

"We'd love to have you, but maybe another time," joked Dusty.

"Really, that's fine with me. Let me give Terri a call and, if it's okay, I'll just pack a few things and Sammy and I can go."

Cassie called Terri and, after she explained what happened, Terri was more than happy for the company. The rain had cleared up and the sky was a whitish-gray as they drove to Terri's. It kind of suited her mood. Sitting in the back seat of Mike's truck, she looked at the back of Dusty's head as they drove. He really didn't have a bad side. Mike was a nice-looking guy too. He had short hair and a ball cap on. She noticed that most outdoor guys always had a hat on of some kind. So far she'd never seen Dusty in a ball cap.

They pulled up in front of Terri's house and Cassie and Sammy got out. Sammy was able to walk around and the only telltale sign of the blow was a bandage on her head. She was recovering quickly. Dusty grabbed Cassie's overnight bag and walked her up to the front door. Terri lived in a double-wide mobile home on a few acres outside of Eagleclaw. The door flew open and Terri exclaimed in one breath, "Oh, Cassie, I can't believe this is happening. I just knew there was something wrong with that guy. Come on in. Hi, Dusty," she managed in one breath.

Dusty stepped in behind Cassie and set her bag down. "We'll head over to your house later today."

"Call me if anything happens," she said.

"Will do. I'll call you, anyway," Dusty reassured her. He wanted to fold her in his arms and tell her she would be safe—he'd make sure of it. But with Terri standing there and Mike waiting in the car, he settled for, "Take care."

"You too. Keep me posted." Cassie stood at the door watching him leave.

As they drove back to his house Mike had a big grin on his face. "What's up with you?" Dusty asked.

"Oh, you got it bad!"

"That obvious, huh?"

"I've never seen you like this before. It's a new side."

"Wonderful. So glad to make your day." Dusty turned down the road to his place. "So you want to meet up later tonight at Cassie's? I've actually got to go to the office today. I have a couple of appointments."

"I have things to do too. I'll catch up with you later." Mike walked to his truck in the parking area in front of Dusty's log cabin.

The morning sky was steel gray and the trees were dripping from the deluge the night before. Dusty glanced up at them as he walked to his house. *Funny, they always look like they are weeping with their bowed branches and water slipping off the leaves.*

Chapter Forty-Five

Freshly showered, Dusty drove into town and sat at the desk in his office working.

"You look tired today," Mrs. Phillips observed, as she sat a cup of coffee on his desk.

"I had kind of a late night." He sipped the coffee. "And thank you for the coffee."

"You're welcome. You had a number of calls this morning. I put them on your desk." She gestured to the small pile of pink *While You Were Out* notes laying in a small pile on his desk. "You may want to take special note of Paul Wolfe's call."

"Paul Wolfe. What now?"

"He didn't leave a message other than to call him." Mrs. Phillips turned and walked back to her desk in the front room.

Dusty stared at the note on his desk. He glanced at the clock as he dialed the number, about 11 o'clock.

Paul picked it up on the second ring. "Dusty?"

"Yes."

"I need to talk to you." His voice sounded urgent.

"What's your lawyer situation? Because if you have one, I don't want to talk to you. Did you hire anyone else? Barker called me and said he was done."

"No, that's it. I don't have a lawyer any longer."

"So what's this about?"

"I don't want to talk on the phone. Meet me at my office as soon as you can."

Dusty thought it over. He didn't trust this guy one bit. He knew Paul could be violent, but he needed to get Julie out of this marriage. Paul representing himself was going to make it that much more difficult. There was too much at stake for him to not get a lawyer involved. "Paul, you should have your own lawyer. I represent Julie in this case. I want to make that clear in any discussions that we have."

"I don't want another damn lawyer," said Paul, his voice rising slightly. "I don't even want a divorce. But if that's the way it's going to be, I would like to talk to you about it myself."

"I'm not going anywhere unless you're going to stay calm. I'm not in the mood for another office trashing—at your office or mine," Dusty said firmly.

Paul lowered his voice and fought to regain control. "I'm sorry, Dusty. I won't do that again. Would you please come to my office? I have some things I want to go over with you. It will remain professional. I promise."

Dusty sighed. He didn't believe Paul, but he had to see what he could do to resolve the case. "I've got some things to do first. I'll be over there about one-thirty."

"Great." Paul sounded relieved. "I'll clear my schedule."

The sun was beginning to peek out through the clouds, and as Dusty drove to the business on the outskirts of Eagleclaw, he felt a little bit more optimistic. The parking lot was empty by the front office of the old paper mill, but the buildings in the back were full. Smoke was pouring out the chimney and things appeared to be operating at a full clip.

As he came in the door, the receptionist looked up and smiled faintly. "Good afternoon."

"Good afternoon. Dustin Rose."

"I'll let Paul know you're here." As she got up, Dusty noticed she was an attractive woman, probably in her early twenties. She wore a very, very short skirt, no nylons and flip-flops. The style these days, he supposed. Mrs. Phillips always wore sturdy oxfords and sensible high collars. This must be Paul's girlfriend. How convenient to *hire* your own date.

"Hey, Dusty. Thanks for coming." The short, stocky middle-aged man hurried out of the open office door, hand extended. Paul wore dark slacks, a white shirt and a green-and-black tie.

Dusty hesitated for a minute and then shook hands. *The things I do for clients.*

"Come on back." Wolfe turned and walked back into his office. Dusty followed and the receptionist closed the door behind him.

"Hey, I'm really sorry about your office." Paul looked at Dusty contritely.

Dusty watched him. He was used to Paul's anger, but this was a new approach. He wasn't sure where this was going. "Yeah, I don't think Mrs. Phillips wants you back any time soon. She had to clean it up."

"She's absolutely right and I owe her an apology."

Dusty decided to get right to the point. "So why am I here?"

Paul seemed to gather himself. He straightened his sleeves and looked at Dusty. "I wanted to talk to you about settling the case. I have an offer."

That was not what Dusty expected. This guy was full of surprises. "Okay. I can listen to your offer, but we've still got the small problem that there is a warrant out for your arrest. You violated a no-contact order with Julie. You've got assault and battery charges, so before you can appear in a court of law, you may want to get that straightened out." Paul blinked as Dusty spoke, and sweat appeared on his forehead.

Paul went into his salesman mode. "Yeah, I kind of lost my temper again the other night. But you know how it is with women. They get so emotional. I never have been able to handle that."

"No, I don't know how it is." Dusty wanted nothing to do with being included in Paul's understanding of women. He felt his annoyance grow. Paul's voice and confidence was really grating.

"Look, I came over here since you wanted to talk to me in person. My client is Julie. I am here to represent her and her best interests. Whatever you want to say to me, you need to put in writing. You can email it to me. Please don't stop by." Dusty's tone was matter-of-fact and he looked directly into Paul's face.

Paul reddened and more sweat dripped down his brow.

"You need to get some help for your rages. And you need to stay away from my client."

Wolfe jumped up and slammed his fist down on the table. "I want to settle this case."

"So do I. But you make it really difficult when you keep violating the restraining order and beating up my client. We're done here. You need to find a lawyer." Dusty calmly stood, towering over the smaller man, and turned to walk out of the office.

Paul stood, momentarily rooted behind his desk. Dusty had seen plenty of guys like Paul before—he wasn't used to losing. What he couldn't win by orders he won by rage. Neither was working anymore, it seemed. Dusty knew he was terminated by his Seattle attorney Barker, and now Dusty wasn't going to play along. He had a strong feeling an eruption was imminent. As he put his hand on the doorknob, the smaller man shot from behind the desk after him.

As Dusty stepped into the reception area, Mike was sitting in a chair waiting. Paul grabbed Dusty's suit coat. "You just hold on for a minute. I'll tell you when I'm done," he roared. Dusty turned to peel Wolfe off his jacket. Mike shot out of his chair and crossed the room in two leaps. Within seconds they had Paul pinned, and Mike snapped handcuffs on him. The young receptionist's face was a mask of horror. She instantly began crying.

"You pop up in the strangest places," said Dusty.

"Yeah. When I called your office and Mrs. Phillips told me where you went, I decided you might need some backup."

"Thanks. You called that right."

Mike pulled his cell phone out and called 911. Over the sobs of the receptionist, he gave them the address.

Paul Wolfe lay on the floor. "You sons o' bitches! I'll get you for this!"

Dusty ignored him. "Mike, you got this? I'm going to head back to my office. I've got one more appointment today."

"Sure thing, Boss. Catch up with you later."

Dusty left the melee and walked out the door to his car.

Chapter Forty-Six

Mrs. Phillips flashed Dusty a concerned look as he entered the office. "Are you all right? I was so worried about you going to see that horrible man."

"Yes. I'm fine. Thank you for letting Mike know. He was in the waiting room when I left and it turned out to be very helpful."

"Oh, thank goodness." Mrs. Phillips looked relieved.

"I don't think we'll be hearing from him for a while, anyway. The police were picking him up. He's probably going to be cooling his heels in jail for a couple nights."

"And that's exactly where he should be," his secretary answered firmly. And then, business as usual, "Would you like me to make a pot of coffee for your four o'clock appointment?"

"Yes, that would be great. Thank you." Dusty walked into his office.

At promptly 4 o'clock the office door jingled. A portly woman maneuvered herself through the door and stood in front of Mrs. Phillips' desk.

"I'm here for my appointment with Dusty Rose," she announced in a strident voice.

"Have a seat. Can I get you some coffee?" Mrs. Phillips asked.

"No, thank you. I'm fine," the big woman said, reorganizing her large handbag on her arm.

Mrs. Phillips picked up the phone. "Mr. Dustin Rose, Mrs. Brubaker is here."

She replaced the phone in its cradle. "He will see you now."

Dusty opened the door to his office. "Come on in, Mrs. Brubaker."

The large woman waddled firmly into his office. She carefully lowered herself into one of the two chairs that faced his desk.

Dusty asked politely. "So you want to change something on your will?"

The woman's fleshy face turned red and then the floodgates opened. "That lazy, no-count varmint of a son of mine. I'm writing him out of my will. I don't want to leave him anything." Her plump cheeks flushed and her fists balled in her lap.

"Okay. We can change your will," Dusty soothed. "Where will we put his inheritance?"

That seemed to stump the woman. She was so intent on writing her son out of the will, she hadn't thought where the money should go. She pursed her lips in thought.

"Do you have any other family you would like to assign as an heir?" Dusty prompted.

"Well, my sister, but she's older than I am," Mrs. Brubaker answered slowly.

"Okay. A charity?" he suggested.

"Hmmm. Yes, I could leave it to the local dog rescue commission." She brightened. "Yes, I would like to do that."

"Okay. I would like to point out that it would be better to leave him one dollar, so that at least he got something. If he tries to overturn the will because of being overlooked as the heir apparent, he will have been listed."

"One dollar. Well, he certainly doesn't deserve that, but if that's the rules, well, then that's what I'll do." She gathered herself. "He is a worthless son. He has not visited me or called me for over a year. Nothing. Her chin began to quiver. Tears gathered at the corners of her eyes and she swept them away, but more quickly followed. "If he doesn't remember me, by gosh, I don't remember him, either. When I have to rely on the help from other people, kind strangers even, to help me around my place because he's too busy, well, that's the final straw. They're better at being family than he is." She took a shaky breath.

Dusty felt his stomach clench. He waited patiently for her to finish. He knew coming to an attorney's office was anguishing for people. They came to straighten things out legally in their lives, and even though courts were non-emotional, the participants had plenty of emotion. They didn't really get you ready for this in law school, and it was something he had had to teach himself. It was hard to be detached when you watched your clients go through so much pain.

After erupting verbally, Mrs. Brubaker's massive shoulders shook and she began to sob. Dusty scrambled up from his desk and got a box of Kleenex. He handed her the box and patted her awkwardly on the shoulder. "Don't worry. We'll get this straightened out for you."

Mrs. Phillips came to the rescue, entering the office quietly with a glass of water. "I thought you might be thirsty, dear." She sat the glass of water in front of the wailing woman.

"Thaa—thank you," she managed to stammer, and took a big drink of water.

After getting Mrs. Brubaker calmed down, they finished the codicil to the will and Dusty told her Mrs. Phillips would call her when it was done. As she walked out of his office, Dusty noticed her shoulders sagged and the purpose seemed to have lessened in her step. She had accomplished her goal, but it didn't make her any happier. It appeared to have the reverse effect.

Dusty sighed and sat at his desk. Leaning forward, he put his head in his hands. He could feel it inside of him. The stress and tension of the job was getting to him. He had to get out. Thinking over what he had to do the next day, he had no court appearances.

"Mrs. Phillips," he called from his desk, "Please clear my schedule tomorrow. If I have any appointments, could you please move them to next week. Tell them I'm sick."

"You're sick?"

"Yeah, sick of work. I need a break."

"Oh, yes. Well, it has been a tough week for you," Mrs. Phillips said with an understanding nod as she stood in the doorway of his office. "I'll take care of it right away." She paused. "Monday is Labor Day."

"It is?" Dusty realized he hadn't even thought about it. "Thank you."

He was heading up to the mountains first thing in the morning. Just the thought of it made the stress begin to lessen in his shoulders and the small of his back. Dusty packed up his brief case and headed out the door. The bell jingled behind him.

As he pulled into the Safeway parking lot, his cell phone rang.

"Hey, Boss."

"How did it go?" Dusty turned off his truck.

"Mr. Wolfe is spending the night courtesy of the county. And it may be a few nights, depending on what happens tomorrow at the prelim. But odds are they aren't going to talk about bail with an assault charge until next week. Everybody is always in a hurry to start their weekend."

"So true. Good job, Mike. Thanks for being there," Dusty said, with heartfelt gratitude.

"That's my job." Mike brushed off the compliment.

"Above and beyond." Dusty leaned back in his seat. "I'm heading out tomorrow morning."

"Oh, yeah? Where?"

"I thought I'd park at the trailhead at Mesatchee Creek and pack into Cougar Lake."

"Want some company? That sounds like somewhere I would really like to be."

"Sure. I'm just picking up some food now. We can talk about it more tonight at Cassie's, but I wanted an early start, maybe nine o'clock at the trailhead."

"Sounds good. I'll pack and then meet you over there tonight." Mike said, his voice lifting in anticipation.

"Oh, and Mike, I'm staying through Monday. It's Labor Day weekend."

"It is?"

"Yeah, my sentiments exactly." Things had been moving way too fast lately, Dusty marveled. Neither one of them knew what day it was anymore, let alone the time of year.

"Well, that's even better." Mike recovered quickly. "See you tonight."

Chapter Forty-Seven

Dusty headed up the two-lane highway as it wound through the mountain pass. The sun was just starting to hit the tops of the trees and the snow-capped peak of Rainier towered before him. He knew he was lucky. A lot of people didn't know where they needed to be. They looked for it and often never found it. Sometimes they looked in drugs, sometimes alcohol. He winced at the thought. He had come really, really close to losing it all. Alcohol was so deceptive. Insidious. He thought he was a reasonably intelligent person. Oh, he may have a drink now and then. No big deal. How the amount he drank and when he drank slipped by him he'd never know. There was always a good reason to drink—and drink a lot.

Scout lay on the truck seat next to him. Dusty patted him on the head as he drove. When Sarah left was when he finally hit rock bottom. The kids were grown and gone. Their differences came much more into focus without the sporting events, the Boy Scouts, the school activities. It was just the two of them. Her dream had always been to live in the city. She never missed the chance to remind him that they had, after all, met in Seattle, and he had cruelly pulled her from the life she knew and loved. When she finally packed up and moved back there, she was happy and he didn't have to hide his drinking anymore. He'd drink all night in front of the TV, pass out, and try to make himself well enough to go to work. Nobody was fooled—least of all his dad.

One spring day, Dustin Rose, his dad, called him up and invited him over for Sunday dinner. Dusty remembered being confused at all the cars there. He hadn't realized his dad was having a dinner party. Turned out he wasn't. That's when Dusty found out what an intervention was, and he thanked God he was able to really hear what they had to say. Both of his kids, Nick and Katie, were there; his ex-wife Sarah; his dad and his latest girlfriend, who was much younger and attractive, of course; and then one other person who Dusty had never met before, but soon learned was a drug and alcohol counselor.

The whole thing was kind of a blur. He remembered really wishing he had a drink. The one he had at home just before leaving had left his mouth tasting like dried-up pinecones. As he walked in the door, everybody was sitting in the living room. His dad offered him a cup of coffee and asked him to have a seat. And then it started. The counselor introduced himself. Katie began talking. His beautiful little princess. Her big brown eyes looked into his and told him how his drinking affected her. Her sporting events he never attended. When she got homecoming queen in high school he was *working*. He never realized it. He thought they didn't know. Katie was never really good at hiding her emotions, and after a couple of sentences she became lost in her own grief. Sobbing, she crumpled in her chair. He remembered feeling like he was shrinking. He wanted to run over and throw his arms around her and tell her it never happened. And if it had, by some weird chance, it never would again. He couldn't move. Sarah ran over and pulled Katie into her arms.

Nick was next. Dusty looked at his own likeness. Clear blue eyes, athletically built and suntanned. Nick pushed his hair back and looked like he was trying really hard to be calm. He was his father's son. Dusty was shaking and he couldn't stop. Looking into his son's eyes, he saw himself. The person he never, ever wanted to let down. He wanted to be the best dad any boy ever had, but he had to listen to the truth. The excuses Nick had to make for his dad's absences. And when Dusty was there, he was so drawn and moody, Nick never felt like he had anyone he could talk to about his decisions.

Shame burned deep through him and the kids would have been enough. Dusty was ready to turn himself in to wherever he needed to go at that point. But then it was his dad's turn. Their relationship had always been so conflicted. His dad didn't understand him and always had a better plan than Dusty. But hell, at this point he was pretty sure he didn't understand himself anymore. His dad laid out his feelings the best he could. Displaying feelings father-to-son wasn't a real strong point for his dad. Dusty listened because he was immobilized. He felt the familiar anger as his dad listed the business failings and missed events. But Katie's and Nick's eyes were on him and what they said had seared his soul.

Then Sarah. She sat quietly holding the still-sobbing Katie. A diamond ring on her hand flashed in the light; he idly thought it must have been a full carat. He had heard she remarried. Then she began to speak. Their relationship had long ago died, as each of them had realized their true foundation of spirit didn't exist. They had coexisted for years as parents and living partners. The good thing was the mutual respect had survived. It took a beating the last year or so before the split, but it was resilient. As Dusty listened to Sarah, he could hear the pain in her voice and he felt worse. She told him she had been a single parent for most of their marriage. *A paycheck doesn't make a partner.*

At the end of the afternoon, Nick assured Dusty he would take care of the animals and they went back to the farm to grab Dusty's things. He had a bed date in rehab that night.

Breaking over the top of Chinook Pass the sun was so bright Dusty blinked. He reached over on the dash and put on his sunglasses. He knew everything about where he came from was what made him who he was today. Time was the great healer. Actually—he corrected himself—time and horses. This was the best part of his life, and he knew it. The marriage, the career, the kids, all that was achieved. Now it was his horses and the mountains. Dusty thanked God for that. He knew a lot of people didn't make it. If he needed proof, the people he had met in treatment gave it to him.

Once it cleared the top of Chinook Pass, the highway wove down the east side of the Cascade Mountains. Now he was in Eastern Washington, known for its pine trees and drier climate. The hillside gave way steeply on one side and he could see the sweep of green trees and, off in the distance, Clear Lake. Mount Rainier passed behind him like a large snowy beacon. Mesatchee Creek trailhead was the first opportunity to turn right at the bottom of the hill. He turned in and was immediately surrounded by deep-green fir trees, and the bumpy dirt road led the way into the small camping area and trailhead.

Mike had not arrived yet. He had the whole camp to himself. Kind of unusual for Labor Day weekend, but it happened sometimes. Everyone thought everyone else was going to be at a trailhead, especially a small one like Mesatchee, so no one went at all. Scout bounded out behind him, and he walked around the back and unloaded Muley and Cheyenne. The rich soil and fir tree smell filled his senses and he felt relaxed for the first time in what seemed like weeks. As he brushed his horses, he thought about the prior weekend.

Having Cassie around did something to him. He could not ever remember feeling quite the same way around a woman. He had such a great time—right up until Roy showed up. When Roy approached Cassie, Dusty went into a blur. He could have easily killed him. It was a protective instinct that he had never experienced in himself before. The intensity of his feelings for her kind of scared him. He did not want to get into another relationship when he didn't know if he could do it. Dusty did not want to screw up anyone else's life. Actually, if he were to be rigorously honest, he wasn't scared at all. *Terrified* was a much better word.

He had called Cassie before he left. Mike and he had spent the night at her house, but it turned out to be entirely uneventful. Dusty told her he was going packing for a few days. She was still at Terri's house and Sammy was doing a lot better. Cassie was going to sit out Labor Day until her dog was well. She thought she would be heading home over the weekend. Dusty told her to be careful. Cassie laughed and told him, "That's why God made firearms." If she was disappointed that he left, her voice didn't show it. It wasn't something he could apologize for, anyway. It was who he was. He needed some time in the mountains.

Dusty brushed Muley's back so intensely that his horse turned his prominent head around and stared at Dusty. "Oh, sorry, boy." Dusty let off a little on his pressure. Muley sighed and faced forward.

Mike pulled in with his truck and trailer just as Dusty was tightening the girth on his saddle. After replacing the latigos from being cut on Tumac a couple weeks ago, he had to deal with the new leather. It was stretchy for a while, so it was a matter of tightening, waiting and then retightening. He knew after using them for a while they quit stretching.

Mike jumped out of his truck. "Sorry I'm late."

"You're not late. I just got here." Dusty straightened up. "Besides, now we're off the grid." He grinned.

"And it feels so good." Mike let his horses out the back.

"Boy, does it."

Chapter Forty-Eight

Muley led the way through the deep forest, followed by Cheyenne, Mike and his packhorse behind. Their hoofbeats were muffled by the thick carpet of pine needles on the forest floor, and the rain in the past week had gotten rid of any dust. As they wound through the trees, they came to a huge pool that covered the whole trail and more. Muley didn't even hesitate and plunged through the middle to the other side. Dusty often wondered how backpackers got through all that water without being soaked. As it was, he had to lift his feet up in the middle to avoid getting soaked.

The trail became steep switchbacks and the sound of a waterfall took over the forest silence. Every once in a while they caught a glimpse of the rushing water as they rounded a corner. It was a huge waterfall and he couldn't see the top. The only thing Dusty didn't like about the trail was the ground bees. They were particularly nasty on this stretch of trail up to American Ridge. He had heard that Lydia McCorkle had hit a bad patch with her Missouri Fox Trotter and had broken her leg. It was a bad wreck. All horses react differently to bees. Some just stood there and took it, while others went from zero to sixty and put miles between them and the bees in a short time. Those were the hat-loser kind of rides. Muley didn't like bees any more than anyone else. He chose to buck and run to show his displeasure.

Riding down the trail, Dusty thought again about his old horse Diamond. When he had just gotten back into riding again, he picked up Diamond from some people not too far from where he lived.

Diamond was a project. He was five years old and the family pet—not the family horse. He had never been ridden and didn't know what to make of the idea. Dusty just wanted a horse, and he was a good price, so they wound up together. He smiled to himself—he'd never forget one of the first rides with Diamond. He had boarded the horse at the time a few miles away. They had to go by a stretch of highway. Diamond was so upset by the cars that Dusty had to walk with him on the road. Diamond literally hid his head in Dusty's back, shaking, as the cars went by. Dusty talked to him, petted him, and eventually they were able to go by cars on highways without Diamond thinking they were going to kill him.

Diamond had a lot of strong points as he made the transition from family pet to an amazing mountain horse. At sixteen hands, there wasn't much he couldn't clear, and if he couldn't walk it, he had an enormous leap that would clear anything. Sometimes he used his leap just for entertainment value, Dusty was pretty sure. If a creek was narrow and very deep, that didn't look right to Diamond, so he would give that an extra five feet in the air, just to be sure. That's where the hat losing would come in, so he had to make sure it was clamped down extra tight or that he had his stampede string on. Dusty didn't usually wear a stampede string, but an old cowboy one time showed him how to cut a two-inch flap in the back of his hatband. When he flipped that down, it seemed to hold his hat on even in twenty-mile-an-hour winds.

The reason he thought of Diamond with bees was the unique way he dealt with them. When other horses would run or buck, old Diamond would find the source, put his head down there, and stomp. Dusty chuckled. He had never had a horse do that before or since. It didn't matter what the rider thought Diamond should do—Diamond was busy stomping and wouldn't listen to anything or anyone until he was done. If the bee stings hurt, Diamond never showed it.

Dusty smiled. He had been such a great horse. Another thing

was thistles. In summer, when the trails were full of flowers, occasionally they would pass the blooming thistles. As he rode down the trail, all of a sudden Diamond would snake his neck out and snatch a flower right off the top of the thorny plant. Just that quick. Dusty was shocked. He wasn't sure he'd seen that right. But the more thistles they passed, the more Diamond snatched them up. Talking to other horsemen, Dusty later learned that it was something that a few horses liked; the sweet nectar of the flower. Most wouldn't put up with the thorns to get the flower, but Diamond was always willing to take the bad with the good.

Muley traveled up the steep hillside barely breaking a sweat. He and Dusty had put on so many miles this summer, he was in great shape. He heard Mike behind him traveling in companionable silence. Dusty's mind drifted back to Diamond, and the end.

It was funny with animals that are part of your life. There reaches a point where there is no difference emotionally between them and humans. Dusty shifted in the saddle. It still hurt to think about it. One day Diamond had stopped eating. Dusty had to literally force him down to his trough to eat the hay. That was not a horse thing to do and he should have realized it immediately. But he didn't. It went on for a couple of days, and it took one of the girls who kept her horse in a pasture nearby to point it out.

Dusty immediately called the vet. She came out that day and did some tests. Dusty turned Diamond loose and let him graze around the cabin in the thick green grass. He put out a big tub of water and threw a horse blanket on Diamond. The horse would vary between shivering and sweating. He would lie down and get up. Most hauntingly, he would walk over to the hitch rail by the barn and wait to be tacked up. It was like, *Come on, Boss, saddle me up so I can do my job.* Dusty would talk to him and lead him back to the grass. When he'd look out the window later, there would be Diamond, waiting patiently by the hitch rail.

On a beautiful day in late spring, Dusty had still not gotten the results back from the vet. He walked outside, surprised to find the old horse waiting for him. Dusty walked up to him and Diamond laid his head on Dusty's chest. He remembered it to this day, it had never happened before with a horse he'd owned, and never since. They stood like that for a few minutes, Diamond's head on his chest and Dusty's arms around him. The horse pulled his head back, turned and walked into the trees. As Dusty watched, he lay down in the thick green grass and died. Just thinking about it made Dusty's chest ache. He felt his eyes start to tear. Diamond had said *good-bye*.

Dusty shook his head. "Come on, boy. Let's go." He booted Muley. His horse faltered a step as if to say, *I thought we were going.* Then he gathered himself and forged up the trail faster.

Chapter Forty-Nine

Dusty and Muley broke over the top of the hill on American Ridge where the ground leveled out. Mike was right behind him. They followed the trail through the thick trees along the ridge top with only an occasional view between the branches of the mountain ranges around them. After a few miles, it opened up and they were in thick meadows with occasional trees. A small creek babbled through and they stopped their horses to water. Scout joined in and immersed himself completely in the creek while lapping up the water.

"Now, that dog knows how to get a drink," Mike said. The horses plunged their noses into the fresh, clear water, drinking deeply. It was thirsty work pulling up the hill they just climbed. Dusty felt a lot lighter. His tenseness had been released. As Muley finished drinking, he raised his head and looked intently into the trees. There was another trail that forked the one they were on. Dusty followed his gaze. He couldn't see anything, but he knew Muley well enough to know that look. Something was there. Sure enough, in a matter of minutes he heard the jingle of packsaddles and the striking of hooves. He heard a deep laugh and a large mule appeared in the trail, five riders and assorted pack stock following.

The man in front wore a well-worn gray cowboy hat, short brimmed, a brown saddle coat and well-broke-in-chinks. He had light-brown hair and a weathered, suntanned face. He pulled two pack horses behind him. The five men were in line behind him.

Dusty could tell by the way they rode that they had to be dudes. They were wearing the latest Cabela's camo clothes with hiking boots, and compound bows strapped over their saddles. They sat stiffly in the saddle. It looked like it had been a long trip for them.

The lead rider's face split into a wide grin and his blue eyes twinkled. "Well, hey, it's Dusty Rose."

"Hi, Pat."

"I haven't seen you for a while. How's your Uncle Bob doing? I just saw him this year in Winthrop at the WOGA Rendezvous."

"He's doing well. Mike and I were just up there a few weeks ago."

"Hey, Mike." Pat nodded to Mike. "Long time no see."

"Good to see you, Pat."

Pat sat back on his mule, completely relaxed. "I heard about what happened up there in the Pasayten."

Dusty wasn't surprised. Being in such a small community, word traveled at lightning speed among horsemen. Pat Webster was an outfitter in the Chinook Pass area. He owned the Bumping River Outfitters. His job was horses and mules. He and his trail hands packed in people ranging from first-time riders to time-worn hunters. They all had one thing in common: they wanted to experience the beautiful Cascade Mountains of Washington state.

"Sometimes these mountains can be a lot like the Old West," Pat added.

The way he said it, Dusty got the distinct feeling he wasn't sad about that aspect of it. "That's true," he agreed.

Pat laughed. "I still want to meet that woman who put the guy down. That's my kind of woman." He laughed raucously. The men between him joined in. One of them said, "Pat, they're all your kind of woman."

"Can't blame a guy for trying." He winked at Dusty.

The minute Pat said it, Dusty fought down annoyance. Anybody else, but not her. The inexplicable feeling of possessiveness hit him again. He willed himself to keep a lazy grin on his face as he talked to Pat.

"Where you guys headed?" Pat asked, oblivious.

"We're going down to Cougar Lake for a few days."

"That's a beauty. I love that spot. Hey, we're going to be camped just about a mile from here. Why don't you two join us for dinner tomorrow night? We're going to be doing some hunting and then we got a big dinner planned. It would be great to have the company and catch up on your big adventure this summer."

Mountain hospitality alive and well in the Cascades, Dusty mused. "What do you think, Mike?"

"Sounds good to me," said Mike.

"Okay, we'll come."

"About six, mountain time."

"Cascade Mountain time," agreed Dusty.

Pat explained where the camp was and the two groups headed down the trail in separate directions.

As they made their way through grass and trees, the rocky trail began to switchback down into a lake. At the bottom they lucked out—the best spot was empty. It was a grassy area set back from the lakeshore with a flat spot for their tents and trees in the back for their highline. The lake rippled with a slight breeze and sparkles of sunlight reflected in the small waves. Mount Rainier dominated the background. The snow was a startling white, fading to blue in the crevices.

They rode in and unloaded their packhorses. In no time at all they had their camp set up. They walked down the trail to check out where it went.

"That's Little Cougar Lake over there." Dusty pointed to another body of water through the trees. The trail stopped abruptly and dropped off. A footbridge lay torn up at the bottom of a steep creek bottom. The bridge appeared to have been dismantled—every other plank was removed. Now only stringers lay across the creek. The walls were washed out and jagged; too treacherous for horses.

"We used to be able to ride through here. There's a beautiful sand beach on Little Cougar Lake in the back part and there's some great camps down there," Dusty said, as they walked. "They pulled this bridge out and never put it back in. I heard they wanted to keep horses out of there, but that's okay. I know another way to get around it."

"I had assumed," said Mike.

"Yeah, we could take that tomorrow, cut around to the back of the lake and pick up the old trail. It's pretty cool. You go up over the top and wind up on the PCT."

"Sounds great."

"It's a good loop. It will take us by American Lake, and then we can hit Pat's camp on the way back."

"Sounds like a plan."

They walked the short distance back to their camp. The horses grazed in their hobbles, knee-deep in thick green grass. Scout barked, happy to be in the woods again.

While Mike was putting the coffee on, Dusty walked out to pick up some firewood. Scout trotted along. Dusty got the feeling he was being watched again. It was odd. It could have been an animal, for all he knew—but he doubted it. If animals were watching him, which he was sure they often did, he didn't have the hair on the back of his neck stand up. He took a quick look at Scout. The dog panted and seemed oblivious. It had to be him then. For sure Scout would have let him know. Dusty loaded up his arms with blow-down limbs of all different sizes and shapes. He'd brought an ax, but it didn't look like he was going to need it.

Walking back into camp, he saw that Mike had stoked the fire. A good flame was shooting up. Dusty could hear some frogs down by the lake, their voices ricocheting off the shore in all directions.

"Coffee's on." Mike set the pot down on a rock by the fire. Dusty dug his coffee cup out of his pack box.

Sitting in his chair by the fire, with a hot cup of coffee in his hand, Dusty said, "It doesn't get any better than this."

"No, it doesn't."

Dusty hadn't realized how stressed out he had been, until now.

He could feel the peacefulness of the high mountain country pull it right out of him. Whatever problems he may have in town weren't here. The only job he had was to just be himself and take care of his horses and dog.

They ate dinner and sat by the fire until the blaze had burned down to bright coals. The week had been pretty exhausting for both, and they didn't talk much. Dusty felt his head get heavy and he had to fight to keep it off his chest. "Guess I'll turn in now before I fall asleep in my chair."

"I'm going to watch the fire for a little longer. See you in the morning," said Mike.

"Come on, Scout." Dusty always brought Scout in the tent with him at night. With the rise in mountain lions alone, it was not as safe as it used to be. Dusty unzipped the tent, Scout and he piled in, and he closed the flap. Taking his hat, boots, pants and gun off, he crawled into his sleeping bag. The canvas, wood smoke and horses were a balm to his soul. Dusty fell into the first deep sleep he'd had in weeks.

Chapter Fifty

Dusty felt heat on his eyelids. As he opened them he was greeted with the canvas of his tent lit up with bright sunshine. He wasn't sure what time it was, but daylight was well on its way. Scout looked at him expectantly. Dusty reached over and opened the tent door. The dog bounded out in a flash. He heard the fire crackling and smelled the coffee—a good time to get up.

"Wished I'd brought my fishing pole," Mike greeted, as Dusty walked out to the fire. "I've been watching them hit the lake all morning. There's some big suckers out there too."

"Always something, right?" Dusty poured his coffee. Then he stood up and looked down at the lake. Sure enough, the clear, calm surface rippled every so often with fish feeding just under the surface. "Busy place."

"Yeah," Mike said glumly.

"When I was a kid I used to have a drop line. Ever have one of those?"

"Yeah, but you kind of need to be fishing off a dock or a boat for one of those," said Mike. "I think the casting is kind of limited on them."

"Well, then there's always the Popeil Pocket Fisherman."

"Geez." Mike eyed Dusty. "You really wake up on your feet, don't you? I haven't thought of those things for years." He set his cup down. "I actually used to have one."

Dusty looked at him with interest. "Oh, yeah? How did you do with it?"

Mike picked up a small stick and threw it in the fire. "Not too bad. I could cast it. Trolling was a little awkward, though. But yeah, I caught plenty of fish with it."

"Those would be the thing to pack, if they worked." Dusty took another drink of coffee and sat down.

"Yeah, save room that way." Mike agreed. "Well, since we don't have the Pocket Fisherman this go-round, how about bacon and eggs?"

"That will have to do. How long have the horses been out? I could gather them up while you're cooking," Dusty offered.

"It's been a couple of hours. You were really sawin' logs."

"I think that directly correlates with how much better I feel today." Dusty ran his hand through his hair.

"Good. It's been a crazy couple of weeks." Mike split open a package of bacon. Scout watched him intently in case he dropped anything.

"I'll go get the horses. Come on, boy." Scout looked from Mike to Dusty. It was a no-brainer. He could find food anywhere, but for Scout there was only one Dusty. He barked and ran after him.

By the time breakfast was done, Dusty had the two packhorses highlined, Muley saddled, and Mike's horse brushed.

"Breakfast is served." Mike flourished the pan containing bacon and eggs.

"Coming right down. I better hurry. I read somewhere that wild animals can smell bacon from up to two miles away."

"Wow. That's a long way. Guess we better not cook bacon when we get to the Bob Marshall. I don't want to accidentally be inviting any griz to our camp."

"No, you don't," agreed Dusty. "I always did wonder how that worked, though. You have a designated cooking area, and when you're done you leave your clothes you cooked in there, then hang up all your food in boxes that are bearproof.

"You walk half naked back to your sleeping tent, and in the morning you cook bacon."

"I see your point," said Mike. "What's to stop them from coming to breakfast?"

"Exactly."

The men finished eating and were in the saddle in no time. Instead of trying to scale the walls on the steep creek, they went the opposite way around the lake. It was grassy, but underneath were a lot of logs the horses had to step over. They saw multitudes of old fishing lures laying alongside the shore.

They saw the narrow spit that divided the two lakes. As they made their way around the halfway point, they came upon a white sand beach on the other side. "No wonder the backpackers didn't want us around. They didn't want to share the beach." Mike gazed down at the sand meeting clear lake water with an incredulous stare.

"It's sure pretty, isn't it?" The men sat on their horses admiring the sand and the clear lake water for a few minutes. Scout plunged in for another swim.

"He's never one to waste a water opportunity, is he?" observed Mike.

"No. I think one of his biggest regrets was not being born a Labrador retriever, but he just makes do."

They turned and headed up out of the valley on the overgrown trail at the untraveled end of the lake. The mountains stood behind them. The sunny skies were clear blue and a hint of fall was in the air. The flowers were still tenacious and fields of lupine dotted the sides of the hills.

The small trail alongside the beach narrowed and came to what looked like an old waterfall bed. As they rounded the corner, there was a faint trail. It was hard to tell whether it was human or game. There were bleached-out rocks to cross, and the thin, barely-discernible path remained. Muley gathered himself and jumped up a three-foot rock and Mike followed. The trail wasn't long, but it was steep. As they rode over the top, they were confronted by a wide-open expanse of trees as far as they could see and the Cascade Mountain range in front of them. Dusty picked his way down the mountain slope, and after about half an hour came to a trail.

"Pacific Crest Trail."

"Pretty good, Dusty."

"I've been here before." Dusty turned his horse down the trail. "You know, what a lot of people don't know is that the PCT is the steepest trail and has the most drop-offs of any trail in the state of Washington. There's a lot of romanticism in the idea of taking a trail from California to Canada, but boy, you better be ready."

"Yeah, I have heard that before. It was something I had fantasized about when I used to backpack," Mike said.

"Yes, hiking over twenty-six hundred miles is definitely an accomplishment for anyone. I'd thought about that too," said Dusty. "Doing it with a horse seems like it would be easier, but it's a lot harder. When you come to areas that are impassable due to snowfall and other unforeseen hazards, you can't just hitch a ride with someone to get around it. You have to have horse people contacts so you can get your horses and all your gear trailered around to the next access."

Dusty adjusted himself in the saddle. "There was a vet a few years back, in the nineties, Ben York. He made history riding a horse and pulling two pack mules from Mexico to the Canadian border."

"Really?" Said Mike, "How did I miss that?"

"You probably hadn't joined BCHW yet. It was a big deal all up and down the coast with chapters. The word went out and we helped him along the way. Chapter members in all the states met up with him, brought him food, camped with him and kept him company."

"Wow. That is really impressive," exclaimed Mike.

"Yeah. I knew some people that rode with him from White to Chinook Pass. He had a lot of trouble in the north part of our state. Lots of bridges were out and the trail was in poor repair."

"Even back in the nineties?" said Mike.

"Oh, man, that spotted owl controversy started in 1986. I'll never forget that. Things changed so quickly," said Dusty. "The timber sales and logging industry had been going full bore. The Forest Service had money to clear trail and keep full crews on. Then in June, 1990, they declared the spotted owl an endangered species."

"I hadn't realized that was when it actually happened."

"Yeah. It's affected our Forest Service severely with lack of funding. They have full stands of timber they are no longer able to harvest. A complete waste." Dusty shook his head. "They are pretty much down to skeleton crews and running on grant funding."

Mike ran a hand over his chin. "That's why they depend so much on the Back Country Horsemen and the other volunteer groups to provide trail maintenance."

"Yes. Not to mention the impact it's had on our logging communities, like Greenwater, Packwood and Randle."

"They do look kind of depressed now," observed Mike.

"Yeah. The only time they get busy is from tourist travel or fire season. Fires are another problem. All the untended forest stands are prime targets for forest fires. There is no longer any thinning done. They used to be able to do selective logging, but that's just about come to a halt. Forest fires have been increasing in size and intensity in the Pacific Northwest in the past few years. It's really a shame. Especially since they found spotted owls living in a K-Mart sign. I guess they really didn't need all that old-growth forest to nest in after all."

"Crazy. I never knew." Mike carefully reined Toby through a couple of close boulders.

"You would probably have made it backpacking, but you might as well forget it with a horse. There are areas that have not been repaired up north; bridges out. More than one horseman has lost a horse over the side up there. They actually have posted strict warnings that the trail is too dangerous for horses. Of course, horsemen go, anyway. As a bunch we're pretty good at doing what we want, regardless of what we're told," Dusty added wryly.

"I can see that, but no thanks. " Mike fondly patted his horse's mane. "I'd just as soon keep Toby."

They picked their way along the side trail. After not very long, the trail turned sharply and their horses had to pivot and jump down a two-foot rock drop with a steep drop-off on one side. Dusty doubted that this part of the trail got much attention. The local Back Country Horsemen groups did work parties on the PCT at least once a year. They had even tried to divide it up amongst the chapters in the state. It was a difficult task with miles and miles of trail and not much time to do the work. A good part of it often remained impassable.

As the afternoon wore on, Dusty and Mike passed a placid lake back in the trees with large rocks around it. As Dusty glanced over, he noticed a naked man and woman enjoying the sun on a sandy beach by the lake. He quickly looked away. Scout was undaunted and ran past the sunbathers to jump in the lake. Dusty whistled to him and, after a brief plunge, he shook himself off and charged back to Dusty. The people were not too pleased at the shower of dog water, but Scout was oblivious. They seemed more upset about that than Dusty and Mike riding by. Dusty grinned. People always thought they were in a lot more remote location than they actually were. Although there were thousands of acres of wilderness in Washington State, Chinook Pass and White Pass were popular areas and they were in close enough proximity to the urban areas that they got a lot of use.

"Sorry about that, folks," Dusty said, keeping his eyes on the trail.

After a few minutes, Mike trotted up behind them. "You didn't get any response to your apology there, Boss."

"I really didn't expect one."

Passing the turnoff to Cougar Lake, they continued down the trail for another mile. The area was full of thick mountain grass and wildflowers. Occasional streams gurgled past.

Dusty turned off onto a barely-visible trail, followed it for a couple hundred yards, and it opened into a clearing.

A couple wall tents were set up with chimneys poking out of the top. Saddles perched on a makeshift hitch rail. A group of men sat around a big roaring campfire, and in front of one of the wall tents sat some large Dutch ovens, stacked and cooking on briquettes.

"About time. Dinner's almost ready," called Pat, clapping his hands together. Dusty and Mike dismounted, pulled their bridles off and tied up their horses.

Chapter Fifty-One

The fire was huge and crackling with large rounds of tree stumps burning as Dusty and Mike walked up to the fire ring. Any possible chill was extinguished by the massive flames. Pat was in the middle of one of his favorite hunting stories. His tanned face was flushed by the fire—and probably whatever sat in the metal cup on the log next to him, Dusty surmised. He and Mike sat on a log to listen.

"We had been hunting all day long tracking that bull elk. It had started to get dark and the snow began to fall. We got off to give them a rest and check the tracks on the ground. We had a blood trail, I could see that, but it was just getting covered up about as fast as it was being made. Me and Jeff started tracking on foot. It didn't take us too long before we came out into a clearing, and there he was—a full six-point right in front of us in all his glory." The hunters sat around the fire with their full attention on Pat. "Wow." One of them exclaimed. "Did ya get him, Pat?" another one urged.

The outfitter paused for a minute and took a drink from his cup, the firelight reflecting in his face. "I quick took out my rifle and finished him off. All of a sudden—I don't know what it was. Don't think it was the gun. Heck, they were used to that—but those horses took off out of there like the devil himself was after them. I told Jeff, 'You better go ahead and catch them or we're never getting this elk out of here.' So Jeff hot-footed it out of there and I sat down to get that elk cleaned up and ready to go.

"Well, time went by and Jeff never came back. The snow kept falling." Pat savored the thought and took a big swig out of his cup. "So I started getting cold. I couldn't leave the elk and I didn't have anywhere to go. So I finally just pried open those rib bones and crawled in there. Damned if I wasn't as comfy and warm as I could want to be. I slept all night that way in that old elk. The sun was peeking over the mountaintops as I woke up. I could hear horses and I thought I'd get up and take a peek. Damned if I could pry those rib bones apart. They were frozen solid!"

The dudes had their metal cups in hand, spellbound by his tale. The fire patterned off their faces and gleamed off the cups as they drank. Finally, the dark-haired younger one of the bunch said, "So what did you do, Pat? How'd ya get out of that?"

"Well, old Jeff showed up just in time. As he rode into the clearing, I started hollering at him.

"'Hey, Pat,' he said, peering into the elk carcass, 'You in there?'

"'Yes, I am, Jeff,' I said, 'and I'd be much obliged if you'd get me out.'

"He got off and tied up his horse. It took two of us to get those ribs peeled apart, they were frozen so tight." Pat took another drink from his cup. "And boys, that's just one way you can stay warm if you get stranded out on a hunting trip." A rumble of guffaws resounded from the group. Then he turned to Dusty and Mike.

"So how you been, Dusty?"

"Not too bad, Pat. Just busy."

"Well, I guess that's a good thing, all right. I've been pretty busy too. The weather's been a little warm for the animals, but by the look of the stars tonight, looks like we might be getting a little frost."

"Let's hope so," said one of the other hunters. "I'd like to at least shoot an arrow after all this."

"Don't worry about that, Duane. I haven't even taken you to the good spot yet." Pat winked at Dusty.

Dusty laughed. One never knew with Pat what was fact or fiction. But one thing was always true—he was entertaining. Even if running an outfit was getting more and more difficult with rising costs and insurance, he knew Pat would always have a full house on his rides. Mike and Dusty relaxed by the huge fire and listened to the banter of the hunting group. Mike didn't say a lot and just stared at the fire. Dusty soaked up the heat, the smell and the camaraderie.

An older couple was working at the cook tent with the Dutch ovens. After the men had a few drinks, the gray-haired woman banged on a metal triangle hanging by the wall tent.

"Come and get it," she called. They had put the large Dutch ovens on the log table for serving. The men lined up picking up plates from the table.

As they filed by the younger hunter asked, "What do you call this stuff?"

Hunter's stew. The woman ladled him a big helping. "There's rolls and salad on the table. And save some room. I have a fresh pineapple upside-down cake to top it off."

The white-haired man with her said, "And you better believe it's good!" He handed out more plates and silverware.

Pat, Dusty and Mike took the end of the line. "So, Dusty, what is the deal with the tumble you took off Tumac, anyway? Is that equipment or a two-legged problem?"

"That's what I'm trying to figure out."

"It's looking more and more like a man-made problem," added Mike. "The confusing part is trying to figure out which one it is."

"Oh, you got more than one nut case, huh? I have to say, I sure don't miss that part of being a cop." Pat had been a deputy sheriff in Yakima County for several years. Nut cases were not a new concept for him.

"Yeah, that works out pretty sweet for you. If you get one on a pack-in with your outfit, at least you have the training to deal with them," said Mike.

"One would hope." Pat picked up a plate and held it out for stew. "Looks great, as always, you guys."

Dusty and Mike followed behind and resumed their seats by the fire.

Everybody was pretty quiet eating. You'd think they hadn't eaten for days, but the fresh air and exercise did that to a person, Dusty reflected. He didn't waste any time in cleaning his plate.

Mike stood. "I think I'm going to try out that pineapple upside-down cake."

"Man, I love outfitter cooking. Right behind you."

They walked over and the woman had just pulled the lid off the Dutch oven, revealing a steaming hot, still bubbling pineapple upside-down cake. The top was golden and the cherries were perfectly placed in each pineapple ring. Dusty's mouth watered.

"Would you like some whipped cream with that?"

"Bring it on." Mike held up his plate.

"I think I'm going to need a bigger horse when I leave," said Dusty.

The sky had turned dark and the stars were starting to come out with an occasional sparkle in the deep velvet of the sky. The fire was warm on his face and Dusty was full. So full he was afraid he was about to fall asleep. Pat pulled out his guitar. "So anybody want to hear any music?"

"Oh, yeah," said Mike, shifting in his seat on the log. Pat and his friend Sam performed every year at the Outfitters' Rendezvous in Winthrop. Sam did cowboy poetry. Pat was known for his singing and even had a couple of CDs out.

Scout had been quietly lying by Dusty's feet the whole time they were there, snatching a few table scraps. As soon as Pat began to sing, Scout raised his head and looked at him intently.

Dusty knew his dog. "It's okay, Scout." Scout looked at Dusty and threw back his head and joined in. It only caused Pat to hesitate momentarily, then he accompanied Scout by drawing out his words at the end. It made quite a combination with Pat singing and Scout howling. Everybody was laughing so much, it was hard to hear the words. When Pat yodeled, Scout looked at him and increased his volume. By the time the whole production was done, everyone was doubled over. It took Scout a few seconds to realize it was over, but then he laid his head back down and looked at Dusty expectantly.

"Good job, boy." He reached down and scratched his dog behind the ears.

"Hey, Dusty, what would you take for that dog? Jeff's getting a little long in the tooth, and I might be in the market for a new partner pretty soon."

"Sorry, Pat. His excellent singing aside, I just can't part with him."

"That's a shame," said Pat with mock sadness.

"We need to be heading out, anyway," said Dusty. "We need to get back and get the horses some feed before we turn in."

"Well, a pleasure to see you, as always." Pat shook hands with Dusty.

"Well, thanks for an outstanding dinner." Dusty glanced over and included the cooks. They smiled at him.

"Tell Bob *Hi* for me. I always enjoy seeing him at the Rendezvous."

"I will. I'm thinking about joining his hunting camp later this fall. Hopefully before the snow flies."

"Guess you're going for deer then; there's no elk up there," observed Pat.

"Hunting's good, but for me, Pat, it's really the ride." Dusty grinned in the darkened evening.

"Isn't that the truth," agreed Pat.

Chapter Fifty-Two

They rode out of the outfitter camp and picked up the trail. The moon was just beginning to come up and created more light than Dusty had anticipated. He knew he wasn't going to use his flashlight. The last time he did that he ended up blinding his horse worse than helping him see. He'd just let Muley figure it out. They were on a split-off trail from the main path, so Dusty timed in his head how long they'd gone. He was figuring about twenty minutes to hit the main trail. The only sounds were the clomping of horseshoes on the dirt and the jingle of bridles and spurs as they walked down the trail.

Sure enough, Dusty glanced down at his watch and approximately twenty minutes had passed when he heard the sound of the creeks babbling in the grassy meadow. He knew this was the trail intersection that went down to Cougar Lake. They turned and picked their way along through the trees. As they got just above the lake and their camp, the trail turned to gravel and some large boulders. As the horses hit the gravel, the sound of their shoes striking rock bounced off the rock walls surrounding the lake.

"Guess we're not sneaking up on anybody," observed Mike.

"Hopefully there's nobody to sneak up on," said Dusty. The thought brought him back to Roy and Cassie. He hadn't thought about that for a while, and now it bothered him. Cassie had said she was going to stay at Terri's for a few days while Sammy recuperated, so that should be okay. When he left Eagleclaw,

Dusty was about at the end of his rope. Now he felt much better. The mountains seemed to do that for him. In the city things became so complex. Once you got away from it, you realized that it was really quite simple. The only complex thing about a problem was overthinking it. Roy wasn't going to be able to hide forever. He should be pretty easy to track down when they got back. After all, he was injured. If he went anywhere at all, they would pick him up.

They rode back into camp. Quickly stripping the saddles off, they hobbled the horses so they could eat.

"You want me to build a fire?" asked Mike.

"I don't know. I don't plan on being awake any longer than it takes for the horses to eat."

"Me, either."

Dusty walked the short distance down to the lake. It was flat and dark. The rock walls were shadows with the moon illuminating the most prominent apertures. The frogs tonight were quiet. *Kind of a contrast to last night.* Looking across the lake, he thought he saw the dim light of a campfire flicker. He strained and looked again. Sure enough. It was a small one. *That's odd.* He didn't remember seeing anyone come in. They had ridden all day, though. *Shoot, it's Saturday. Hikers could have come in at any point.* So what was it about the fire that made him feel so uneasy?

Scout stood next to him looking across the lake at the fire. A low growl rumbled in his throat. *That is really not a good sign.* "Come on, boy. Let's go back up to camp." Scout wagged his little stub of a tail at Dusty, but continued to stare at the spot where the fire flickered. The fur on the back of his neck was standing up. Dusty hesitated a moment and then headed back up the trail at a fast walk with Scout following.

Mike had a small fire going. "I figured it was better than just sitting in the dark while we waited for them to finish eating."

"Yeah, good idea." Dusty sat down by the fire. "I thought I saw another fire across the lake."

"Really? I didn't know there was another camp area over there."

"That's the interesting part; there's really not. Oh, I guess you could camp anywhere, but it's not really set up for a regular camp. A light backpacker camp could fit in there. But Scout didn't like it. He growled and his hair stood up."

"Really." Mike's full interest was on him now. "How often has he done that before?"

"Never."

Both men sat quietly in front of the fire digesting that information. They were uneasy. Something felt wrong. Dusty looked at the camp. They were set back from the lake and their tents were hidden by the trees. They weren't just sitting ducks in a large open area, at least. It would be kind of hard to hide horses, though.

Mike said nothing. They were both armed, so someone surely wouldn't just try to come in and open fire. Dusty considered their situation. The only possibility was that someone would attempt to ambush them. Having surprise in their favor would make up for the lack of backup. He shook his head. Maybe he was overreacting. Dusty could only hope he was. Scout was lying calmly in front of the fire now. It was pretty easy to think it was just his imagination.

Dusty felt the long day's ride and big meal beginning to take their toll. He was tired in a good way. It was what he came up here for: the mountains, the horses and sometimes the camaraderie. Thinking back over his day, the bright sun reflecting off the bleached white rocks, the vibrant wildflowers and the mountains that stretched out before him was a balm to his soul. Sitting before the small fire with the darkened lake and rock walls around him, he felt full. He knew he had it all. There was nothing else that could give him this feeling, and he was thankful he had been able to finally learn that—even if it took him awhile.

Mike poked the fire. "Hey, have you ever had one of those card readers tell you your fortune?"

"Can't say as I have," Dusty said with surprise. "And where did that come from, anyway?"

"I don't know. Just thinking." Mike said wistfully.

"So what did yours say?" Dusty knew Mike well enough to

know that he wouldn't have brought it up if he hadn't done it.

"An old girlfriend drug me along one time. We had our auras read."

"Interesting. Never heard you talk about dating before."

Mike got a sly grin. "Yeah, well, I guess it's happened once or twice."

"So what did you find out?" He had Dusty's interest now.

"I was a mountain man." Mike said it with such finality, Dusty knew it was a statement of fact for Mike.

"That's pretty good."

"Yup. In the 1820s, a mountain man in the Pacific Northwest. For what it cost me, I wished they would have told me something I didn't already know." Mike stood up and stretched. "I'm tired. I think I'll turn in."

"Yeah, go ahead. I'll gather the horses—you're always getting them."

"Oh, man, I got so into my past life I almost forgot the horses. I'll get mine."

The shadows of the trees were dark as they picked their way through to the grass. It was hard to distinguish between a horse and a rock. Scout trotted ahead of Dusty and behind Mike. The lake sat in a pocket with steep rocks on one side and grass and trees on the other and with intermittent boulders ejected from ancient volcanic activity. There was plenty of graze, but the horses had to look for it. Horses were funny about that. You could have beautiful green grass and, for their own reasons, they would bypass that for something farther away. As he trudged on, Dusty wished they wouldn't have picked tonight to shop for greener pastures.

His earlier apprehension had pretty much dissipated and he was just thinking about getting the horses and going to bed. The bullet whizzed in front of him and hit the rock a few feet away. "What in the hell? Gunfire, Mike!" He saw Mike drop to the ground and heard some more bullets zing by. He wasn't sure which happened first, but he prayed Mike wasn't hit.

Chapter Fifty-Three

Cassie pulled into her driveway. The rain had stopped the day before and the sun was out. Sammy was still a little stiff, but she was getting back to her old self. Terri had helped her with feeding and hadn't wanted her to leave yet, but Cassie wanted to get back to her own home. She felt like she was strewn all over the place and she just wanted to get things back to normal.

As she drove in and parked, her house stood dark and silent. Even in the late-summer sun, there was a distinct feeling of foreboding that she had never felt before. It made Cassie angry. She had been coming out here since she was a little girl, and no low-class thug was going to take that away from her. Her .38 was in the holster under her coat. She had always taken her gun riding, but with the way things had been going, she was wearing it all the time now. The rifle was her gun of choice, but it was a little bulky to carry around all the time.

Opening the door of her truck, she got out and Sammy bounded out behind her. Prince and Murphy stood at the pasture fence nickering to her. Grabbing a couple flakes of hay from the barn, she fed the horses and checked their water. She got her overnight bag from the truck and headed to the house. She dreaded what she would see. Walking in the back door into the kitchen, she breathed a sigh of relief. It was clean. Any disarray from the last week had been cleaned up. Bless Terri's heart. She was an amazing friend. Terri had gotten up before Cassie the last couple days to feed her horses, so Cassie wouldn't have to leave her dog.

Walking up the stairs she felt a chill on her neck. The house wasn't cold, but the events from a few nights ago were fresh in her mind. At the top of the stairs she passed the spare room and went down the hall to her bedroom. The door was open. Cassie still felt a hint of dread in the pit of her stomach, but forcing herself ahead, she turned into her bedroom. Terri at work again. The bed was made and the dressers that Cassie was certain had been turned over were righted and sat neatly where they always did. Just like it never happened. She sat on the bed and pressed the heels of her hands into her temples.

It had been a long week. Roy had turned out to be more than a coincidental meeting at the trailhead; she was sure of it now. The way he had relentlessly pursued her told her it was a lot more than that—he was a stalker. She had always felt pretty confident in herself and her ability to handle situations. How many times had she ridden up in the high country alone? She couldn't even count them. But she had never encountered a person like this—at least at a personal level. Sure, she had had clients with situations similar to this—and a couple with true stalkers. Why was it when it was at a personal level you were always the last to know?

Cassie considered what she knew about stalkers. They surveilled their victims for a long time before they acted, anywhere from days to years. From her legal experience, they were like a pit bull—once they had their victim, they did not let go. In her mind she could not think of ever meeting Roy before, but that really didn't mean anything, either. She could have had him in a college course. He could have been a relative, a friend of a friend, or a client—or heck, he could have seen her picture in the paper. It didn't matter—he was locked in now. And obviously dangerous. She didn't know when, but she knew he'd be back. That kind of disorder did not cure itself. Whatever fantasies he had about her— and she knew he had them—were not going to cure themselves. She was going to have to be vigilant.

As she lay on her bed thinking, Sammy curled up on her rug next to the bed. Cassie's thoughts drifted to Dusty. She hoped that Roy's behavior was only limited to her and he wasn't going to turn it towards Dusty. She wasn't sure how that worked with stalkers. She knew there were different reasons for why they did what they did.

When Roy had confronted them up at the Tin Shack, his flat affect mixed with rage had truly been frightening. The whole scenario could have had a really bad end if Dusty had not been so capable at handling himself. When Roy had been hit, it hadn't seemed to faze him. Kind of like a zombie, or something, he just kept coming. She shuddered to think what would have happened if the deputies and Dusty and Mike had not shown up the other night.

She sat up. She wasn't going to be a victim. She had things to do around her place and work from the office to take care of. Top of the list was she'd buy bear spray. She would keep her firearms close by and she was going to live her life. If anything, Roy was going to get more of a welcome than he bargained for if he decided to stop by again. She walked downstairs, pulled her Muck boots on and grabbed her barn coat. The weight of her gun felt reassuring under her jacket. She had chores to do and no Roy was going to stop her.

Cassie felt a lot better as she shoveled manure out in her front pasture. Murphy and Prince were milling around picking up the last of the alfalfa grass hay lying around. The physical exercise helped to clear her head. She thought about Dusty and how approachable he'd been up at the Tin Shack. He was attracted to her; she was certain of it. She knew he wasn't the kind of guy to invite a girl to go riding, kiss her, and call it a day. In fact, even though she didn't listen to the buzz around the Back Country Horsemen women, she had heard that he had never asked anyone out. Ever. They often complained about how he always just rode with Mike. There were a lot of women there who really wanted to change that, she'd heard.

Dusty was an enigma to her. One minute he was totally there for her. He looked honestly concerned when he rushed into her house the other morning after Roy broke in. When they'd gone to breakfast she'd gotten electricity from him as he sat next to her. She definitely got the impression that he wanted to sit as close as possible. But then, all of a sudden, he needs to leave. He has to go to the mountains. Right now. Crazy. He was definitely a man of mixed signals and she really didn't know what to think of him. On the other hand, she knew that feeling all too well herself.

Cassie threw another load of manure on top of the wheelbarrow and, with a grunt, pushed the heavily-laden cart towards her manure dump. However it worked out, she hoped Roy stayed off Dusty's tracks. She closed the pasture gate behind her and pushed her wheelbarrow toward the pile. She had a lot of chores to catch up on from being gone, and the always-waiting files to go through. She knew it was going to be tough to sleep tonight, but she had to start somewhere. No one was going to make her afraid to sleep in her own home.

As darkness began to fall, Cassie lit a fire in her woodstove. Sammy lay on the carpet next to her curled in a ball. Her recovery was rapid now, and if the concussion bothered her at all, it didn't show. Cassie felt a renewed flash of heat go up her back and her stomach tightened, thinking that Roy would kick an innocent dog. She sat in her recliner and flipped through the files in her lap. Every once in a while she would glance surreptitiously at the phone. It remained silent. *Of course it did. It's a land line.* That was another weird thing about Roy; the fact he called her on her land line. Just about no one did that, and she'd only given Dusty that number because she sometimes left her cell phone in the car and she hadn't wanted to miss his call. The only reason she even kept the land line was really because it was tied in with a package on her internet and cable TV, and she used the fax from time to time. She needed to look into that. It was probably a big waste of money. And that was the number Roy had used because it was accessible to the public. Another red flag of his stalking. It was much harder to get her personal cell phone number, but somehow he'd done it.

Cassie doubled-checked her alarm system and headed up to bed, Sammy on her heels. She felt apprehension and she hated it. It was just another violation from Roy. A person should feel safe in their own home, and she always had before.

Lying in the dark, Cassie listened. She heard the wind gently blowing through the trees. She heard a bump on the porch and her stomach tightened. She looked down at Sammy. Her dog's breathing was even with no sign of alarm. Cassie willed herself to relax. It was going to be a long night.

Chapter Fifty-Four

Dusty couldn't tell exactly where the bullets were coming from, but judging by where they hit the rocks, he thought it was somewhere off to his right. "Mike, are you okay?" he whispered.

"Yes," Mike answered quietly.

"You have your gun?"

"Always."

It was silent. Dusty racked his brain. They needed a plan. He heard a movement not too far off in front of them, followed by a crashing and struggling. It only took him a minute to figure out—it was one of their horses. The shooting had spooked him and it sounded like he was hung up and fighting it.

"Easy boy," Mike called out softly.

The thrashing subsided and then renewed with more vigor. The horse freed itself and then they heard the thundering of hooves as the horses spooked and ran wildly away from the shooting.

More shots ricocheted above their heads on the rocks. They sank lower into the grass and dirt. Right now they were sitting ducks. They needed to figure out his position. Dusty turned his head carefully to the right and looked out. There in the trees he saw a small red light. It was a laser. *Perfect. This gets better all the time.*

"Hey, Roy," Dusty said in a loud voice. Since the shooter obviously knew their positions, there was nothing to lose.

"You couldn't leave her alone, could you?" came a cold voice.

"She was my woman, and you couldn't leave her alone."

"Well, that explains that," whispered Mike.

"Now you're gonna pay." Another volley of shots hit the rocks around them.

Dusty flinched. He needed Roy to come out into the open so they could get a shot at him.

"You're going to shoot two unarmed men?" Dusty tried. It was a white lie. Only for special circumstances, he told himself quickly, like life or death.

"Liar!" charged the shooter furiously.

Dusty reached for a calm voice. "We were just going to get our horses. We didn't need our guns."

More shots rang out. "Don't lie to me, you piece of shit!"

Another whisper from Mike, "That seemed to work really well. Maybe you should try something else."

Before Dusty had time to think, Scout handled it for him. Recovering from the initial attack, his dog took off like a streak toward the shooter. "Scout!" Dusty called out, but Scout was locked in. A vicious snarl emitted. A string of swear words followed. Dusty sneaked a look up and he saw the red light move around erratically and then go down.

"Let's go," he whispered urgently. "Those big rocks up there." Both men scrambled out from behind the rocks and, keeping low to the ground, they ran behind a huge rocky formation on the side of the hill. It wasn't perfect, but it afforded them a lot more shelter than where they were before. Once behind the rocks, Dusty looked down where the light was. He could hear dog snarls and swearing. Finally, a yelp.

"Come on, boy, that's enough," he called. Dusty was worried. Scout would die defending him. He was the best dog Dusty had ever had, and he didn't want to lose him now, not like this. The silence was deafening. As he pushed down the pain in his gut, a wet nose nudged in his hand. Relief flooded through him. "Scout!" He patted his dog and pulled him close. Scout licked his hand.

"Is he okay?" asked Mike.

Dusty ran his hand along Scout's back; he appeared to be. "I don't know how you did it, boy, but you made it."

"He's getting up again," Mike whispered, as he watched the red light scrambling in the copse of trees below them.

"We're going to have to try to surround him. If he won't stop shooting, at least he'll slow down," said Dusty. "I have my Ruger with six shots and about twenty on my belt."

"I've just got my Colt cap and ball. Only five shots."

"Dang, Mike, I was hoping you'd got a newer one since you quit dressing mountain man."

"I hadn't got to it yet. And honestly, it wasn't utmost on my mind when all I was doing was gathering up horses before bed."

"You sons o' bitches!" screamed Roy from below. "You're going to die and so is that flea-bitten mutt of yours." More shots rang off the boulders.

"You work your way around behind him and I'll cover you. The darkness ought to help shield you." Dusty pulled out his Ruger and checked the cylinder to see how many shots he had left.

Mike dropped down and slowly began to work his way around the rock. Dusty flattened himself against the boulder and took a shot as close as he could at the red light. The shot split the night air and rang in his ears. Scout cowered close to Dusty. He hated gunfire. "Sorry, boy." Dusty could feel his dog shaking against his leg.

"You son-of-a-bitchin' liar! I knew you was lying. You don't have no guns, huh?" The angrier Roy got, the more his vocabulary slipped into street slang. A volley of shots rang out of the blackness. Roy finally figured out to shut off his laser.

Mike was out of sight. Dusty could only hope that he was able to make it okay in the darkness. The moon hit the tops of the rocks and the trees threw shadows on everything else. Dusty waited. He didn't want to use up all of his rounds. Roy knew he had a gun now, so it was a matter of seeing what he'd do next. The guy was crazy—no doubt about that. Dusty felt calm and resolute. He'd do what he had to do.

Another shot pinged close to the side of the rock. Roy was moving up. Dusty flattened down more, stuck his gun out to the side and fired again. His shot whizzed into the meadow. *God, I hope Mike is keeping under cover.* It was pretty hard to shoot in the dark at somebody you couldn't see.

"You goddamned lawyers are all alike," hissed Roy. "I'll show you sons o' bitches what I think of you for good!"

"Cassie's a lawyer, Roy," offered Dusty, trying to buy time for Mike.

"Don't you say her name," Roy screamed, like the lunatic he was. "She's going to pay too. I ain't done with her. She just needs to be shown who's boss. Then she'll act like a good woman."

The words made Dusty's skin crawl. If they didn't get this guy now, one way or the other, Cassie was never going to be safe. Dusty heard Roy's harsh intake of breath below him as he labored over the rocks. Dusty tried the other side of the boulder, and fired down at Roy. More shots rang out. He hoped Mike got around Roy pretty soon, he was running out of time. The nutcase just kept right on coming, bullets or no bullets. Dusty was starting to sweat, he could feel it trickle down his arms, despite the chill of the night air. More scrambling noise below and then a single shot pinged out and Roy screamed.

"I'd stop right there," came Mike's voice from the copse of trees behind Roy.

"I ain't dead yet, you sons o' bitches! I still got another good arm. And if I'm going down, you're going with me."

Silence followed. Dusty and Mike waited. Until Roy made a move, they weren't sure what theirs would be.

The long night slowly began to turn to light. Dusty was exhausted. He was stiff and sore. The cold seemed to settle in his joints. The immediacy of the adrenalin wore off in the silence and he fought to stay awake. He knew falling asleep could mean the end of him, but as the cold depleted him, he'd catch himself nodding off.

Dusty wasn't sure how long he'd sat there. Dawn had broken and a gray mist hung over the lake. A scraping noise got his attention. He wasn't sure if he'd been asleep or not. The sound came from the other side of the boulder. Dusty straightened up and flattened himself against the rock. Roy was close. He could hear raspy breathing. In a flash Roy was in front of him, his gun pointed directly at Dusty. Scout growled and snarled viciously. Roy took his eyes off Dusty and pointed the barrel of his gun directly at the dog and pulled back the trigger. "You son-of-a-bitchin' dog, you're buzzard meat."

At the same second Roy shot, another shot rang out from behind him. It was low and zinged on the rock right by his foot. "What the fuck?" screamed Roy. It knocked him off balance and his bullet went wide, missing Scout. Dusty didn't waste a second. Picking up Scout, he dashed around the other side of the boulder. Roy crouched down and looked behind him, then fired his gun at the area where the bullet had come. Silence.

Scout squirmed—he wanted to be free. Dusty wasn't sure what his dog was going to do and didn't want him shot. He set him down and whispered, "Stay" in a firm voice. Scout looked up at him intently. Rocks slid as Roy repositioned himself on the side of the hill, now behind the boulder. Knowing Mike was on the other side, the shooter put himself in the middle. Dusty sank down. He was fully exposed on one side and wanted to make sure to put the boulder between himself and Roy. The ground dropped off abruptly on the hillside, and Dusty and Scout took cover. A shot pinged off the edge of the rock, and a couple more hit the ground right by Dusty's side.

Dusty figured Roy only had a couple bullets left, so the lunatic better make them good. He quickly reloaded his gun from his ammo belt. It was quiet on the hillside. That couldn't be a good sign. Peeking around the rock, he could make out Roy belly-crawling towards Mike's location. From his vantage point Dusty could see Mike's blue shirt behind the rock not too far from where Roy was, and he couldn't tell if he was aware that Roy was coming.

Carefully, Dusty took aim at Roy's head as he crawled. As he saw Roy raise his gun at Mike and fire, Dusty fired. In a chain reaction, Mike jerked backwards and fell over, then Roy fell silently to the ground. Dusty waited a minute. No one moved. He jumped up and ran down the hill toward Mike. As he leaped between the boulders, a shot rang out. Dusty was landing as it hit the rock next to him. He fell forward. His gun flew from his hand. His leg came down hard between two boulders. Trying to get up, he found his leg was wedged tight.

Scout licked him and tried to urge him on. "Can't do it, boy. I'm stuck."

Roy got up, his shoulder bleeding, and walked toward Dusty with his gun drawn.

Chapter Fifty-Five

"Well, lookie here, you son of a bitch. Guess you're going be leaving my woman alone after all," Roy gloated. His dark flat eyes were lit with joy, and his mouth slashed back in a cruel smile exposing crooked teeth.

"Roy, don't you think we could talk about this," Dusty said in his most calm and reasonable voice. "I'm sure Cassie can decide who she would like to see—"

"She's my woman!" Roy bellowed.

Scout had taken all he was going to take. With a vicious snarl, he launched himself at Roy. Before Roy could turn his gun to the dog, a deafening roar split the mountain air. Roy's face registered complete surprise. A gaping hole bloomed in his chest. Dropping his gun, he put his hand over the wound, blood pouring through his fingers. He staggered backward and fell over. Scout, still growling, hesitated and watched as Roy's legs kicked and then went still.

Before Dusty could move, a man walked out of the trees, gun in hand. "Dusty, what in the hell are you guys doing?" Pat yelled.

"How did you end up here?" asked Dusty. "Thank God you did."

"Your horses came running into my string sometime in the middle of the night. I figured you'd need them, so I saddled up early to bring them back. I heard the shooting, so I tied the horses up a little ways from here and thought I'd take a look." Pat walked up to Dusty. "You need a hand?"

"I do. And we need to find out how Mike is. It looked like Roy shot him."

Pat helped Dusty pull his leg out and then turned to check on Mike.

"I'm all right." Mike had blood on his shoulder and face, but he was standing up. "Let's have a look at that," said Pat. "Being up-to-date on first aid is part of being an outfitter."

Mike smiled. His usually olive-colored skin was white in the morning light. "Well, that's the best news I've heard all night."

Dusty was relatively unhurt, except for bruising and scraping on his leg from ramming it in the rocks. Mike only had a graze wound on his left shoulder. Roy lay on his back in the rocks, his eyes still registering surprise, staring skyward. His shirt was blood-soaked and his legs were bent at an odd angle.

Pat looked down at Roy's inert form ruefully. "I hated to have to do that, but I couldn't see any other way around it. After copping for so many years, it was one of those split-second decisions. I had been watching, sizing up what to do. When that guy drew down on you, he didn't leave me any choice."

Dusty shuddered as he remembered looking down the barrel with the crazy man on the other end. "I think you did the right thing, Pat."

"I'm going up the hill. I think I can get a signal up there to bring a helicopter in. Plus I need to call back to the outfit and let them know what's going on. Jim can take the hunters out while I help you get this cleaned up." Pat turned and went up the hill.

Dusty and Mike sat on the rocks by the body. The sun was coming up and breaking through the fog. It glinted off the lake in ripples as a slight breeze hit the water. Both men were in shock. Dusty marveled at how such a beautiful place could turn ugly in such a short amount of time. Scout lay next to him, his eyes closed and his breathing regular. *At least Scout is okay.* Dusty looked down at him. *No amount of money could replace that dog.*

"Well, I guess we don't need to worry about Roy anymore," said Mike.

"Yeah, Cassie will be glad to hear that. She'll be able to sleep at night again." Dusty stared down at the lake. He and Mike avoided looking at the body that lay on the ground next to them, the face frozen in a surprised grimace, a bloody hand clamped over its chest. That was going to haunt him for a long time.

A short time later Pat came walking down the hill at a good clip. He wasn't a tall man, but he always seemed large by his self-assurance. "Everything's done. The helicopter will be here in about an hour or so. What do you say we put on a pot of coffee?"

"What about Roy?" asked Mike.

"We'll just throw a mantie on him. He'll be okay for a while," said Pat, turning to go to their camp. Mike, Dusty and Scout—completely exhausted—followed behind.

The three men sat around the small campfire. Dusty felt a lot better from the heat of the fire and the hot coffee. He was beyond tired. Mentally and emotionally drained. It had been quite a weekend and not much of a rest from his hectic week.

Pat took a drink. "Hey, did I ever tell you about the time I packed out a dead body?"

"What haven't you packed, Pat?" said Dusty, glad to put his mind on something else.

"Not much," Pat said matter-of-factly. "But this was a guy who had been with a hunting outfit. He dropped dead from a heart attack."

"Your outfit?" asked Mike.

"No, thank God. I don't need that kind of negative business." Pat cracked a grin. "Anyway, I went to pack him out and they forgot to lay him over a log."

Mike raised an eyebrow. "Lay him over a log?"

"Yeah, so he'd be bent in half and I could put him on a packhorse. As it was, I had to pack him out flat and laid out straight. Rigor mortis had set in."

"Oh, man," said Dusty.

"So I finally got him tied on my packhorse. He really stuck out.

As I went down the trail, he bounced off about every other rock. The trails aren't cut wide enough for the length of a man lying down."

"Never thought about that." Mike shook his head.

"So by the time they did the IME, the doctor couldn't figure out what bruises were before or after he died. It was a heck of a deal," concluded Pat. "The coroner was pretty upset with me. He strongly suggested if it ever happened again, I call the airlift."

The rumble of a helicopter sounded overhead. "Sounds like they're here." Pat dumped out his coffee and started up the hill.

Mike, Dusty and Scout followed wearily behind.

Chapter Fifty-Six

After getting the body on the helicopter, they made arrangements to meet with the sheriff when they got back. Mike and Dusty gathered their horses and then headed back to camp. They hadn't gotten too far away. Mike's packhorse, Duke, only had some minor cuts on his back legs from being hung up in the brush. After taking care of the horse, they were too tired to pack up and leave. Dusty and Mike both went and passed out in their tents.

It was mid-afternoon by the time Dusty woke up. He heard the bees buzzing and the occasional stomp of the horses shifting at their highline. As soon as he moved to sit up, the stiffness hit him like a knife. His leg was really sore and it went up into the small of his back. He slowly got up and stretched painfully. Hopefully he'd loosen up after he walked around for a while. Scout watched him. "You okay, boy?" Scout wagged his tail. *He is an amazing dog. He took quite a beating in the last few days and just kept right on going.*

Dusty walked out and sat in his chair by the fire pit. The afternoon sun was high in the deep-blue sky. It was warm today. It didn't seem like fall by the weather. The terrain was another story. An occasional vine maple burst into fiery red, orange and yellow in the otherwise green stands of trees around the lake. The winter always made itself known up here first. The high country was the last to thaw and the first to freeze. That's why the packing season was so short—but so worth it. Dusty poked the fire with a stick. He stared vacantly when he thought about the approaching winter and the end to high mountain riding for the year.

Staring out at the lake, Dusty knew he needed to start packing up. He didn't have work tomorrow, since it was Labor Day, but he'd need to make an appearance at the sheriff's department. At least the Roy problem was out of the way. That was the major issue. He'd need to let Cassie know. As soon as he thought about Cassie, he felt a tightening in his chest. He really liked her. He really liked his life the way it was now. He thought about the twenty years being married to Sarah and he shuddered. He wasn't getting into anything like that again—he had promised himself that. And he remembered it every time he got up in the morning and decided exactly what he wanted to do, without having to check with anyone. That was huge—he got up and started packing his gear.

Mike and Dusty made it out of the mountains in good time. After turning his horses loose and unpacking his gear, Dusty decided he'd better drop by Cassie's house. The hot shower had gone a long way toward loosening up his stiffness and Advil pretty much took care of the rest. As he pulled into her driveway, Dusty admired the older bungalow-styled house surrounded by flowers and shrubs. It looked like someone had really enjoyed gardening at one point, but it had been a while. Working all the time and having an overgrown garden was a bonus in Dusty's book—it meant you were probably riding more and working in your garden less. And he knew that was true about Cassie, at least by the amount she seemed to ride.

She walked up to the truck with a rake in hand as he pulled in. Her lips were curved in a soft smile and her thick light-brown hair fell around her shoulders. His chest got a catch in it. She was a beautiful woman. That came to his mind every time he saw her.

"Hi, Dusty. What a surprise." She smiled at him warmly.

"I thought I'd come over and let you know what happened to Roy." He got out of the truck. He wanted to pull her into his arms, but held himself back.

A puzzled look passed across her face. "Well, come on in. I'll put on a pot of coffee or tea. I can't wait to hear this." She turned and headed toward the back door.

Dusty followed her into the house. Her silky long hair trailed down her shoulders, and her blue work shirt, tucked into her jeans, showed off her athletic frame. He fought the conflicting emotions and he felt irritation rising in his throat. Why had he even come here? He just wanted to prove to himself he could be like everyone else. And he knew he wasn't. He'd tried. They had a great time on their ride at Crystal. And that kiss—why was he thinking about that now?

"Coffee or tea?" Cassie peered at him. He looked different. She was trying to follow him. *Is he glad to see me or not?*

"Coffee, always," he said shortly. His smile looked forced.

As she turned to put the coffee pot on, she was thoroughly confused. He definitely was a moody person. He seemed almost angry. *How could it be at me? I haven't even seen him long enough to have done anything,* she puzzled. *Oh, well.*

"So what happened with Roy?"

Dusty told her the whole story, ending with Roy's demise. His deep-blue eyes were tired and there were lines in his face. He looked like it had been a long weekend.

Reflief flooded through Cassie. "Well, thank God for that. At least I'll be able to sleep at night."

"That's why I wanted to come over and tell you in person, so you wouldn't have to worry." Dusty sat his coffee cup down and stood up. "I guess I should be going." He was torn between wanting to pull Cassie into his arms and getting out of her house as quickly as possible. He hated feeling the loss of control of his emotions. The best way he knew how to handle that was leave.

Following him out to the door, Cassie said, "Well, thank you for all your help."

Dusty gave her what he hoped was a bright white smile. "My pleasure." He touched her face, turned, and headed out to his truck.

Cassie watched the truck drive away. She stood there for a while. *I'm not going to be seeing him again.* She felt an overwhelming urge to run after him and scream, *What happened? Come back!* Instead, her heart was a lead weight in her chest as she closed the door and went back into her house.

Chapter Fifty-Seven

Dusty sat morosely in Maude's café on Tuesday waiting for his lunch. Mike caught his eye, walked over and sat down. His arm was in a sling and he had some scrapes on his face.

"That good, huh?" Mike looked at Dusty's face. "What's wrong?"

"Oh, nothing. Just kind of tired, I guess." There was no way Dusty was going to talk about it with anyone. As it was, he was working really hard to understand why he behaved the way he did.

"Well, I have good news," said Mike.

"Great." Dusty looked up. Maude approached, refilled their coffee and put Dusty's plate in front of him. A thick Reuben sandwich with golden fries sat in the plate. He was hungrier than he thought. "Thank you. It looks wonderful."

She smiled at him. "Mike, what would you like?"

"That looks great. Ditto for me."

"Coming right up." She turned and headed back to the kitchen.

"So." Mike paused, putting his arms out expansively. Dusty looked at him, head cocked.

"They arrested Paul Wolfe last night. He finally did the big meltdown and brought a gun to Julie's house. Luckily she had the cameras and security system wired and ready to go. A patrolling police vehicle made it there in a couple minutes, fortunately, before Paul could even enter the house. There was a shoot-out, but

Paul managed to get away. He jumped in his car, tore out of there, and apparently wrapped himself around a tree."

"That's convenient." Dusty shook his head and took a bite of his sandwich.

"Yup. Nice and neat. No one was injured but Paul. And now the domestic violence charges have been escalated to assault with a deadly weapon, destruction of public property, endangerment, and the list goes on."

"Wow. Christmas comes early. At least now he'll stay in jail for a while." Dusty felt light and happy in the pit of his stomach. Now Julie and her daughter were going to be safe.

"It gets even better. He gave a full confession once he figured he wasn't getting out. Spilled his guts."

"I can't wait to hear how the books on his business pan out," said Dusty.

"Should be an interesting read."

"I thought you'd be interested to find out he paid that guy that broke into your house. It was apparently supposed to scare you off the case."

"Scare me, huh? That's probably one of the more stupid things I've heard. Anger me, maybe, but scare?" Dusty laughed at the idea. "Besides, how was I supposed to know which client I was supposed to be scared of? I have more than one."

"No one said the guy was intelligent."

Dusty took a bite of his sandwich, "Did they catch him yet?"

"No. But it's only going to be a matter of time. He left quite the cell phone map." Mike bite into a fry, "Plus, our buddy Paul will probably be more than happy to rat out his friend for a lighter sentence."

"Sounds about right." Agreed Dusty.

"One last thing. Apparently, Paul like to just change his name rather than use the legal system to obtain a divorce." Mike said conversationally.

"I knew it." Dusty exclaimed. "That just took care of the dissolution."

Mountain Cowboys

"Yup." Mike bite into a French fry.

As they ate and discussed the case, a woman's voice interrupted their thoughts. "Mind if I join you?"

Shelley stood behind them. She was back to her glitzy jean jacket and low-cut top. Her hair was frosted and her blue eye makeup was liberally applied.

"Help yourself," said Dusty.

She pulled herself up on a barstool next to him. The strong smell of perfume wafted into his nostrils. She played with her bracelets as she talked. "I heard on the news about Roy. At least I figured it was Roy by the description."

"Yes, it was Roy," Dusty confirmed.

"I was sorry to hear that. He had some serious problems. I'm really glad you two are all right."

Mike laughed. "That makes three of us."

"You guys are my friends," she said sincerely. "And I don't have a lot of them. People don't seem to like me very much."

"Yes, we *are* your friends, Shelley." Dusty patted her arm.

"Yeah," said Mike.

"Thanks. That means the world to me." She beamed at them. "How's Cassie, anyway? I heard about Roy stalking her place."

Dusty's sandwich stuck in his throat and he coughed. Grabbing his water, he took a big drink. "Oh, she's fine."

Shelley looked at him, puzzled.

"Hey, Boss, where do you want to ride next weekend?" Mike jumped in to the rescue.

"The fall colors are great in the Teanaway," offered Dusty. "And then we have to plan the hunting trip back to the Pasayten. I think Uncle Bob's expecting us."

"That sounds good. I'll check with my boss to see about getting some more time off."

"If it's for riding, it's probably a good enough reason," said Dusty.

Shelley watched them banter back and forth and shook her head. "You guys are just too much."

Dusty smiled. "So little time and so many rides to go."

"Well said, Boss."

As they made plans for their next ride, Dusty got a light feeling in the pit of his stomach. Once they started talking about riding, he could see things more clearly. He winced when he thought about how he'd left Cassie standing in the driveway. It wasn't what he'd really wanted to do—it was just a reaction to his own turmoil. He couldn't leave it that way between them. *Damn it. I can't stop thinking about her.* Dusty abruptly stood up and grabbed his coat.

Mike stopped mid-sentence. Both he and Shelley looked at him. "Where are you going?" Mike asked with a puzzled look on his face.

"I've got to go take care of something. I'll catch up with you later." Dusty turned and strode purposefully out of the café. Cassie was either going to think he was crazy, or she was going to give him another chance. Dusty was beginning to doubt his own sanity when it came to that woman. As he headed to his truck, he felt uncertainty contract in his stomach—it was followed quickly by a firm resolve. *I am not going to screw this up. Everything is going to work out just fine.* As he put the truck into gear and pointed it toward Cassie's ranch, he added, *By God in Heaven—I'll see to it!* He flashed a confident smile at himself in the rear-view mirror for emphasis, and drove a little faster down the road.

Glossary

Angora Chaps – Long woolly leg coverings, made from goat hide that belt around the waist.

Decker Pack Saddle – is a pack saddle with two metal arches on the front and back of the saddle to lash to.

Flakes of Hay – A flake of hay is 3 to 4 inches thick (typically, but can be thinner) and is made as the hay is baled.

Garcia Spurs – Spanish spurs with large round, blunted-point rowels (rowels are a small wheel with radiating points, forming the extremity of a spur.)

Hay Bags – Snapped onto the highline to allow the horses to eat and move around while tied onto the highline.

High Hunt – A special hunting season for deer in September, occurring in specific high elevation areas.

Highline – Two straps made of seat belt material looped around trees to protect the trees, and a rope pulled taut from the straps.

Hobbles – A one-piece restraint with a buckle strap on each end. This is buckled onto the two front legs of a horse so he can only take small steps. In most instances it keeps him near camp. Some horses are still able to cover ground with them on.

LQ – Living Quarters Horse Trailer.

POA – Pony of the Americas. Average measurement is 11.2 to 14 hands (46 to 56 inches) to the withers. A large pony or small horse.

PCT – Pacific Crest Trail runs from Canada to Mexico via the Sierra Nevada Mountains and Cascade Mountains

Pulaski – Special hand tool developed for use in wildland firefighting. It is a single-bit axe with an arched mattock blade extending from the back.

Romeos – Leather slip-on shoes.

Sawbuck Pack Saddle – A pack saddle with two crossed pieces of wood (sawbucks) in the front and back of the saddle, used to lash to or hang pack boxes from.

Sorels – A leather topped boot with a rubber bottom. Comes with an insulated liner that allows the boots to keep you warm in below zero temperatures.

Product Names:

Carhartt – Insulated one-piece coveralls.

Marie Callender – Food chain with restaurants and frozen dinners.

Muck Boots – Thick rubber knee boots

Stetson – Brand of Cowboy Hat.

Stetson Silverbelly – a grayish white Stetson hat color.

High Hunt

Book 3, Dusty Rose Series

Dusty and Mike return to the Pasayten Wilderness to help out Uncle Bob in his outfit. Dusty feels he's finally getting things figured out with Cassie. When he arrives at Bob's camp, it is full with hunters excited to take part in the September high hunt. The fall weather is unpredictable—Dusty knows from experience—but other things are beginning to seem out of place.

Dusty's shoulders felt tight and he moved them. He felt the hair on the back of his neck raise. Suddenly, the metal slide of a rifle bolt being cocked sounded through the trees; over the rustle of brush and thuds of Cheyenne's hooves hitting the earth. Dusty came to an abrupt halt. Did he hear that or was that his imagination?

Check on my website www.SusieDrougas.com for the release of **High Hunt**. Sign up for my Newsletter (announce only) and be the first to know the release date!

About The Author

Powerful new novelist, Susie Drougas, rides with her own Greek packer, husband Mike.

Susie has written a series of exciting new books set in the high country. She is a long-time court reporter in Eastern Washington and has been packing horses in the mountains for over 25 years. She is the mother of two grown daughters. She and her husband Mike are active members of the Back Country Horsemen of Washington.

Susie is passionate about educating and sharing the beauty and bounty of riding and packing horses. She has effectively put us in the saddle to experience firsthand a rugged backcountry pack trip in the Pasayten Wilderness of Washington state with first novel, "Pack Saddles and Gunpowder." And has carried on the ride in her latest novel "Mountain Cowboys."

Made in the USA
Middletown, DE
03 March 2015